MARVEL

A NOVEL OF THE MARVEL UNIVERSE

INFINITY

NOVELS OF THE MARVEL UNIVERSE BY TITAN BOOKS

Ant-Man: Natural Enemy by Jason Starr

Avengers: Everybody Wants to Rule the World by Dan Abnett

Black Panther: Who is the Black Panther? by Jesse J. Holland

Captain America: Dark Designs by Stefan Petrucha

Captain Marvel: Liberation Run by Tess Sharpe

Civil War by Stuart Moore

Deadpool: Paws by Stefan Petrucha

Spider-Man: Forever Young by Stefan Petrucha

Spider-Man: Kraven's Last Hunt by Neil Kleid

Thanos: Death Sentence by Stuart Moore

Venom: Lethal Protector by James R. Tuck

X-Men: Days of Future Past by Alex Irvine

X-Men: The Dark Phoenix Saga by Stuart Moore

X-Men: The Mutant Empire Omnibus by Christopher Golden

X-Men & Avengers: The Gamma Quest Omnibus by Greg Cox (January 2020)

ALSO FROM TITAN AND TITAN BOOKS

Marvel Contest of Champions: The Art of the Battlerealm by Paul Davies

Marvel's Spider-Man: The Art of the Game by Paul Davies

Obsessed with Marvel by Peter Sanderson and Marc Sumerak

Spider-Man: Hostile Takeover by David Liss

Spider-Man: Into the Spider-Verse – The Art of the Movie by Ramin Zahed

The Art of Iron Man (10th Anniversary Edition) by John Rhett Thomas

The Marvel Vault by Matthew K. Manning, Peter Sanderson, and Roy Thomas

Ant-Man and the Wasp: The Official Movie Special

Avengers: Endgame – The Official Movie Special

Avengers: Infinity War – The Official Movie Special

Black Panther: The Official Movie Companion

Black Panther: The Official Movie Special

Captain Marvel: The Official Movie Special

Marvel Studios: The First Ten Years

Spider-Man: Far From Home – The Official Movie Special

Spider-Man: Into The Spider-Verse – The Official Movie Special

Thor: Ragnarok – The Official Movie Special

MARVEL

A NOVEL OF THE MARVEL UNIVERSE

INFINITY

ADAPTED FROM THE GRAPHIC NOVEL
BY JONATHAN HICKMAN WITH NICK SPENCER

JAMES A. MOORE

Avengers created by Stan Lee & Jack Kirby

TITAN BOOKS

Marvel's Avengers: Infinity
Paperback edition ISBN: 9781789091649
E-book edition ISBN: 9781789091632

Published by Titan Books
A division of Titan Publishing Group Ltd
144 Southwark Street, London SE1 0UP
www.titanbooks.com

First paperback edition: November 2019
10 9 8 7 6 5 4 3 2 1

FOR MARVEL PUBLISHING
Jeff Youngquist, VP Production Special Projects
Caitlin O'Connell, Assistant Editor, Special Projects
Sven Larsen, Director, Licensed Publishing
David Gabriel, SVP Sales & Marketing, Publishing
C.B. Cebulski, Editor in Chief
Joe Quesada, Chief Creative Officer
Dan Buckley, President, Marvel Entertainment

A CIP catalogue record for this title is available from the British Library.

Printed and bound in the United States.

MARVEL

A NOVEL OF THE MARVEL UNIVERSE

INFINITY

This novel is dedicated to Tessa Moore, my beloved,
and to the memory of Heidi Ann Saffel

Author's Note

The source material for this story was vast and complex, yet our
mission was to produce a single cohesive novel. As a result some
things needed to change, while others had to be rearranged. This
is in no way meant to reflect on the efforts of the talented people
who wrote the original comics. We hope the end result is uniquely
entertaining, and does justice to their work.

ACT ONE
FIRST STRIKE

PRELUDE

IN THE beginning there was the universe.

How it came to exist was a mystery that might never be solved—at least, not in its entirety. For the majority of the inhabitants, it was enough simply to accept its existence and the infinite number of parts that made up all that was known, and all that remained enigma.

Unknown to most, however, a key influence in the development of the universe had crisscrossed the cosmos for unknown eons, shaping worlds, creating and eliminating life, controlling the structures of space and time in ways that seemed incomprehensible. The Builders had always been there, seeding and molding entire civilizations in the name of the entity they knew as "the Mother."

The sum of the universe, personified.

Even after they ceased to revere the Mother, the different species that constituted the Builders continued to impact the ebb and flow of the universe, operating in this reality and in all realities. They moved through the Multiverse as a driving force—ageless, eternal, and unconcerned with the consequences.

Until that changed.

The vast elements of the Multiverse warned the Builders that all of their realities were in danger of failing, of collapsing, of dying.

This could not be allowed…

CHAPTER 1

SELF REPAIR

MOST OF the world did not see the objects as they approached. Only the most advanced cameras and telescopes caught sight of the seven projectiles as they streaked down from the heavens.

High above Earth, the space station known as the Peak peered down toward the planet and outward into the cosmos. Acting as a base for the multinational Sentient World Observation and Response Department, its sole purpose was to address extraterrestrial threats to global security. S.W.O.R.D. saw the beams, and immediately issued an alert.

Too late.

○━━━━━○

"WHAT ARE we dealing with?"

"It's difficult to tell, sir," Nathanial Byrd replied. When the president just glared up at him, the secretary of defense continued. "Wherever an object strikes, power goes out instantly, along with communications—including computer systems. It's like an electromagnetic pulse, and the majority of the power grids go out each time it occurs. Each blackout only lasts eight seconds, as far as we can measure, but system reboots take time."

In some cases a reboot only took a matter of minutes, Byrd knew, but in others the software that had to reload took longer and longer with each pulse as failsafes and protocols went into overdrive, attempting and failing to regain and restore vital information.

"From what S.W.O.R.D. has reported," he continued, "the power outages are occurring across the globe, clearly visible from orbit. The damage is minimized where there are defenses set up to deal with electromagnetic assault, but a lot of locations have been crippled entirely."

The president sat back, but didn't reply.

Disruptions to the power grids were bad enough, but they were only the tip of the iceberg. Aircraft in flight suffered those same failures. Controls went dark. Radar systems fluttered and failed. Some of the planes managed to land safely, but far too many did not. In a very short time, the body count began to rise.

The Avengers and other superhumans across the planet did what they could. Not all were successful.

The crisis rocked through urban and suburban areas alike. Electronics failed. Backup generators attempted to function, but in some cases they remained dormant as a result of complex computers designed to make them more efficient. Those were compromised again and again.

Information that was buffered and saved became corrupted after repeated attempts to restart and restore that data. Fail-safe systems designed to protect the populace—and indeed, the very world—from critical situations faltered and died.

The most sophisticated technologies managed to pull through the worst situations, because they were designed with catastrophic failure in mind. "This year's model," as it were, had all the bells and whistles.

The designs from a few years earlier, however, were lacking.

THE NUCLEAR plant in Ulchin County, North Gyeongsang Province, South Korea, began having issues only an hour into the interstellar assault on the planet.

At first the technicians and workforce at the plant tried to handle the matter themselves. They were trained for just such situations. When they realized they required outside help, they made the appropriate calls. Further attempts were made to resolve the crisis by following all the appropriate protocols.

Without success.

Dr. Kim Jae-Yin oversaw the running of the Ulchin Nuclear Plant. He sent the majority of the workers away as soon as he safely could, and decided to call in a favor from an old friend. Ignoring the rising radiation levels, and despite the rising tide of ice that tried to freeze his stomach and his heart, Jae-Yin remained calm and efficient. He did not want to die. He suspected, however, that it was already too late for him to have any say in the matter.

Dr. Bruce Banner was an old college friend. They'd debated many times over games of chess or the occasional beer. They had never agreed, but it was an amiable sort of conflict.

When he finally reached Dr. Banner, it was through a S.H.I.E.L.D. communications center— perhaps the only reason his struggling communications got through. Foregoing any pleasantries, Kim begged his acquaintance to use his influence and send the Avengers to the area in an effort to save as many lives as possible. Bruce promised to do what he could. The connection ended.

Dr. Kim Jae-Yin then began to make peace with death.

AT FIRST it was only the monuments.

Chhatarpur District, India, wasn't a vastly populated area, and that proved to be for the best. The signal that struck near the Khajuraho Monuments did not care whether people were in the way.

The signal did not feel.

It simply did what it was meant to do.

It changed the world.

There was an extensive collection of temples around Chhatarpur, including the Khajuraho temples dating back a thousand years and more. None were spared. The ground around them was saturated with alien radiations that began their work immediately upon impact, altering not only the landscape, but also all life in the area.

The temples stood near the town of Khajuraho, boasting a population of over twenty thousand people. The ancient structures and the land around them were quickly overwhelmed by huge, twisted, vine-like growths and a dark viscous substance beneath which every living being disappeared.

A strange mist fell over the land, resembling a starry snowfall—and with it came utter silence.

Then the ground began to move, *writhe*, as new human-like forms rose up and freed themselves from the dark substance. These humanoid forms were muscular giants, naked and genderless, with dark-blue skin and standing twenty feet in height. Each monolithic being had a grotesque, cube-shaped head with four expressionless faces, one pointing in each direction.

Rising from the alien muck, moving without any noticeable form of communication between them, the creatures set about building a large circular structure. Each individual carried huge stones that seemed too heavy to lift. These they assembled with uncanny precision. When complete, the structure's configuration evoked the symmetries of the Nazca lines of southern Peru as seen from high above.

Their task complete, the blue figures formed a living ring around the construct. As one they reached out, placing their hands against its outer wall. For the first time an expression appeared on their many faces—an expression of pain... or anger.

DR. BRUCE Banner peered at the screen, studying the feed sent to him by the S.W.O.R.D. telescopes located aboard the orbiting Peak. It revealed what was occurring in India, and elsewhere across the globe.

As terrifying as the images were, he couldn't help but be excited. This was what he lived for. The mysteries of the world made him feel vital and alive.

Yet excitement wasn't always the best idea where he was involved. There were very few people who could argue with the merits of keeping Bruce Banner calm. When aroused, his anger tended to result in catastrophic property damage.

However, in times of crisis like this one, he didn't exactly have a choice. Steve Rogers—Captain America—was counting on him for answers. Banner was an Avenger, after all.

The more he studied the digital feeds, however, the more excitement gave way to horror...

IN PERTH, Australia, the effects of the impact were similar to what had occurred in the Chhatarpur District. The land and buildings in the city were violently transformed, the ground giving way as massive plants pushed their way out of the fertile soil and up through concrete and asphalt alike. Heavy cloud cover stretched overhead, lightning arcing through the sky.

The vines moved with deliberate design, covering structures, roads, and bridges, and quickly developing a network of organic cables that in turn rose in rapidly growing towers. Along all of those alien structures, heavy pods bloomed like cancerous growths. Swelling quickly to maturation, these bulbous eggs spewed forth cyclopean, beetle-like crustaceans that moved with efficiency as they scurried along the alien vines.

As each reached its destination and faced upward toward space, the creature's head opened, flaps peeling back to reveal a glowing eye. Beams of unknown energy joined the lightning above.

ABOARD THE Peak, technicians worked tirelessly to locate the source of the assault coming from the stars. Scanners swept the heavens, yet found the answer surprisingly close to home.

The source was none other than the red planet, Mars.

The strike zones in Japan, India, and Australia

were followed by impacts in the Savage Land beneath Antarctica; in Split, Croatia; in Regina, Saskatchewan, Canada; and in Holjanmyaa, Norway. In each location the changes to the atmosphere and environment were immediate and violent. Millions of people were *altered*, the land transformed beyond recognition.

Time was running out.

Most terrestrial space agencies didn't even have launch capabilities. Those that did—including NASA, the CNSA of China, Russia's RFSA, and even the privately owned organizations—didn't possess the technology or equipment needed to mount a mission from the third planet in the solar system to the fourth without taking more time for preparation and travel than was feasible.

The good news for everyone involved was that the Avengers had other methods of arranging transport.

CHAPTER 2

LIFE ON MARS

"WE ARE NOT HERE TO RECREATE, EX NIHILO," the Aleph asserted. "WE ARE HERE TO PURGE."

Like the others of his species, Ex Nihilo considered himself a Gardener. His purpose was simple: find life and either help it become what it should become, or pull it like a weed from the garden. In the beginning he'd preferred to pull weeds, but as time passed he started wondering about what could be, what should be—and so he became determined to change things.

That did not sit well with his companions.

The Aleph was taller than he was, and made entirely of metallic alloys that defied analysis. Though not completely indestructible, it was close. There had been a time, in ages past, when both Ex Nihilo and his sister, Abyss, had been seeds carried by the robotic form. Still, it was not their father—more like an equal.

The three of them stared impassively at the massive organic cannon that fired pulses at the Earth, trying—thus far without any success—to reform the planet that lay 34 million miles away at its closest. Ex Nihilo wanted to reshape the garden of Earth. His sister remained aloof regarding her preferences, and the Aleph disagreed and continued to argue its case.

"**THE EARTH IS CORRUPTED**," it said. "**OUR DUTY IS TO RAZE THIS WORLD**."

"Nonsense!" Ex Nihilo shook his head, the great horns scraping the air as he did so. "We have a rare opportunity, Aleph. We can reshape the world, help it correct itself and become something greater than it is now—as great as it was meant to be when it was first seeded and shaped."

"**DECLARATIVE: OUR OBJECTIVE IS TIME-SENSITIVE**," the Aleph persisted. "**THE EARTH IS A DANGER AND MUST BE ELIMINATED**."

"Perhaps, but first I prefer to see the correction. They are living creatures with great potential. The world is rich and fertile, and deserves a chance to first be nurtured and directed." He turned to gaze at the dot of life in the sky. "My signals will give the Earth that chance."

"**DECLARATIVE: WORLD-RAZING. OUR OBJECTIVE IS TIME-SENSITIVE**."

Ex Nihilo shook his head, moderately annoyed that the robot would not listen to him. It was sentient.

It could think and reason as well as any organic creature. Still, it remained intractable in its solution to their problem.

"I prefer to create life, to guide it." He waved his arms, trying without words to express his frustration. "I am weary of destroying anything that might have the potential to be a threat. What of the potential to be something better, rather than something worse? What of the possibilities for redemption and growth? We're Gardeners, not destroyers. Gardens need to be tended, weeds pulled, yes—but not every life is a weed."

Ex Nihilo gestured, and a form manifested in the air beside him. It was a human form; though mature, it was pulled into a fetal position.

"Observe, even as we speak I am completing the creation of one of their kind—a human without any of the flaws inherent in the species. He will be our new Adam. He will be the first of a perfect race that can replace the flawed."

His sister spoke softly.

"They've sent some of theirs," she announced. "They send their best fighters to stop us."

"APES," Aleph responded. "THEY SEND APES."

Ex Nihilo nodded. "Perhaps, but they are apes with which we can reason."

"WANT TO explain to me how it is we have green vegetation on Mars?"

Captain America frowned as he looked at the

heavy forest in which they had landed. The ship settled gently, yet a palpable tension gripped everyone on board. Thor and the Black Widow nodded silently. Hawkeye just glared.

"Why *wouldn't* it be there?" Iron Man shook his head. His red-and-gold armor glinted in the dim lighting of the ship's cabin. "The first bombs that hit Earth completely changed the biospheres of the impact zones. Whoever we're dealing with, they've altered billions of years of evolution in minutes. That's very nearly godlike."

Thor snorted in contempt. Iron Man ignored him and turned to address another passenger aboard the quincruiser, a modified Avengers quinjet. With this craft, they could even reach faster-than-light speeds.

"Bruce, you're better at this sort of thing than I am. Anything you can suggest? How could someone produce a forest out of nowhere?"

Banner scanned the area. Ever since the *Curiosity* and *InSight* landings, mankind viewed Mars as a desert landscape—always red, flat or with rolling hills, and dotted with rocks. Where they stood now, it was thick with vegetation—jungle-like with trees and twisted vines and dense undergrowth.

"Tony, two of the first bombs hit Perth and Regina. Those alone affected over two million people." His voice began to change, growing deeper. His body morphed, as well, growing in size at an alarming rate—even as his skin went from a pale peach hue to a shade of green as deep as the darkest emerald.

"I think we're done talking," he growled.

The Hulk left the ship through the rear port. He was walking when he exited, and then broke into a run. Tony Stark sighed inside his armor and moved after the green goliath.

Three figures stood not far away. The first was a woman, dressed mostly in black, with long, thick black hair that seemed made of living shadows. Next was a humanoid male, with golden skin and an Omega sign painted across his chest. He had no hair, but two mismatched horns perched on the sides of his head. His eyes were solid blue, with no pupils, and a third one sat in the middle of his forehead directly above his nose. Off to one side a humanoid figure floated in the air, unmoving.

Even as the Hulk charged, the golden-skinned man smiled warmly.

"Visitors!" he exclaimed. "And not the boring kind."

Some people just aren't very bright, Stark mused.

Before the Hulk could reach the smiling horned man, however, the woman made a gesture. A thick dome of black shadows appeared in his path. Carried by his own momentum, the Hulk vanished inside.

"Well, damn," Stark muttered. "That's not a good sign." Quickly running through a set of protocols, he prepared to launch an assault. Abruptly he felt a tugging, and a warning alarm sounded inside his armor.

"Armor integrity compromised. Systems failing. Power levels at twenty percent… thirteen percent… six percent…"

"What the hell?"

The tugging continued as the plant life around him wormed its way into his armor.

"Powering dow—"

All systems ground to a halt.

"Come to me, metal man!" The voice came from the golden figure, who was still smiling as he gestured. "Thank the Goddess in all her splendor… I am dying for some entertainment."

The plants responded to him, hauling around Tony and his inactive ninety-five pounds of inert armor like it was nothing at all. Before he could respond, the plants began stripping away the metal shielding. It shouldn't have been that easy. There were redundancies in place, yet it was like peeling an orange.

"You have an exoskeleton!" the golden man exclaimed. "Only three percent of races possess exoskeletons. You are a rare find indeed!" He sounded so cheerful as the armor continued to peel back. "Let's see what you look like after we speed up your evolu—"

Abruptly he screamed in pain, his teeth clenching past bared lips as explosions erupted from his back. All traces of cheer dissolved as he turned to face his attackers.

"Step away from the man with all the money," Black Widow said tersely.

Hawkeye finished with, "Please."

Regaining his balance, the golden man crackled with energy.

"You dare violence?" he said. "Violence for the *sake* of violence? When I offer so much to your people and your planet?" Such was the energy that his skin was obscured in the glare of power that surrounded him. "This is the thanks you offer, for all I would gift you?"

The energies around him coalesced and flared outward into a blast that struck where the two Avengers stood, shredding the trees and plants alike. Stark couldn't tell whether they were alive or dead.

To his relief, as the flash and debris of the attack diminished, the Black Widow and Hawkeye emerged from cover to either side. Beyond them there was motion as the woman with the shadows in her hair slid into the sphere of darkness that surrounded the Hulk. An instant later the green goliath burst out of the shadow sphere and shot straight toward Thor, one massive fist forward.

The golden man struck a second time. This time the impact caught both of his targets, sending them rolling across the ground and trying their best to absorb the force of the assault. When they skidded to a stop, they lay there, unmoving. Stark hoped they were only unconscious.

The Asgardian had just long enough to be surprised before the Hulk's massive fist made contact with his head and sent him sprawling backward. He hit a tree and knocked it down, bounced off a second tree, and then crashed into the dense foliage. His assailant went after him, roaring like an animal. As Thor slowly but surely rose to his feet, the Hulk crashed into him again, roaring his fury for all to hear.

As he did, the woman in black emerged from the dome, which faded away.

The golden man started to turn from his defeated foes when a disc-shaped shield cut through the air and smashed into his face. It ricocheted off and into the back of the shadow woman's head, knocking her to the ground.

Still gripped by the vines and unable to move, Stark noticed the third figure standing impassively not far away. Distance made a trick of the thing. At first he thought the newcomer was the same size as the golden man—largish, but roughly the height of a human.

No. It was much larger.

Reaching Captain America in four strides, it seemed to *grow* as it moved closer. The shield was flying back toward Cap's waiting hand when the robot moved and intercepted it, catching the object before it could reach its owner. As it stepped up next to the star-spangled Avenger, the thing stood at least twelve feet tall.

It looked like a grown man addressing a third-grader.

"YIELD?" The thing looked down and asked once.

"No." Captain America spoke just as softly.

Its free hand was a blur, moving too fast to follow, as the alien pounded a fist into his opponent's face. Something in its movements convinced Stark it was entirely mechanical.

"YIELD," it said.

"No."

Cap tried to block the next blow, but the robot was merciless, unyielding, and *fast*. He slammed the

Avenger's head into the ground with the second blow, and then a third, a fourth. He was ready to strike again when the golden man stopped it.

"Enough, Aleph. We have no need to kill him. We will send him back home with a message. We will let the Earth know that resistance is a futile waste of time. They will adapt to the changes we make, or they will die."

Sounds of carnage indicated Thor and the Hulk were continuing their fight somewhere out of sight. Through it all, Tony Stark strained to turn his head to see what was occurring. He tried to incite his armor to work, tried to break free of the vines that held him and his armor alike, and through it all he failed miserably.

Without warning, all was silent.

The Hulk and Thor, both unconscious, were gripped in the vines and brought toward him, wrapped in greenery. The same was done with the Widow and Hawkeye—all except Captain America. When the vines lifted his badly battered form, it was moved into their ship, followed by the golden man.

Moments later the alien left the vessel and nodded his satisfaction. The hatch shut with a metallic *click*, and the vessel launched into the atmosphere of Mars, receding until it was little more than a bright glow.

And then it was gone.

The golden man smiled.

"You see?" he said, his cheerful demeanor returning. "We choose not to harm you. We want only what is best for your Earth. We want to make you better." He smiled at Tony as he approached. "We will reshape your planet as it should be."

The woman was up and standing now, alongside the towering robot.

What now? Stark thought, his mind racing. *Well, where tech failed, maybe communication will work. If it doesn't...* He couldn't bring himself to finish the thought.

"So what happens now..." he began. "I'm sorry, Goldie, what's your name?"

Goldie smiled. "I am Ex Nihilo. This is my sister, Abyss"—he gestured—"and this is Aleph. We are here to change your world, to save it from itself."

"Yeah, well, we've seen how that works," Stark replied. "It's not that we don't appreciate your concern, but no thanks. We'll pass."

Goldie laughed and spoke to him as if he might be addled.

"We are not here to ask if you want our help," he said. "We are here to change you before the Builders decide to change you." His expression went serious. "They will not be as kind, or as forgiving."

"What do you mean?" Stark responded, and he had a feeling he wasn't going to like the answer.

"Your world has two choices," Ex Nihilo said. "Adapt or perish. We are here to help you adapt. Your people will not survive, but what comes after them will be much better for the effort, and your world will continue on. If we fail in this, your world will die. The Builders will see to that."

Tony smiled grimly. "Okay, work with me here

and assume I've never heard of these 'Builders.' What are we dealing with?"

"At the dawn of everything, there were the Builders. They were the first race, the oldest living things in the cosmos." Goldie smiled again and looked warmly at Tony. It made his skin crawl. "They were a perfect people, and for a while they worshipped the Goddess, the Mother maker herself. The universe."

He stepped back and gestured. "Eventually they grew beyond this way of life. They abandoned the old ways of reverence for a new path of, well… of relevance. As expansion and evolution occurred, the Builders created aggressive systems to direct, control, and shape the very structure of space and time. The first of these systems were the Gardeners." He pointed toward the robot. "Alephs sent out into the wild to purge species unfit and unsuitable for the Builders' new universe.

"This is our Aleph," he continued. "For countless millions of years, it razed world after world, destroying all it deemed unfit for progress, until finally it found a world with potential. One worthy of keeping. One worthy of evolution. Then the Gardener released the seeds it had kept inside of itself for all that time."

Goldie looked around, seeming to forget Stark was even there, and spoke with a subtle awe in his voice.

"No two seeds are the same. The Builders, in all of their wisdom, knew that creation is chaos and embraced this inconstant constant. This Aleph—our Aleph—yielded my sister and myself. From that day until now, whenever we encounter a world that is living or has the potential for life, we either offer it change or we end the life that exists. Here we are, ready to offer your planet the chance to transcend all that it is, and offer it far greater potential than currently exists. Aleph says we should destroy your world. I disagree, and so we approach with evolution in mind."

"And whatever happened to the idea of free choice?" Stark demanded. "What say do we have? It *is* our planet, after all."

"There is no free choice here," Ex Nihilo said, again as if to a simpleton. It was beginning to get on Stark's nerves. "Your world will evolve, or it will be destroyed."

Stark closed his eyes and took a deep breath. It was going to be a long argument, but talk was all he had to work with.

CHAPTER 3

A GATHERING OF FORCES

STEVE Rogers woke in Avengers Tower in Manhattan. That was where the ship had originated, and where it had returned. It took twenty minutes to bring him up to date on what had transpired. The rest of the away team had not returned.

He had been sent back as a warning.

Cap was urged to remain in bed, to allow his body to recuperate from the vicious beating he'd received. He listened to the medical staff, then responded in the only way he could. There were calls that had to be made, and he made them. Then he took a brief shower, and suited up.

His face ached where he had not yet fully healed. Thanks to the Super-Soldier Serum, he was faster at recovering from injuries than most people, but still he was only human.

As he prepared for the return mission, those he had contacted answered his call. There were more of them this time—they would not be caught ill-prepared again. Some of those who arrived were mutants, others had been altered in ways that couldn't easily be explained. They were humans and superhumans alike, and they answered the summons because it was more than just a call to arms.

It was a call from Captain America.

"SO THE signal originated from Mars?"

Cannonball frowned and peered at the display in front of him. He had been off-planet before, yet the very prospect remained both exhilarating and frightening at the same time. Hailing from Kentucky, Sam Guthrie been raised among coal miners and had expected to live his life with them. Then his mutant powers had manifested. The world since then had never been quite what he'd been raised in, but it had always been… interesting.

"Well, it didn't come from Planet X."

Guthrie pressed his lips together to avoid making a comment. He admired Spider-Man. He had seen footage, watched videos, heard stories from any number of people who had worked with the man, but he didn't much like him. He was too sarcastic. He lacked manners.

The guy standing next to him was an Aborigine—

an indigenous Australian. His name was Eden, though they called him Manifold. A teleporter. Never in a million years would Guthrie have expected to meet someone like him.

"We are going to Mars," the man said. Manifold's accent was different than what Sam might have expected, but he couldn't have said just how. Really, sometimes the world just seemed incredibly large, even after all he'd seen.

"Thank you, all of you, for coming." Captain America looked around and nodded. They all knew the situation, and the mood in the room was grim. "This isn't going to be easy. We're going to have to go very fast, and take these people out before they can pull any of the tricks they did on the first wave of Avengers. I don't know if any of that team is even alive—I just know that we have to stop these people before they can cause any more damage down here."

Guthrie stared at him, stunned. There were people who just had a kind of presence, and Captain America was one of them. He seemed larger than life. Sam had met heroes and villains aplenty, but few of them came close to making him feel like he was in the wrong room. And yet the Captain had called him and invited him to join the Avengers.

You just don't say no to that.

"You ready, Sam?" Roberto tapped him on the arm, and he jumped a little. He'd known Sunspot ever since he'd become a super hero.

Guthrie nodded. The team Cap had chosen

gathered together—Sam himself, Sunspot, a massively muscular man called Hyperion, Smasher, Captain Marvel, Captain Universe, Shang-Chi, Spider-Man, Spider-Woman, Wolverine, and Manifold—and began to *glow*. It lasted only an instant, and there wasn't any of the vertigo Sam had expected to experience. One moment they were standing in Avengers Tower—

—the next moment they were facing their targets. Targets they'd only seen in surveillance images taken by the quincruiser.

The photos hadn't done them justice.

CHAPTER 4

RESCUE MISSION

THEY'D had all the talks they were going to have. Each time it came down to the same thing.

Evolve or die.

Near as Tony understood it, Ex Nihilo—the Golden Child—wanted to save the Earth by forcing evolution. Aleph wanted to end the whole thing, and Abyss didn't care either way. She was just going with the flow. The new human Ex Nihilo had created didn't seem capable of caring about much of anything. Yet it spoke, and when it spoke Goldie was like a proud papa excited to discover his new life-form had developed speech.

He wasn't sure what the language was, but gathered it was the same language the Builders spoke, so Tony did his best to memorize the words, even if he couldn't understand them. The other Avengers were nearby, still unconscious and held firm by a gargantuan, unnatural tree-thing.

"Did you hear that, Abyss?" Goldie said, gesturing toward his creation. "That was life. *Life* happened. Unforeseen, uncontrollable, wild, unfettered life!" He laughed. "I know because this is who I am, sister. I've created something new. Something unexpected."

For all the world he sounded like Victor Frankenstein.

"Something—" Ex Nihilo was cut off by a blast of energy that came down from above and knocked him into the ground. He hit hard enough to leave a fourteen-foot trench in the dirt.

Tony couldn't help but smile.

"APES," the Aleph said, then Captain America drove his shield into the robot's face and broke part of it. From far above two shapes looked down. One was a female form in black and white. He knew her from the files. Smasher. She was a relative newcomer with a serious power boost from alien tech.

Next to her was Hyperion, who was—as far as they could figure—one of the most powerful beings currently on the Earth. *Well, on Mars now.* He hovered in the air, his body floating effortlessly, his cape billowing in a wind Tony couldn't feel. His uniform was black and gold, and he watched as Goldie tried to get up. Without warning, Hyperion shot eye-beams that struck Ex Nihilo hard enough to make him scream.

That made Tony chuckle more than it should have. Then Abyss woke the Hulk.

"Kill him." She pointed at Hyperion. Freed from the vines the Hulk launched himself into the air like a green missile, swinging a fist bigger than Hyperion's head and connecting with his face.

Hyperion hit the ground hard, but was back up and soaring toward the Hulk at a speed almost impossible to catch with the naked eye. When he hit his target, the impact was enough to shake the air around them and send his enemy flying back a few hundred yards.

The fight was on. The group Cap had selected appeared out of thin air, and again Tony smiled, secure in what the outcome had to be.

Ex Nihilo gestured, and the landscape exploded into activity, birthing wolf-like creatures that rapidly matured and attacked the Avengers with feral ferocity. The lupine things were six feet at the shoulder, and came out of the ground with an attitude that made Wolverine seem like a Cub Scout by comparison.

Without hesitation, Captain America dove into the thick of combat, moving with deliberation toward the robot Aleph. With his attention diverted, Carol Danvers—Captain Marvel—called out instructions, directing the Avengers in their counter-assault. They followed those commands without hesitation.

One by one she hauled the wolflings into the air and threw them away from the center of the fray. The entire time she focused on the three sentient creatures that to all appearances had instigated an attack on Earth.

Stark could only watch the chaotic melee from his vantage point, wrapped to the side of a very large tree that had been formed for the sole purpose of holding the Avengers captive. The vines were powerful enough to restrain even Thor, whose hammer rested only a few feet from him on the ground.

The vines were tough.

Adamantium was tougher.

While many of the new group fought the wolf-things, Wolverine moved through the fight, easily dodging opponents and making a beeline for the tree. Then he began cutting the vines that held Thor in place. Metallic claws carved away the vines easily, and within moments Thor fell to the ground, remaining there a moment, recovering from his captivity. Stark noted his expression, and a ripple of anticipation shivered through him.

The God of Thunder did not look amused.

There was a flash of red and blue as Spider-Man moved across the field of battle, his webs covering wolfling after wolfling, pinning them in place. Roberto da Costa, now in his ebon Sunspot form, lashed out, and the things obligingly broke on his fists. Hyperion continued his assault on the Hulk, moving at superhuman speed and forcing the gamma-spawned brute back again and again, seldom letting himself get hit.

The Hulk raged, but was unable to get the upper

hand. Tony prayed the man didn't get cocky. The green goliath had caught more than one person off-guard with a sudden fast move, as Stark knew from personal experience.

Spider-Woman launched into the air and targeted wolflings with her bio-electric "venom" blasts. Smasher tracked the creatures and shot them from the air, incapacitating them. Cannonball blasted through at full speed and crashed into the giant robot fighting Captain America, his indestructible form staggering the thing.

Suddenly the vines holding Stark went loose around him, and he found Wolverine slicing through them with deadly precision. The mutant said not a single word, but a low rumble came from the man's chest—and then he was gone, back in the thick of combat.

Another rumble, this time from a different direction.

Thor stood now, holding the hammer he called Mjolnir up into the air. Above him clouds formed in an instant, blackening the sky over an impossible forest that never should have existed on Mars.

Hyperion paused in the air. The Hulk was below him, on the ground and tensing to leap up and renew his assault. Aleph and Captain America were momentarily separated. The siblings Abyss and Ex Nihilo stood close to each other, poised to attack.

The lightning that came down was selective.

First it speared Ex Nihilo, then tore through

Abyss and danced across the surface of the Aleph, leaving black burn marks across his metallic form. The thunder born of the lightning was explosive, and so was the roar that came from the Hulk as Hyperion unleashed a haymaker across the brute's face.

An instant later the Hulk crashed to the ground, sending out shockwaves in all directions. His skin smoked as if he'd been struck by the very lightning that assaulted the others, and despite the ringing in his ears Tony heard Abyss speak.

"I've lost him."

She fell gracelessly to the ground.

Then the Hulk disappeared. He shrank down into the form of an unconscious Bruce Banner—a transformation that never ceased to fascinate Tony.

As the ripples and debris settled, new motion attracted his attention. Half a football field distant, Captain Universe hovered in the air and looked down at the new "Adam" Ex Nihilo had created. She spoke, and it was in the same gibberish language he'd heard from the Gardeners—and from Adam himself.

Closer still, the Aleph rose to his feet. *Dammit,* Stark raged inwardly, *I should be out there helping them.* Once again he tried to reboot his systems, but nothing worked. He was forced to remain an observer, watching for anything that might grant them an advantage.

"Not again." Captain America faced the thing and shook his head. "Not this time," he said. "Yield."

"**NO.**"

The Aleph started forward—when it was struck from one side. If there was a weapon, Stark didn't see it, yet Shang-Chi drove his fist through the robot's knee as if he were punching through balsa wood. The Aleph let out a squawk and fell forward, catching itself on its hands.

Immediately the damage done to the thing—by both Cap's shield and Shang-Chi's fist—began to repair itself. Stark was unable to look away, trying to understand exactly how the repairs were initiated.

With a bellow of rage, Ex Nihilo rejoined the fray, his demeanor completely altered now that his little pipe dream was falling apart. His third eye opened wide, and a blast of energy shot toward Captain America. His shield—a unique alloy combining Vibranium and Adamantium in a way that had never been duplicated—took the blast. It was as close to indestructible as anything could be, and it absorbed impacts that should have destroyed the bearer with ease. Cap stood his ground and barely grunted.

The Aleph clambered back up, fully repaired.

It also grew larger.

Captain Universe turned away from Adam and rose into the air.

They knew very little about Captain Universe, Stark thought to himself. "She" wasn't a person, per se, but a power that made use of people. The current host for the power was a woman who had few memories of her past—perhaps none. At times the force acted on the side of humanity, yet there were long periods when

Captain Universe was nowhere to be seen. There was little they could do to influence its decisions, but for the moment the woman hosting that power chose to aid them.

In the next instant every living creature in the combat zone was bathed in a pure white light that was nearly blinding in its intensity. Ex Nihilo and Abyss looked into that light and immediately prostrated themselves on the ground.

What the hell?

They remained there, cringing.

"Please. Equilibrium." Captain Universe spoke, and the siblings listened. "You recognize me in this form? You know who I am?"

"Legend," Ex Nihilo said. "You are the Mother."

"Goddess," Abyss added. "You are the universe itself."

"**ERROR**," the Aleph countered. "**DEITY NEGATIVE**."

Captain Universe shook her head. "No. Deity positive. My children—your Builders—are adrift. They flail. They and you have become insufficient. The cycle is broken. The systems are broken."

Then Captain Universe's voice changed. It became uncertain and took on, for lack of a better term, a more human tone.

"When I was a girl, my momma always made me pie. Is there pie?" She shook her head as if to clear it, and the uncertainty departed. "Destroy no more worlds that possess life. Transform no more inhabited planets." Her words were infused with a powerful presence that was far beyond human.

"Mother, are you certain?" Abyss asked. "It's who we are."

Ex Nihilo... *smiled.*

"It is who we *were*, Abyss," he said, animation creeping back into his tone. "This is change, the very stuff of life. Now we fly into the unknown, as we should." He turned his head toward the metallic man who had carried him as a seed and birthed him into the world. "What say you, Aleph?"

The towering robotic form looked at Captain Universe, then down to Ex Nihilo and Abyss. After a long moment, it looked back to Captain Universe where she floated in the air.

"DECLARATIVE: NO."

Oh, crap...

The mechanical form changed. It grew even larger as sections of its exterior armor moved and revealed a series of assault cannons hidden underneath. Tony gaped. He didn't want to consider the raw firepower.

"THIS ALEPH HAD DETERMINED THAT THE HUMAN WORLD MUST BE DESTROYED. THIS ALEPH MUST PERFORM ITS DUTIES."

Captain Universe rose higher into the air until she stared into the face of the massive machine, now towering some twenty feet tall.

"There are seemingly infinite mysteries within my expanse, machine," she said. "This is not one of them." She shook her head as she spoke. "What good is any system built by children—even my own—if the children refuse to mature?"

The Aleph looked at her, weapons continuing to crawl free from its interior. The damned thing had more extras than a Swiss army knife, but Captain Universe didn't seem to care much.

"Stand down," she said. "The end is not what you think it's going to be."

Suddenly Tony's attention was grabbed by a familiar voice. "Back away." Not far off, Black Widow was gesturing. "We need to back away." Though he still wore his powerless armor, he felt the fine hairs on his body rising. He nodded his agreement and retreated.

Ex Nihilo shook his head. "Aleph, please…"

"**DECLARATIVE: I CANNOT OBEY.**" At that, the mechanical cut loose with several cannons, all firing simultaneously. The powerful barrage burned the air and completely engulfed Captain Universe. The assault lasted for three full seconds before it stopped.

From the center of the carnage, Captain Universe moved forward. Her finger touched the Aleph…

…and it ceased to be. Its entire gargantuan structure, all the amazing machine was, vibrated into dust in an instant. Even as the flecks of debris drifted to the ground, so too did Captain Universe.

Cap was close by, and Tony leaned in. "When we get back," he said, "remind me to put 'get pies' on Jarvis' to-do list."

Cap nodded, and said not a word.

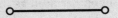

THE COMBINED Avengers away parties gathered together. What few wolf-creatures remained now disappeared, their purpose removed. Left untended, Ex Nihilo's "new Adam" had died, never truly having lived.

Captain America, Iron Man, and Captain Marvel conferred, then joined the rest. Within short order the decisions were made. Ex Nihilo and Abyss would depart with the Avengers. Captain Universe would destroy the cannon with which they had sought to transform the Earth. Stark suspected that, had it just been the Avengers who made the proposal, the fight would still be raging. But Captain Universe spoke with the authority of a god or a grandmother.

He wasn't sure which was more powerful.

CHAPTER 5

BUGS

"IT'S never easy, is it?"

Back on the Peak, Bruce Banner spoke mostly to himself. His hands moved constantly, encountering new textures, the constant input balancing the tempest that existed in his mind. It was a method he'd tried over the years to calm himself when he found that he was becoming too excited. He thought he could have written a master thesis on how to meditate, to remain focused.

The nuclear physicist's narrow shoulders held burdens that would have terrified Atlas. He had saved the world, yet destroyed entire towns. His allies trusted Bruce Banner, but not so much the Hulk. So for the most part Banner had to remain calm, centered.

"It's Perth, Cap," he said. "The Perth site is where

all of this is focused. Whatever these damned pulses are supposed to do, it's all with the goal of making Perth the epicenter."

"What do you mean 'epicenter,' Bruce?" Captain America replied. "Epicenter of what?"

Steve Rogers had been employing military strategies and fighting to make the world a better place since before most of the Avengers had been born. A veteran of World War II, he spent years in a state of suspended animation, literally frozen. He was one of the best when it came to deploying his forces. That said, the Avengers were spread thin.

"Each site has experienced the pulses, the power outages," Banner replied. "Like the Ulchin Nuclear Plant. If we didn't have a team on the ground there, we might be facing a catastrophic meltdown. But the greatest concentration is coming from one site. Perth." He rubbed the back of his neck, adjusted his glasses. "There's something unique happening there. Whatever the nature of this assault, that's where you need to be."

Cap nodded. "Stay on it, Bruce. Keep us apprised of anything new." His voice was steady. "You're doing an amazing job, and I need you here and calm, got me?"

"I hear you."

"'COME WITH us,' the men in brightly colored clothing said. 'We will show you the wonders of the universe, and have great adventures,'" Eden Fesi said. "Didn't you just convince me to leave Australia, Captain? And now you want me to go back?"

Manifold was an Australian with the ability to warp space. For many teleporters, the ability to shift from one place to another was exhausting. Worse was the notion of moving others in the same fashion—it could be the stuff of nightmares.

Fesi wasn't like other teleporters. He had yet to find a limit to his ability to move himself and his companions over vast distances. It was as easy for him as breathing. As talents go, it was the sort that made Captain America glad to have him as an Avenger.

"Afraid so," Cap replied. "We need to get to Perth now." He stepped closer, accompanied by a handful of others. Wolverine, a fighter with bones coated in nearly indestructible Adamantium, and claws covered in the same incredible metal. His ability to heal from almost any injury had saved him countless times. Like Eden, he was a mutant, considered by many to be the next stage of human evolution.

Cannonball and Sunspot, new recruits to the Avengers, were also mutants. Sam Guthrie could fly at incredible speeds and generated a force barrier around himself while he was in flight. Sunspot—Roberto da Costa—was a human solar battery who could convert his stored energies into raw physical power.

Spider-Man, however, was not a mutant. He'd been in the super-hero business for years, and had a reputation for beating the odds. The remaining member of the away team was a martial artist with incredible skills and a family pedigree that would have terrified most people. Shang-Chi was quiet, enigmatic and deadly.

"Keep alert once we land," Cap said. "There's no guarantee that we'll be able to communicate with the Hub, so we might be on our own."

"Pretty sure—" Cannonball began.

Manifold lifted his spear—a modern take on a traditional aboriginal weapon. The tip glowed, and the glow surrounded the entire group. In less time than it took to take a breath…

…they were in Perth.

"—we'll survive it," Cannonball finished. Then his eyes went wide.

The capital of Western Australia, known as the "City of Lights," was a hellscape. Vast organic structures rose to terrifying heights above the streets. These alien structures were connected, woven together over buildings, bridges, and roads alike.

Everywhere the Avengers looked, cyclopean creatures crawled over everything. Looking like gargantuan pill bugs, they possessed hard, layered carapaces, too many legs, and antennae waving above wicked-looking mandibles. The smallest of the creatures was more than four feet in length, but some looked closer to the size of a school bus. They were everywhere, swarming over buildings and climbing the vast vines and constructs that were growing from the ground, stretching into the skies above Perth.

The sight rendered the newcomers speechless.

Even Spider-Man, ever ready with a quip, just crouched on a pile of rubble, peering this way and that. Cap hoped he would hold it together.

"Where are the people?" Sunspot looked around, frowning.

"They might not be here anymore," Cap replied.

"What do you mean?"

Spider-Man answered, his voice shaky. "Nothing comes out of nothing. I mean, there has to be a source for all the physical material being grown here."

Roberto da Costa looked around, his eyes round with horror, and shifted, letting his innate powers come to the surface. His body remained the same shape, but a thick caul of black energy crawled over his skin and sputtered around him in a Kirlian dance. The reaction was purely instinctive: He was better defended against attacks while allowing the solar radiation to shield his body.

"You mean the people are the bugs?"

"Maybe." Spider-Man shook his head. "But they might also be in the plant stuff growing everywhere."

"We don't have all the information we need," Cap said, his voice remarkably calm. He needed to put a lid on it before panic set in. "We just know that there are no people here. That means we proceed with caution—and if anything attacks, defend yourself with appropriate force."

That was when the bugs noticed them.

The things had been crawling this way and that, seemingly oblivious to the newcomers. Then one of the creatures turned their way. As if on cue others noticed them as well, perhaps directed by the first. Several of the creatures that were higher off the ground and moving along vines abruptly dropped down, spreading wings that rose from beneath their carapaces. They descended in a swarm.

Cannonball launched himself toward them, flying along a blast of concussive force that surrounded his body. He collided with the closest of the insects and knocked it aside. The creature fell to the ground with a sickening *crunch* and lay unmoving.

There were plenty more.

The rest of the nightmarish things were upon them, attacking in a fury. It was just a matter of moments before the area erupted into full-blown combat. One of the things landed on Wolverine, its many legs grasping. Adamantium cut through organic armor with ease, coming free with a trail of green ichor and ropy innards.

Another landed on him, then a third, mandibles cutting away a part of his thigh before he could pull back. Wolverine let out a growl of pure rage and attacked even more viciously, tearing through the creature even as the wound in his bleeding thigh began to shrink. By the time he had dispatched the third assailant, the cut had sealed, the scar already fading.

Sunspot moved to intercept another of the things before it could land on his feral teammate, tossing it to the ground hard enough to shatter the body and crack the asphalt beneath it. Still his eyes were wild and his breathing came out in loud gasps. The next one that attacked moved straight for him and met the same fate. The bugs seemed to realize that, like Wolverine, he was a serious threat, and they came in even faster.

A familiar voice sounded in their ears. "Cap, whatever you're doing down there, it got the attention of the things in India—they must have some sort of telepathic connection." Bruce Banner's words came in loud and clear despite the communications issues most of the world was experiencing. No telling how long that would last, though. Their tech was only so good. "They're moving away from their work and gathering together. You might have a problem coming your way."

Manifold gestured, and a dozen of the bugs disappeared. Knowing Eden, it would be nowhere on Earth. Hopefully the things couldn't survive the vacuum of space.

"No sign of anything yet," Cap replied, "but thanks for the warning."

"They're gone," Banner replied. "No warning, just vanished."

There was an explosion of displaced air, and the creatures appeared. Blue giants with cubed heads and multiple faces—all of which looked angry. Surveillance footage had made it seem as if they were roughly twenty feet in height.

They were bigger.

"Thanks for the warning, Bruce," Cap said. "They just showed themselves."

The giants came in hard and fast. A massive foot came barreling down, landing with an impact that shook the ground, cracked pavement, and scattered Avengers as if they were dolls. More of the gargantuans followed suit—there seemed to be a half-dozen of them.

"Are you kidding me?" Wolverine's voice was low and loud, and he dodged out of the way as one of the things tried to stomp him into the ground.

"See? This is what I've been living with my entire life. Bugs trying to eat me and guys trying to squish me." Spider-Man's voice was sarcastic, and he seemed to have regained his cavalier cheerfulness. Wolverine ignored him as he swung his claws at the nearest blue leg.

From the midst of the melee, Captain America assessed the situation.

As he did, Spider-Man's webs blocked a behemoth that was reaching for the Super-Soldier. The thick strands of synthetic webbing stopped the arm in mid-motion, and the web-slinger hauled back with enough force to stagger the giant. Cannonball saw the opportunity and took it. He struck at the leaning giant and knocked it back. It crashed to the ground, taking part of the closest building with it.

An instant later the bugs swarmed in again, moving between the giants, crashing against the heroes, engulfing them with their sheer numbers. Sunspot bellowed as several of the things crawled over him, pressing down. A moment later they sailed backward, knocked aside by his desperate attempt to defend himself.

"This is getting worse, not better," Manifold called out. He nodded his head and sent three of the giants away, destination unknown to anyone but himself. "There are more of the bugs showing up every second."

"They're multiplying," Captain America said. "At the current rate, we're going to drown in them soon. We need help." He spun and threw his shield. It cut through the air and shattered a face of the closest giant, then arced back to his waiting hand.

"Captain, I don't know if you're going to have time to bring in reinforcements before it is too late." Even as Shang-Chi spoke a giant struck out at him, trying to swat him away. The master of the martial arts carried a perfectly balanced bō staff, and he lashed out with it, ruining the towering attacker's knee. Spinning, he planted the staff in the head of one of the van-sized bugs.

Cap nodded, and scanned the area to find one person in particular. "Manifold, I need you to go get the team from Ulchin."

Fesi frowned.

"They're dealing with a nuclear reactor."

"They've had enough time to address it," Cap replied, adding silently, *I hope.* "Right now, Perth is the priority."

"A wise course, Captain," Shang-Chi offered, "but do we have the—"

Before he could finish, Manifold was gone.

IT WAS the beginning of a biological disaster of epic scale. The Ulchin County Nuclear Power Plant was dead. Whatever defenses it had were gone, the radioactive waste it produced was going to kill everything for miles around, and there seemed to be nothing they could do about it.

Thor was the God of Thunder. He had walked the planet at varying times over centuries, and battled creatures of myth and legend—more often than not leaving his enemies beaten into submission.

This, however, was something he could not fix. Hyperion stood by his side and looked equally frustrated. Hawkeye, Captain Universe, and the Black Widow stood with him as well, though he doubted any of them could hope to repair the death coming from those reactors.

Rage played across Thor's features.

"We're too late." Natasha Romanoff was a trained assassin, a spy and infiltrator who had found herself in the employ of more than one nation on any number of high-risk assignments. That time was long past, but the gravity of their current situation was all too familiar.

"Stage-seven reactor meltdown," she continued. "There won't be any survivors. We should—"

"Enough!" The thunder god peered at the reactor as if it were a living enemy. "This should not be happening. The lightning and thunder are mine to command, and I can do nothing to stop this."

Like Natasha, Hawkeye was a mortal. He stood currently with two men who really were godlike in their abilities, and with a woman who had powers that might even dwarf theirs. He wasn't worried about being their equals: He was worried about all of them surviving. The radiation levels would be rising soon, and there wasn't a damned thing they could do about it.

"Let it go, Thor," Hawkeye replied. "We lost this one." The archer stood close by, and the Black Widow could tell that he was just as frustrated as Thor. He just had a grip on his emotions.

"We can't win every fight." The voice held a soft, sing-song quality. "Grandma said that to me a long time ago." It wasn't the voice that chilled Natasha, however—it was the power that rested beneath it. The speaker wasn't a large woman, she did not carry herself as if she had great purpose, but she held power on a level that had seldom been seen in the universe.

Indeed, that was her name. Captain Universe.

The ramifications were mind-boggling. The universe itself was an Avenger. Her host, Tamara Devoux, nearly died in an automobile crash, only to be chosen by the mysterious "Enigma Force." The mission to Mars has been her first outing with the team, and without her it might have ended in failure.

"Captain Universe?" Hyperion said, shooting her a curious look.

"Grandma always said that everyone gets sick, sooner or later." The outfit she wore was white from her toes to her ribcage, and then the ebony of deep space spotted with interconnected circles of white. Only her head was bare, allowing for a full display of tight curls. As she spoke, that too was covered in blackness, and her eyes shone with an indecipherable glow. She gestured, fingers dancing in the air like those of a concert conductor.

As if answering a silent call, the raw energies spilling from the reactors coalesced into a loose sphere of dancing green. She gestured again, and they were lifted from the earth, moving higher and higher.

"You did it." Even Hyperion, who possessed Thor-level strength, looked on with awe. "You stopped the reaction."

Captain Universe nodded. "We'll all be together again someday, Grandma and Grandpa and all the children." With a flourish she sent the radiation out of their sight, beyond the atmosphere. They didn't know where it went, and Captain Universe didn't say. It was tempting to be terrified by the tone of the woman's voice, by her disconnected words and the sheer power she displayed.

If ever we needed to stop her, Natasha thought, *could we do so? Would any of us stand a chance?* She didn't say the words aloud, however, and with some effort she discarded even the thought. Someone with that level of power might be able to read minds.

Hawkeye seemed as if he were about to say something, and the Black Widow silenced him with a look. This wasn't the time for an emotional outburst.

Thor opened his mouth to speak.

Manifold appeared from nowhere.

"We need you. Now."

Before any of them could respond, his energy glow surrounded them. An instant later they were elsewhere.

"—time to... Oh... never mind." The speaker was Shang-Chi. He stood in the midst of mayhem and violence. They were surrounded by enormous bugs and walking blue giants with four faces.

One of the giants drove Wolverine into the ground with enough force to send the vibrations through the soles of Natasha's boots. The Canadian growled deep in his throat and thrust his metallic claws through the thing's forearm. To her surprise the giant *broke*, pieces chipping off like stone.

They're not alive!

Quickly scanning the scene, she took stock. Spider-Man had covered several of the large beetle-like bugs in webbing, and they struggled to peel it away from their bodies. Captain America used the edge of his nearly indestructible shield to break the stone hide of one of the giants.

There was a shout. Thor's hammer went sailing past Cap and struck the giant dead center, knocking it back into one of its companions. Both of them fell to the ground, but were quick to rise again.

Another gargantuan figure reached out to grab Sunspot. Roberto wasn't a large man—he was on the thin side and only a little taller than Wolverine. Still, he shattered the arm of one of the giants as it reached out to grab at him. Cannonball plowed a line of carnage through several of the insects, moving like a bullet through their forms.

Hyperion caught one of the giants and hurled it away, sending the stone man soaring until it was out of sight. He threw another one toward the growing alien structure that actively dwarfed the human parts of the city, rising several hundred feet into the air. It looked as if it were working at becoming something else. Near the top the organic structure was separating, not unlike the opening blossom of an enormous exotic flower.

Or a claw.

The hurtling stone giant punched through one of the cables leading up to that blossom, and the strands snapped away from one another. Immediately bugs moved to rebuild the thing, crawling over the form and each other to make the necessary repairs.

One of the bugs noticed Natasha and skittered her way. She pointed her wrist blaster and delivered a "Widow's Bite." The explosion reduced the disgusting creature to wet ruins across the ground.

The bugs completed their repairs, and high above the giant tower let loose a pulse of energy that lit the skies and bleached the entire area white. Natasha reacted quickly enough to shut her eyes. Even so, the flash left a residual blotch against the insides of her eyelids.

"Of course," she said.

"Thor! This thing is an antenna," Captain America shouted to his teammate. The thunder god was occupied with shattering the four-faced head of a giant.

"Captain?"

"Lightning rod."

Nothing more was needed—the two of them had worked together for years. Thor just smiled and dispatched his foe with a single devastating blow. Then he gestured, and the lightning listened. The skies erupted, sending spears of electrical discharge through the entire structure, leaving deep burn marks in the vines and bursting the bug-things that walked across the extraterrestrial strands. The air shook with a dozen peals of thunder, and again the Widow shut her eyes.

Even so, she had to deal with blue afterimages long after the structure was destroyed. Most of the bugs died in the barrage; the few that hadn't kicked and struggled, upended by the force of the storm. A couple of the giants were still standing, but Hyperion punched his way through one of them while Cannonball hit the last one like a torpedo.

"CAPTAIN? ARE you there?" It was Bruce.

"I hear you, Dr. Banner… go ahead."

"I think we might have something—buy us a couple more minutes."

Their enemies defeated, the Avengers assembled among the rubble. There were cuts and bruises, but no casualties.

"No need," Captain America responded, fixing his shield to his gauntlet. "I think we're done here."

Hawkeye looked his way. "So that's it?"

"No." The answer came from above.

The ebon-and-white figure floated down toward the gathered group, looking more like a ballerina than a super hero.

"It never ends until it has to end," Captain Universe said, "and then too late to begin. Now is a time for beginnings, and so we have to start—and the start is what happens before our very ends." She landed gently on the rubble, touching down without a sound.

CHAPTER 6

THE POD

A.I.M. Island was the sort of place most people didn't want to know existed.

Those who did know found it unsettling, or infuriating. Advanced Idea Mechanics believed in science for the sake of knowledge, and damn the consequences. Through the history of the group, they had committed numerous crimes—usually to finance their experiments—and had evolved to keep up with the times.

They'd purchased an island, formerly the republic of Barbuda, modified it to suit their needs, and arranged for formal political status. They became a sovereign nation, and the world dealt with them as they did with other such entities. A.I.M. had developed many new technologies over the years, and most governments were willing to overlook a few "transgressions"—as long as the advances were shared properly.

A.I.M. Island had political clout.

So groups like the Avengers, who required certain concessions to be made if they wanted to move freely across the globe, could not trouble them without very good reason. In turn A.I.M. made sure to keep their illegal operations to a minimum, and performed most of those where prying eyes couldn't see.

When the energy pulses came from the stars, A.I.M. scientists were quick to respond. Without distractions like keeping the world safe, and with access to the best technology, they had a distinct advantage. While S.H.I.E.L.D. and other agencies scrambled to keep damage and casualties to a minimum, A.I.M. went on a hunt for anything they might exploit.

They found a pod.

"MINISTER SUPERIA!" the scientist said. He wore the A.I.M. uniform and helmet, which looked a lot like a hazmat suit. "We were not expectin—"

The dark-haired newcomer held up a hand. She wore a skin-tight black uniform with gold details.

"Status report on the pod, Doctor," she said. Spiked and looking like a vaguely organic obelisk, the pod stood in the center of the chamber. Retrieved from Holjanmyaa, Norway, it had an extremely dense exterior layer, and had resisted their best examinations.

"Until the last hour, there wasn't anything to report at all, ma'am."

"And now?"

"We're detecting activity," he replied. "We tried pretty much everything we could think of—started with laser scalpels. Then it was thermal torches, and we tried partial phasing."

"All unsuccessful, I assume," Superia replied. "So what caused the change?"

"We think it's the result of the signal interference coming from Perth." Something in the pod was moving, however slightly.

"You suspect a message?" the minister asked.

"Something like that," the anonymous scientist replied. "We recorded the signal, and we've been projecting it back to the pod."

"What?" Superia shot him a doubtful look.

"I got the idea from my wife," he elaborated. "You see, we're pregnant, and she does this thing to make the baby kick. She plays music for her, so I thought if the pod reacted to the signal once—"

Crack!

The sound echoed off the walls as the alien shape split open. In the next moment, all hell broke loose.

"CAPTAIN UNIVERSE," Cap said, "we could've used your help here—" Shang-Chi gestured to cut him off. If she had heard, however, she gave no indication.

"How can we help *you*, Mother?" the master of kung fu asked.

"Did you see my fuzzy slippers that I accidentally

misplaced?" she asked. "I think someone put them in the trash one winter. I wish I had a winter coat. It's cold out there.

"And you're not coming…" Captain Universe turned and gestured toward Manifold, while still talking to Shang-Chi. "Just him, for the trip."

"Great," Eden said, and he didn't look thrilled.

"You don't have a winter coat either," she said to him. "You should get one."

"Why?"

"It's cold in space."

CAPTAIN UNIVERSE pointed at Manifold, and before he had time even to blink, he was moved to another part of the cosmos.

That's what it must feel like for the others, he thought. *She was right. It's cold.*

"So where are we now?" He frowned. "I can usually tell, but this is… this is different." They stood atop a building that looked to be at least a hundred stories high—one of many in a futuristic cityscape. Most of the buildings seemed at least that tall, and spread across the distance before them. The sky was a deep rust color, though stars could be seen. This wasn't a place on Earth—he'd have felt it. Equally important, it wasn't anyplace he had traveled before, and he had traveled to a great many places since learning how to move through space.

"Galador." Captain Universe turned her head a

bit and looked his way. "This is where it begins."

"Where what begins?" In the distance, far above the planet, something moved, too far away for him to identify.

"The end," she replied. "The end begins here."

"Doesn't seem so bad to me," he commented, his eyes still on the distant object. It moved closer.

She sighed. "You see it as it is," she said, "and not what it will soon be." The shape coalesced into that of a ship. It was a massive thing, several city blocks in length. "They come," she added.

"They?" Her words confused him until motion, off to one side, drew his attention away from the leviathan. Five smaller forms rose from the city— humanoid forms, with eerie red light glinting off gleaming armor. "Are they part of the problem?"

"No," she responded. "They are knights. The guardians of this place. They will be the first to stand—and the first to fall." The ship came closer, dwarfing the buildings. "My children. My lost little children… How did you stray so far?"

When the ship was directly overhead, she turned to him.

"You should go now, Manifold. This is no place for you."

"So you brought me here just to see this, didn't you?" he replied, and she nodded almost imperceptibly.

"The others wouldn't trust it coming from me," she said, staring into the distance. "They confuse damaged with delusional. But they will listen to you."

She paused, then added, "Next time I want you to wear your coat."

"I'll try to remember that," he said. "This is going to be bad, isn't it?"

"Beyond your comprehension, Eden." As he began to glow, she added, "Tell the Avengers they have not done enough. The machine is not complete. To protect a world you must possess the power to destroy a world." She looked over her shoulder at him. "Go now—use words they will understand. They have to get bigger."

The last thing he saw was the five figures, sheathed in metal, each one unique, though similar enough in design to let him know they shared an origin.

Then he was gone.

"RUN!" THE masked scientist screeched. "Runnnn!"

He and the other staff from the A.I.M. lab bolted down the hallway past a group of security personnel whose armor was fashioned to look much like the scientific uniforms. The leader of the three-man squad was the first to enter the corridor.

"Lockdown has been initiated, sir. Code Black," one of his men said. "That means a full island quarantine."

"Yes, but what's the meaning of this?" the squad leader demanded, snagging the fleeing scientist. "Explain yourself, Doctor… Why have you abandoned your lab?"

"Not worth it," the frantic man babbled. "Just not worth it."

"I suppose not." The squad leader gestured, and one of his men shot the scientist. "Coward." He headed down the corridor toward whatever had caused the panic. "Follow me, gentlemen. Let's see what scared those weak men so badly."

Turning the corner, he stopped short. A dark-haired woman in a black-and-gold uniform leaned weakly against the wall. The uniform was tattered.

"Superia?"

"Sh-should never have brought it here," the woman muttered.

"What happened?

"There's a price to pay for it," she said, looking up with unseeing eyes. "It heard the call and broke free… Now it's loose."

"IT'S MOVING very quickly, Doctor," the S.H.I.E.L.D. technician said.

"Or we're moving too slowly," Banner replied.

"Sir, we did as you asked," another tech said. She was seated at a console. "Gamed out the trajectory based on the times it's slowed down enough to be picked up by satellite." She locked eyes with him, and he saw fear there. "You're not going to believe this," she added. "It's headed for Perth."

Banner went to activate his comm. "Captain, are you still there?"

"Sir," the first tech said, "we've lost the signal."

"Well then, get it back," Banner replied. His head was tight with tension, and he began to sweat.

"Yes, sir—attempting to reconfigure. But we need you to—"

"Yes, I know, I know," he said, rubbing the bridge of his nose. "Just give me a moment."

"Work-around did it—we're coming back online," the tech said.

"Good," Banner said. *Keep it together, Doctor…*

"Sir?"

I am not here… he thought. *I am standing in a meadow, surrounded by nothing but peaceful—*

"Oh, hell," Banner said aloud. "Run."

PETER PARKER—SPIDER-MAN—LOOKED at the decaying structure that still towered over the city of Perth. He was, at his very core, a man of science and logic. Reality and reason were the things that comforted him, just as surely as his sarcasm was his way of coping when his stress levels got too high, or someone else in a costume was trying to remove his head from his shoulders.

"Whatever that thing was meant to do, it served its purpose." He spoke the words mostly to himself, but Captain America turned to peer at him. He resisted the urge to cringe.

"What do you mean?" Cap said.

Spider-Man shrugged. "Whatever that life-form

was, it existed to serve a purpose, and now it's done."
He gestured around. "I mean, we beat those things—
okay, *Thor* beat those things—but they went down
because they were done with what they had to do." He
shrugged. "First rule of life is that it's persistent. It'll fight
to survive at any cost. But all of those things stopping
at the same time? Not one of them even twitching
anymore? It's done with whatever it was doing."

"So what was it doing?"

Now and then, when he felt down about the
way his life was going, Peter Parker considered
what Captain America had overcome, what he'd
accomplished, and felt better about the world around
them. Though he would never say so out loud, he
admired the Super-Soldier more than he could easily
admit—even to himself. So when Cap asked him a
question, Peter dropped the sarcasm.

"Honestly? I don't know. I mean, we can guess
that it sent a message, but there's no way of knowing
where that message went or how long it'll take to get
there. Maybe S.H.I.E.L.D. sensors can tell us if there
was a tachyon stream in that energy burst. If so, the
message would get where it's going a lot faster."

Cap nodded, and then punched the communication
tab on the earpiece buried under his helmet.

"Dr. Banner? Bruce? Can you or one of your
technicians tell me whether or not there was tachyon
radiation in the burst that came from the Perth tower?"

They all heard the response through their comms.

"This is Technician Henwright," said an

unfamiliar voice. "Dr. Banner has gone to Code Green. He's not going to be able to help you." In the background they could hear the sounds of carnage. That Henwright remained calm was a sign of how well trained he was. Most people would have been justifiably terrified.

"Drop him if you can," Cap ordered.

"Already on it. Got a Hulkbuster team en route." A pause, then the tech added, "Sir, before he lost it, we spotted something big heading your way. Probably responding to the same outgoing call as your recent opponents."

"How big, Henwright?"

"Based on the readings it's giving off, it's on a power level much greater than the things you were dealing with there in Perth."

"Thanks for the heads-up. Do you have an E.TA.?"

Spider-Man's head buzzed, and the fine hairs on his body stood on end. He called the sensation his spider-sense. It was actually a culmination of all his senses, which had been enhanced in unique ways when a radioactive spider bit him years earlier.

"He's—he's on top of you now," Henwright said.

"Incoming, Cap!" Spider-Man shouted. "Whatever it is, it's fast!" He didn't bother to turn his head but he pointed.

That was enough for Hyperion. He moved into the air at a speed that would have shamed the average bullet, and aimed himself for the thing coming their way.

Whatever it was, it was fast, it was metallic, and it slammed into Hyperion with enough force to send out shockwaves that shook the piles of rubble—many of which were precariously stacked—and shattered the few windows that had somehow survived the earlier battle.

Hyperion was strong enough to face off against Thor or the Hulk with little effort, and he could fly besides. Now he plowed into the ground and left a trench that stretched for several city blocks. In the process he tore through cars, trucks, and solid walls, adding to the ruins.

The thing that had smashed Hyperion into the pavement lowered itself to the ground with all the speed of a gently settling autumn leaf.

"Oh, man," Spider-Man said, mostly to himself. "This is not good." His spider-sense was screaming so loudly it felt as if he had a migraine.

Whatever it was, the thing was vaguely humanoid. Two arms. Two legs. It had a torso and a narrow waistline, but was decidedly not human. Its shoulders, its forearms, and other parts of its anatomy bulged in an exaggerated fashion, and it was covered from head to foot in plates of an unidentifiable grey metal. The thing was more than ten feet tall. In the center of its head, where there should have been features, was a glowing, solid-red faceplate that resembled a cyclopean eye.

"What the devil is that?" Spider-Man asked, crouching at a forty-five-degree angle on a slab of rubble.

"Something we weren't ready for," Cap replied. "Everyone still with us?"

"Up you go, 'Berto," Cannonball said, helping his teammate rise.

"You know, we could be at the beach, Sam," Sunspot said. "Little drinks, naps…"

"Just be glad we're still breathing, kid," Wolverine growled. "Count yourself lucky."

"Luck had no part in this," Thor responded, rising from a crouch. "It left us alive for a reason. It's playing with us." He peered at the armored newcomer. "It craves battle."

"Then we give it what it wants," Captain America replied as the rest of the team gathered around him. Hyperion joined them. "You know the drill, people…

Avengers assemble!"

With that he launched himself forward, and the rest followed suit.

Components spread outward from their opponent's forearm. The first blast took out Hawkeye and the Black Widow. The energies that came from the creature were concussive in nature and sent both of them flying back as the force of the blast knocked them unconscious.

Spider-Man, Shang-Chi, and Wolverine were next. Before the heroes could even land a blow, another powerful blast struck the ground at their feet, and they were hurled away. Only Spider-Man remained conscious. Cannonball and Sunspot streaked in, only to bounce off an energy sphere that surrounded their target. Their own momentum knocked them out.

Avoiding concussive blasts, Captain America actually made it to the enemy, only to be grabbed and hurled into a nearby wall. Then Thor and Hyperion launched an assault from the air. The thing's faceplate glowed bright, then erupted in a blast that rendered them unconscious.

The blinding flash was the last thing Spider-Man saw. Spots in his eyes gave way to blackness.

CHAPTER 7

PURSUIT

A.I.M. Island was on high alert. Weapons were assigned, and some of the most brilliant—if questionably ethical—minds in the world went to work on the problem of retrieving their lost prize. Satellite feeds from around the world—those not affected by the pulse—were hacked for data. A.I.M. was skilled at finding shortcuts and covering their tracks.

"WE SHOULD have been better equipped," Superia said. "Even if the thing was exponentially stronger than initially believed." She surveyed the damage where the pod had stood. The bodies had been removed.

"Still, you have to admit…" she added, "quite a specimen."

"Hmmm," the uniformed man standing next to her responded. "And one worth retrieving." As he did, a technician approached quickly and spoke to him.

"Scientist Supreme," the newcomer said. "The tracking system has picked up the entity. It's stopped in… in Perth, sir."

"Of course it has," the lead scientist replied. "Going where it believes it is needed—where the signal called it to." Using a handheld device, the technician called up holographic screens that showed the violence taking place in the Australian city.

"Just look what it has done to these Avengers," Superia said, a hint of glee in her voice. "What carnage. What potential! Breathtaking."

"Indeed," the Scientist Supreme agreed, and he turned to a group gathered around a device that boasted four large rings, mounted on end one after the other. "Doctors! Power up the Auger!" he said loudly.

"You're certain this will work?" she asked.

"It has before," the Scientist Supreme answered, remembering the screams of the human guinea pig. "In a certain manner." Details of that particular test run had been very effectively squelched.

The assault team was ready to go within five minutes. If any members of the group had a problem with the idea of being sent thousands of miles in an instant, using *highly* experimental technology, they never shared their trepidation.

"IT'S ALL right," Superia said, peering up at the huge red eye. "I just want to talk." The towering figure, fully armored, didn't respond. Didn't move.

The scene to which they had arrived was even more impressive than the images had implied. Thor lay smoldering on the ground, his hammer resting against his hand. Hyperion was bruised and unconscious—she hadn't thought that actually possible. Given different circumstances this would have been a gold mine of assets. The vivisection of an Asgardian would teach them so very much that was currently pure conjecture. Just to get her hands on Spider-Man for a few hours would yield a wealth of scientific data.

Even now Thor's breathing was changing and Captain America groaned. They had been defeated but not killed.

Pity.

Still, the harvesting team would gather what they could, for further study. No sense in wasting a unique opportunity, after all.

Above them stood the target of her attention. The thing was magnificent. Organic, yes, but metallic. This was the sort of creation that would change the game, given time—as evidenced by how quickly and easily it had taken out the so-called "Earth's Mightiest Heroes."

The thing's head turned, and she assumed it was studying them, assessing their potential as a threat. Beyond that, the thing did not move, and she decided that was a positive. Carefully she held out a small holographic projector.

"I want you to see something," Superia said, keeping her voice utterly calm. "I would have shown it to you as soon as you emerged, but you left in such a rush." The image that floated in the air showed both the Earth, as seen from a distance, and Mars. "Best we can tell, this is what happened to you," she continued.

"It started on Mars and spread to the Earth. Most people around the world thought it was an attack." She nodded toward the fallen heroes. "After looking closely, we determined it was more like an infection—a way to modify our ecosphere. But it was interrupted."

She walked closer. The head of the thing tracked her and focused, as near as she could tell, on the image she was projecting. Keeping its attention was important. Around her, the assault team shifted, the men and women moving slowly into position. She switched the hologram to show the pod as they had found it.

"When you hatched from your cocoon, it was into a world that didn't really want or need you, and now you don't know what to do," Superia continued. "We can help you. We can teach you. It'll just take time... and a more conducive..."

By her calculations, they would have exactly one chance to do this right. If they failed, the Avengers wouldn't be the only ones lying on the ground, though she was convinced that any blasts the thing might let loose would be enough to vaporize ordinary humans like her.

That wasn't going to happen.

"…work environment."

The instant she uttered the keywords, the first team struck from behind and caught the creature unawares. The sole purpose of the light show was to keep its attention and, happily, it had worked. Their clamps locked onto the thing's neck and arm, and sent low-amplitude electrical discharges through its body, set to a frequency that mirrored the creature's assaults on the Avengers. The devices had been designed to use on Thor or the Hulk, and modifications had been easy enough.

The thing teetered, ready to fall.

Team Two did its part and signaled the Auger. Their prisoner disappeared in a flash, leaving the clamps empty.

"Did we get him?" she said into her comm.

"We have him," the Scientist Supreme responded. "Translocation to the island was successful. Tunneling into trans-universal, also successful. There's little damage it'll be able to inflict there."

Superia nodded to herself. Excellent. A.I.M. had found a space between dead universes, a nothingness they used as the ultimate storage facility. It also served as the perfect prison for a creature that could level all of the Avengers with ease.

"However, there's still work to be done," the scientist reminded her, and she bristled a bit at the condescension. "Are the harvesters ready?"

She looked at her team. "They're collecting what

they need now," she responded. A.I.M. wasn't just made up of testosterone-charged foot soldiers. They weren't Hydra. It was a gathering of inquisitive minds who wanted to understand science in ways no one else could—and to profit from that information. "When they're finished, we'll need a redirection on the lure, to translocate us back to—"

"A machine? That's what you use to teleport?"

She spun to face the newcomer.

"How adorable," Manifold said.

"It's Eden Fesi, ma'am," one of the techs said. "He's their teleporter. He's—" The man's words were cut off as Manifold's spear pierced his shoulder.

"I don't know what you're doing to my friends," Fesi said as he sprinted toward them. "I don't even know what happened here, but it ends now." One by one the A.I.M. personnel vanished in flashes of light. "It's time for you guys to leave."

More flashes.

"And I don't care where you go."

Only Superia remained.

"No!" she said. "Get your hands off—"

Her feet crunched on snow in a dark wasteland.

"—me," she finished. "Damn."

CAPTAIN AMERICA looked up and blinked at the glare above him. The last thing he remembered was being knocked senseless by a new attacker, another threat to the Earth. Now—as he rose to his knees and then his feet, grabbing his shield as he stood—he saw only Manifold.

The man looked to him and nodded. "I have bad news."

"How bad?" Cap looked around and studied the other Avengers. They were breathing. There was that much at least. No fatalities was the best news he could have imagined at that moment.

"Very bad. According to Captain Universe, we have much bigger problems than we originally thought."

That was exactly the sort of news he didn't want to hear, but some things were simply inevitable.

Captain America listened, and then sighed.

Much bigger, indeed.

ACT TWO
GAUNTLETS

CHAPTER 8

MACHINATIONS

THEY were eternal. By definition, they had always been. That was the belief the Builders held. Since the universe was new, having been created by the Mother, they had been there. Her servants once upon a time, now they were masters of their own destinies—and of the fate of the Multiverse.

Not just one universe. All of them. That was the purpose of the Builders: to make certain the Multiverse remained pristine and healthy, regardless of the cost. The Builders did not age. None of them had ever died. They had been created to guide the Multiverse, and they had been created well.

The Builders were many, and were said to be the oldest race in the universe. There were factions within their ranks. Though they considered themselves one people, the Builders fell into two unique groups: the Creators and the Engineers.

The Creators seeded the cosmos. Though creatures existed in many places without their machinations, they often stopped and made alterations to what they found, the better to promote life in the way they felt it best suited the needs of the universe.

The Engineers worked out the designs for the changes. They also created the vessels used to move through the vast void of space and across the Multiverse. Their creations included the robotic Curators, which recorded the changes that were made and the worlds that were touched, making recommendations as necessity demanded to preserve what had been accomplished.

Similarly, the creatures known as the Caretakers nurtured the worlds modified by the Builders, making certain natural events did not undo the important work that had been done.

Where necessary, the mechanical Alephs cleansed the worlds of random life-forms that did not satisfy the Builders, after which the Gardeners replaced what had been removed with new life—organics the Builders would deem satisfactory. The race known as the Abyss judged the success of their work.

Each species had a purpose, and together they worked to make the universe better.

A SIGNAL came to them from a distant spot in the cosmos. It was clear, and they took in the information offered and considered it carefully. Then they made their determination.

Something had gone wrong.

Repairs would be needed before the changes taking place caused irreparable harm to the universe and the Multiverse alike. They would make the repairs as they always did, and always had.

It was their reason for existing.

No matter the cost to the living.

They were eternal.

Nothing would stop them on their sacred task.

Nothing.

T'CHALLA LOOKED at the newcomer, and controlled his anger. Even though it was justified. Despite his passionate desire to strike the man dead, he did not move. As sure as he was of his country and his abilities, he was also certain this opponent could snap his neck as easily as he would bend a blade of grass.

The Black Panther was no longer the king of Wakanda. His sister ruled over his homeland—yet in his heart they were his people, and it was his job to protect them.

They stood in the Necropolis, the City of the Dead. It was a place T'Challa often wandered when he needed to think. Shuri was his sister and the reigning queen, but either she or her advisors had made poor choices. Atlantean leaders had been captured in Wakanda, and they were to be tried for war crimes.

Atlantis tried to return the favor by taking the Wakandan ambassador to the United Nations. Instead of a capture, the ambassador and his people were dead. From there, events had spiraled out of control.

Namor stood several inches taller than T'Challa. He was dressed in a dark-blue, scaled vest and blue pants, with golden bracers on his arms. His face was all sharp angles and brooding eyes. There had been a time when T'Challa had called Namor an ally, if not a friend.

That time was past.

"That's far enough, Namor," T'Challa said. The Sub-Mariner came up behind him, the sound of his footsteps revealing the regal grace to which he had been born. "You tread in a land where you are most assuredly not welcome. What do you want?"

Namor paused. "To offer you something," he replied. "To do you a favor."

T'Challa did not bother to look.

"Are you offering to fall on your sword?" he asked darkly. "If so, you forgot to bring it. Posturing is a bad idea for a dead man."

"So is playing king when one clearly is not." Namor shook his head. "Listen to me, T'Challa. Wakanda cannot possibly win a war with Atlantis."

"I think you overestimate the strength of Atlantis." He stared at the man now, his eyes locked and showing clearly his repressed fury. "And any perceived weaknesses of Wakanda."

"Ah, the fabled technological superiority of the

great nation that has never fallen." Namor shook his head. "And men call me arrogant. T'Challa, your problem is not resources, tactics, or even your army. Your problem is the people."

"How do you suppose?"

"Many do not care for the pretender who keeps Wakanda's throne warm," Namor continued. "The queen—your sister—has enemies. These enemies whisper, and would like to see her fall."

"She is the rightful ruler of Wakanda."

Namor took a deep breath. "How do you think we so easily defeated your elite forces? How do you think we knew they were coming? Enemies from within weaken Wakanda, and will continue to do so as long as your sister sits on your throne."

The man who wore the mantle of Black Panther looked at the man who had made war on the surface world more times than he could count.

"Would you like to hear my favor now?" Namor said.

"If you would have me deliver a message to my sister, the queen, I can do so. Beyond that, I make no promises."

"Very well." Namor nodded. "Tell your queen I want peace. I will offer favorable terms. All I want in exchange is a cessation of violence between our people." He paused, then added, "I will not make the offer a second time."

"She will refuse you."

"Then she is a fool," the Sub-Mariner said without

any trace of irony, "and she needs someone to help her make the correct decision."

"I would refuse you."

"Liar. Regardless of how you feel about me, you know we have better things to be doing than spilling blood, my friend."

T'Challa shook his head. "We are not friends. That time is gone. You have warred against my people, and I will not forgive that."

"*Your* people, T'Challa. Not hers."

T'Challa found himself nodding, and hated the fact. "Make your offer through the normal channels," he said. "If I choose to back it in the council, it's best if the offer doesn't originate with me."

Namor nodded. "Very well."

He began to walk away.

Then he paused. "Oh…" he said. "You're welcome."

T'Challa said nothing.

He was no longer the king.

There was nothing he could say.

SOME THINGS were simply too large to ignore. For example, the city of Attilan—home to the Inhumans, a race of beings created by the aliens known as the Kree. At the time of their creation, Earth was a small, insignificant backwater of a planet.

Attilan had moved several times in recent years. In the early days it was hidden in the Himalayas, secluded and seldom encountered. For a time it had rested in the Blue Area of the moon, home to an enigmatic alien who observed the Earth and its inhabitants. When the Inhumans settled there he—the Watcher—had paid them remarkably little notice, so immersed was he in his mission.

Attilan was hidden no longer. The city hovered in the skies over Manhattan, leaving part of New York in perpetual shadow. There were many who wanted the island moved, but few who could convince the Inhumans it was a good idea. The population of New York itself guaranteed no one would consider attacking Attilan, even if they could penetrate its impressive defenses.

The Inhumans traced their origins back millions of years, when the Kree visited Earth and experimented on man's primitive ancestors. The Kree hoped the research would help them overcome a genetic crisis faced by their race, and they intended to use the genetically modified Earthers as powerful living weapons.

Though the test subjects advanced far beyond the primitives of Earth, the Kree abandoned the experiment. The Inhumans went into hiding and developed a technologically advanced civilization. Among their discoveries were the mutagenic Terrigen Crystals, which in turn yielded the Terrigen Mist.

When subjected to the mist, carefully selected Inhumans developed a wide variety of physical attributes and superhuman abilities.

Black Bolt, the king of the Inhumans, was the son of prominent geneticists and had been exposed to Terrigen while still in the womb. The result was the most powerful Inhuman, an energy manipulator whose slightest whisper unleashed immeasurable destructive sonic energies.

"IT'S FOR the best," Maximus said to his brother, Black Bolt. "You know this and I know this, but if we are wise, we'll keep that bit of knowledge to ourselves."

Maximus was the Inhumans' greatest intellect. He was also quite mad. At the behest of his brother, Maximus had bolstered Attilan's defenses, making them virtually impenetrable. As a result, the devastation that had fallen upon the Earth as the signals from Mars came and went did not have any impact on Attilan.

"I'm spinning the circle, brother," the madman continued. "Cogs in an Inhuman machine. A Terrigen haze, clouding my vision... Maximus the maker is building something wicked."

Wicked, indeed. Black Bolt just sat, watching silently. A part of him thought the weapon too extreme. Certainly the device would, for lack of a better way to express it, help even the odds if the humans decided the Inhumans were too much of a threat. Best of all, the weapon would cause remarkably little harm to the planet.

Humans had their thermonuclear devices, viral weapons, and deadly gases.

Black Bolt had Maximus.

He wasn't truly sure which weapon was the least humane. Even as he thought it, his brother turned to glare at him.

"Don't blame me," Maximus protested. "This wasn't my idea. It was yours." He grinned. "And I'm not going to stop unless you tell me to. Go on…"

Silence.

"No? Nothing?

"Very well."

Maximus returned to his work.

"Let's burn it all down."

TITAN. SATURN'S moon was his home. It was where he was born. It was where he was raised and where he grew to become who he was.

It was not the same as it had once been. It had been shattered, beaten, and broken, then re-formed to suit his needs. In a sense, Titan meant nothing to him. He had no particular affection for the people and no need for them in his world. His mission was more important than any one sphere.

His mission was to transform the universe to suit his needs.

At different times, he had possessed—however briefly—the power to shape the universe as a whole. He had held the Infinity Gems—shards of reality left over when the universe was formed that could, if held by the right person, remake the universe. Gathered together, they offered the power of a god.

Thanos had held the power of a god. Not of a minor deity, like one of the Asgardians, but the ability to create and recreate and destroy and alter the universe on a whim.

Such power was heady stuff.

Thanos had followers—a galactic church worth of followers, led by the Cull Obsidian, the Black Order that followed his every instruction and obeyed him without hesitation. His followers looked upon his throne and were humbled, as well they might be.

"My Lord Thanos!"

Corvus Glaive stood before him—a tall, regal creature with a heavy brow and enough powerful fangs to give children nightmares for generations. He dressed in black and gold. His skin was the color of ash, and his eyes were darker than midnight. Corvus was a loyal follower, devoted to Thanos and eager to please.

"I offer you the Ahl-Quito, called the 'World Cleaver.'" He held a wooden box before him; it contained broken fragments of a sword, drenched in red. "It is all that remains of the champion of the planet Ahl-Agullo. They have surrendered to you, rather than risk destruction."

"Of course they have." Thanos placed his hands together and nodded. "They aren't fools. Merely… optimistic." He shrugged. "Show me."

Glaive gestured, and four of his servants ran forward with an even larger chest. In this one were the heads of fifty of the creatures that had once ruled over Ahl-Agullo.

"Your tribute, Lord Thanos." Glaive lowered his head in a formal bow.

Half a hundred heads. Before, when first Thanos took Titan, it had been hundreds of thousands laid to waste. Millions. These days the population of the planet was only a few thousand. Still Thanos smiled. He could end them, but preferred that they live and worship him properly.

"Excellent work, Corvus. You do me proud." The man swelled with pride, and lowered his head again.

"This one has done you great services, Lord Thanos, and seeks to assist you again." He gestured to an Outrider. The creature was a genetic stew, with four arms, an eyeless, horse-like head and wicked teeth, its other senses serving in place of sight. The Outriders were loyal to a fault, and just intelligent enough to serve without hesitation—powerful fighters capable of great stealth and savagery.

This creature bowed low, facing the ground rather than risk being burned by the glory of its god.

"You would serve me again?"

"Yes, my Lord Thanos." It shivered in a near ecstasy of devotion. "Oh, yes."

Thanos leaned closer and placed a massive hand on the shoulder of the thing. Both of the arms beneath that shoulder relaxed at his touch. Its mouth, filled with nearly as many fangs as Corvus Glaive's broad maw, panted lovingly.

"There is an Infinity Stone on the planet

Earth," Thanos said. "I know this to be true. I need it found."

"I will not fail you, my Lord." It dared much, and all four of the Outrider's oddly shaped hands touched his thick wrist—just for a moment—before letting him go.

"Make me proud, Outrider, and you may yet earn a name granted by me." That was very close to the offer of heaven in the view of the Outriders. To be named by Thanos was an honor few of their kind could ever hope to achieve.

"I will not fail you!" the creature said. "I live only to serve you, Lord Thanos." With that it rose and backed away, bowing several times as it did so. Thanos smiled and rose from his throne. He walked closer to the creature and leaned over it, his mouth nearly touching the side of its head.

He whispered another command, while the thing shivered at the close proximity of its god.

A moment later the Outrider was gone.

Thanos looked around at his followers.

"Prepare my flagship, Corvus," he said. "We shall find what I seek... on Earth. And in the process we will make our presence known."

GALADOR WAS burning. It did not go quietly, however.

"Unforeseen complications, Builders," the Caretaker announced. It stood at a vantage point that allowed it to observe the carnage.

"They all resist," a Builder responded from aboard its vessel.

"As they should, Creator," said another. "What good is a race that would be any other way?"

"Clarify, Caretaker," a third requested. "Please define the obstacle."

"This world, it has heroes." As the Caretaker observed, Alephs moved through the flames of the burning cityscape without heeding the screams of the dying. Laser-thin eye-beams added to the destruction.

"OBJECTIVE: TIME-SENSITIVE," the foremost Aleph noted. "GOAL: WORLD CLEANSING."

"ALERT: ENERGY CASCADE IN PROXIMITY," a second Aleph said. "ERROR: COMPENS—"

Its words were cut off as a blinding flash of light consumed them, marking the arrival of five armored beings. The knights of Galador once were men, sacrificing themselves for a greater good. Their fragile bodies had been replaced by cybernetic technologies that transformed them. They became the champion protectors of their world.

"The invading fleet's command vessel is stationary," a knight with a swirling topknot announced. "We've finally got their attention."

"As we should," responded one of her teammates. "Emergency upgrades from the Prime Directorate have given each of us the firepower of an entire cavalry. We'll burn out, but Galador will stand."

"LOOK, SANNO," a young woman exclaimed, peering up at the Knights. "All the stars in heaven, and none shine as brightly as them."

"Yes," her brother replied. "The Spaceknights will save us, Kiru. They have always saved us."

"This time they will not," Captain Universe said. The softness of her voice belied the certainty in her words. "Everything dies. Even the things you think cannot."

"Who are—" Sanno began.

"I am the universe," she replied without even looking back. "Here at the start, to see how the end begins."

"Well… you're wrong. This is not the end. My father's father was a knight. He fought in the Wraith Wars, stood against the Shadow armies. He, like them, was good and noble, and fought for something greater than himself." His voice cracked. "He had to win, because losing meant the end of everything he believed in."

"They will prevail," Kiru agreed. "Because they must. See, they are not just brave and mighty—they are righteous. They are the very best of this world. They are the sons and daughters of Galador."

"It won't matter."

"Why?" Sanno said. "Why do you seem so sure?"

Captain Universe looked up, and the two young people followed her gaze. A ship, more massive than any that had ever been seen in the skies over Galador, appeared from behind the smoke and flames.

"Because," Captain Universe said, "now my children are here."

An instant later a pure white heat engulfed the city, instantly incinerating everyone who was there.

THE ENERGIES moved across the surface of the planet and drove deep within the crust, vaporizing land and oceans and every living thing that existed upon the surface of a world that had endured for centuries.

Galador died in a series of growing explosions. Where there had been a planet, there was little left but star stuff and the unconscious forms of the noble souls who had given up their humanity to save their world and, ultimately, failed.

CHAPTER 9

OUTRIDER

IT MOVED through space and dropped to the planet Earth like a spare thought, a whisper. The ship in which it traveled was invisible to the eye and to the limited technologies available on the planet.

The Outrider lived only to serve Thanos, and it moved with the careful and meticulous steps of an assassin. It was not here to kill, but to gain information. It would find out exactly what Lord Thanos wanted, and it would do so by following a trail very few creatures in the universe could have detected.

The world was larger than the moon called Titan. There were billions of creatures through which to sift in its hunt for the Infinity Stone—and the other prize Thanos sought. Fortunately the Outrider could sense the residue of the Infinity Stones—where they had been, what had touched them.

Through cities and desolate areas, it followed one of the many trails. There were several Infinity Stones—or there had been, at least—and the strongest trail led to Attilan.

Upon reaching the city of the Inhumans, the Outrider left its ship hovering overhead and entered the structure occupied by the king and his retinue. The hunter scrabbled across the walls, avoiding advanced defenses as a ghost moves through walls. It moved past guards who did not see it, or smell it, or even hear it.

Finally it made its way to the chambers of the king of the Inhumans, where the man called Black Bolt slept in darkness. It dared to perch upon the slumbering form's bed, and did not even disturb the sheets.

The occupant of that bed did not stir. The king was asleep, and his rest was deep. Reaching out with long, delicate fingers, the intruder eased its insubstantial claws into his prey's head.

Now, Inhuman king—give me what I seek.

All of them…

It began sorting through memories—of the king's early years, his ascension to the throne, the necessity of moving his people, again and again. Meeting the woman, Medusa, who became his queen and for the most part ruled with her husband. A son of prophesy who took five wives to gather all of the castes under his crown.

He loves one, hates one, cares little for the rest…

How many secrets were held in a lifetime? When

a man could not speak, he possessed more than most. The Outrider touched memory after memory, looking upon the royal family. Cousins and family who remained loyal to Black Bolt, regardless of internal strife within the kingdom.

Many secrets were sorted. Studied and cast aside.

In time, however, it found the answers it sought.

Something hidden… a brotherhood…

The gems Thanos sought were gone, taken by this king and several others. They called themselves the Illuminati, and sought to protect and guide the various factions of the world's dominant race.

Then even further back, hidden kings, a lost queen—

Get out of my head.

The ruler of the Inhumans woke.

Impossible!

The words were uttered only in Black Bolt's mind. Had he spoken, the Outrider knew, devastation surely would have followed. Yet still the creature knew terror—and *pain*. Its hand, held fast within the monarch's mind, was severed in an instant as the king ripped the entire arm free from his body as if it were the wing on a fly. The Outrider made no sound as the agony tore through it. To make a noise would be a disaster of a different sort, and it would alert others.

The Outrider tried to flee. It could not allow itself to be destroyed or captured. It had information Thanos needed, and his master would have that information no matter what the cost.

"KARNAK," THE Inhuman known as Gorgon said. "An assassin!"

A creature appeared in the corridor, vaguely human but with three arms and an elongated head possessing too many teeth. Where a fourth arm should have been, only a bloody ruin remained.

It seemed vaguely insubstantial, slipping past the two members of the ruling family like a smoking wraith. Though Karnak failed to strike it, Gorgon pounded the stone floor with one of his massive hooves, sending out a powerful shockwave. The intruder became solid and hurtled toward two of the king's guards.

"Be ready, Kirren," one of them cautioned.

"I am not afraid, Tolos."

Then the creature collided with them, tearing the guts from one and the throat from the other before they could do much more than brace themselves. The delay was enough, however, and Black Bolt appeared. As the thing leapt away from his pursuers, the Inhuman king spoke with the faintest whisper.

"Stop."

The air exploded with a storm of vibrations that crashed into the intruder, shattering its armor, pulping muscles, straining bones to breaking point. The creature screamed, but the sound was lost in the cacophony as the balcony on which it stood was destroyed, pulverized into little more than dust.

Blown backward by the force of the sound, it

plummeted toward its death. Then it hit what seemed like solid air, and a strange craft appeared. With desperate strength it reached for the hatch and rolled into the opening with feeble yet frantic effort.

Before Black Bolt and his cousins could react, the craft shot past, roaring into full flight and heading for the stars above. Quickly it dwindled down to a speck, and then a memory.

No one spoke. No one needed to. Black Bolt alone could have expressed how vast their troubles were, but he dared not speak—and even if he could have, what could he have said? How vulnerable was a kingdom that had no secrets?

His people, he knew, were likely to find out.

CHAPTER 10

THE WAR AT HOME

EVERY reserve member who could be contacted had been summoned. As they awaited instructions from Captain America, *something* occurred above the city of New York. Surveillance devices detected unusual activity in Attilan, and the departure of a strange vessel, but the Inhumans chose not to share any details.

But other, more pressing concerns took shape.

Captain Universe appeared on the Peak and fell first to her knees, and then on her face. A being who held more power than any of them could easily comprehend had been bested. Had been beaten down until she lay in a coma.

o———o

"HOW LONG?" Captain America asked. He, Iron Man, and Ex Nihilo had been summoned. The woman lying on the diagnostic bed looked less like a goddess and more like a fragile young human being. The S.W.O.R.D. medical bay held miracles of technology designed solely for restoring damaged flesh and bone, and all of its wonders worked to do so, but so far there had been little evidence of success.

"Captain Universe has been like this since she materialized on the command deck," Commander Abigail Brand said.

"Ex Nihilo, is she—" Cap said.

"Rebuilding. Regenerating." The Gardener peered through the protective glass with an expression of awe. "Mother will recover."

"The last time we saw her, she took off—disappeared, jumped to another part of the universe," Cap explained to Brand.

"Rambling about impending doom," Iron Man added.

"Those were holy words, Anthony Stark," Ex Nihilo said. "Words to be heeded. Mother knows things."

"Super. Then I wish she would wake up," Brand said, "because we could use her input on something else I wanted you to see. We intercepted a Kree omnicast from one of their deep-space outposts."

"An open-channel distress signal," Stark said. "That's not how they do it."

"No, it isn't, " Brand agreed. "On the big monitor," she said to a tech. There were other Avengers waiting in the communications center—including Captain Marvel, Thor, and Hawkeye. More were joining them by the moment.

Captain Marvel brought Steve Rogers up to date. "We've found several nests of aliens on the planet that weren't here a few days ago. They're coming from all over the place, it seems, and doing their best to hide."

He nodded as the largest monitor came to life. Though the equipment was technologically advanced, the signal was grainy and interrupted by frequent static.

"… too late *zkkppzz* … blinded. They came from the system core. We didn't see them until they were already on top of us. *Zpkk* … blacked out the sun. An overwhelming force—"

The speaker disappeared from the monitor as something mechanical struck his head, all but separating it from his shoulders. Another face appeared, and Cap involuntarily looked to Ex Nihilo. The newcomer was a Gardener.

"… take no pleasure in this. It is simply how things must be. *Zpkkk* … path is set. If you see us, choose wisely. Run. There are some of us who would rather you live, and *zpkk* …"

"Looks familiar, don't you think?" Cap said to their golden ally.

"The Builders?" Ex Nihilo said, a look of shock on his face. "This… this cannot be right."

"Here's the thing," Brand said. "We've been listening in. The outpost has gone silent, but the Kree have not. There's a lot of traffic out there, Cap.

You take the uptick of flight from the regional Skrull territories, add to that the location of the not-so-secret Kree base. Plot it all out on a map of the known universe, and you get a cone equaling the projected path of that... Builder fleet."

"I cannot believe this," Ex Nihilo muttered.

"Earth lies in the dead center of it," Brand continued. "They're headed right for us."

They moved now to where most of the Avengers were gathered—including Spider-Woman, Cannonball, Sunspot, Thor, Hyperion, Shang-Chi, Hawkeye, Falcon, Nightmask, and Black Widow. Abyss was present, as well. There were newer Avengers—relative unknowns, like Smasher. Isabel Kane was a human from a farm in Iowa who had joined the Shi'ar Empire's Imperial Guard. She wore alien technology that granted her amazing capabilities including advanced speed and strength, energy beams, and even the ability to travel in the vacuum of outer space.

"So what else do we know?" Cap asked.

Captain Marvel spoke up. "We're still gathering information, but in the hours since intercepting the distress signal from the destroyed Kree moon, S.W.O.R.D. has picked up increasing military chatter from... well, from all of the major empires, confederations, and remote areas governed by regional warlords. Basically, the entirety of the current Galactic Council. Because we have a member of the Imperial Guard here, we have information that those council worlds are mobilizing. What can you tell us, Smasher?"

Smasher stepped forward. "Gladiator, the Shi'ar Majestor, has issued a priority alert. All Superguardians, including me, have been recalled. He's even activating all Imperial Subguardians, who will be on standby to replace anyone who falls in combat. They'd only do that if they were expecting heavy losses."

Captain Marvel spoke again. "Whatever is happening, it's headed in our direction. It isn't here yet, it has a ways to go before it gets here, but there's a real chance Earth is at least one of the targets."

"So there you go," Captain America said. "Understand, people—whatever this is, it's real and it's scary enough to make space empires scramble." He turned to face their new recruit. "Ex Nihilo, these people—your Builders—created you and your sister, Abyss. You know them better than anyone here. What chance would we have if they make it to Earth?"

"Captain," the golden alien responded, "the measuring of probabilities is—"

"The answer is none," Abyss said. "If that fleet reaches this system, the next step in human evolution is extinction."

Iron Man nodded. "Yeah, that's kind of what we were thinking." His armor was dramatically different. Though he often changed the tech to suit his needs, it had been a long time since Captain America had seen him in a suit designed for the vacuum of space.

"Then we have no choice," Cap said. "We take

the fight to them. We stand with the other worlds."

"Other worlds? Are you sure I should be going with you?" The young hero known as Starbrand spoke up hesitantly, softly. "I mean, the Star Brand is a planetary defense system, meant to protect Earth."

Sunspot answered him. They were of a similar age. "Relax, it'll be fun. Like *Star Wars*, only with handsomer protagonists. Tell him, Sam?"

Cannonball smiled, though he didn't look anywhere near as confident as his friend.

"Space," he said. "So awesome."

That prompted a reply from Iron Man.

"Space," he said. "The word should be enough to give any wise person pause, but all of you—everyone assembled in this room—represent the best chance we have of stopping this before it comes here." He was silent for a moment, then added, "I wish I could go with you."

Sunspot frowned. "Wait. What?"

Captain America answered. "Iron Man's job is to stay here and enact certain contingencies, on the chance we might fail, including marshaling the Earth's defenses. Our job is to make his unnecessary.

"We leave in one hour."

CHAPTER 11

THE BLACK ORDER

THE pain was monumental. Its body was pulped in several places, and the lifeblood it had been granted pumped from a dozen wounds. Still, it moved as fast as it could in its ship, desperate to reach Thanos before the end of its miserable life.

It could barely speak, but the dexterous fingers of the remaining hand on its right side tapped in communications as the ship streaked across the space between worlds, once more heading home to Titan.

THE LANDING was not a good one, and the ship and its occupant both suffered severe damage. By the time it regained consciousness, for it had certainly faded into the gray for a time, servants of Thanos were peeling it from the wreckage and speaking of how badly it looked for the Outrider.

"Phow, look at this," one said. "It's all spoiled and missing parts."

"Rotten, not long for the living."

"Come on then—best hurry. Everyone will be waiting."

It ignored them. Thanos was all that mattered. The dreams of a name were nothing now but fading glories. It needed to reach its master, to prove its worth and to give him the information he required. Nothing else was of consequence.

Still, it was honored to find all five of the dreadlords surrounding it as it was carried to the throne. Thanos was a god, to be sure, and these five were his high priests.

"Suc… success," the Outrider said through the pain.

"Yes, creature—so you signaled on your return," Corvus Glaive replied. "And your message was not ignored. The Black Order has assembled."

Proxima Midnight, lean and lovely, her face half hidden behind a mantle that sported ceremonial horns. Black Dwarf, a beast a large as Thanos himself, covered in hard plates of natural armor and adorned with horns and barbs. The Ebony Maw, a male with pale skin and wide eyes that saw much more than most, and Supergiant, who towered over even the great Thanos. With Glaive they ruled beside the god the Outrider worshipped. They were great and powerful leaders.

They were named.

Finally they arrived. Thanos sat upon his throne and looked at the Outrider as it lay dying. He did not speak, but Corvus Glaive did, with a voice that sounded like death.

"You have done well. You have served Thanos faithfully, and your god is pleased." Glaive looked upon its wretched form, his gaze without pity. Pity was saved for the weak—and the Outrider, even dying, had never been weak.

"Tell us where."

"A-Attilan," the Outrider said. "Earth. The… Inhuman king… he hides what Thanos seeks." The words were pain. The words were glory to the great god Thanos.

"So be it," Glaive responded. "You have earned your reward, Outrider. If you wish it, you may have it now."

"I do. I wish it."

It did not face Corvus Glaive, however, but instead turned its head to Thanos, who whispered softly a name only meant for the Outrider's ears.

It learned its name at the exact moment Corvus Glaive drove a blade through the chambers of its heart, granting the reward of death.

THANOS LOOKED down upon the dead Outrider. Death was a release, he knew, and a gift. Corvus Glaive held out the bloodied tip of his weapon as if making another offering.

"This is how it is supposed to be," he said. "Does this please you, Master?"

"No," Thanos sneered. "Earth would please me."

Several of his followers muttered their displeasure at the notion. He had heard it all before.

"Earth?"

"Madness."

"On Earth even the very best plans fail and fade."

"On Earth even the darkest night always yields to day."

"Last stop for the foolish."

"A waste of time and energies best spent elsewhere."

Thanos said nothing, but marked which of the fools dared challenge his opinion. Glaive spoke for him, turning to the naysayers and hissing.

"Yes, we all know of Earth," he said. "But this is an Earth more favorable than accustomed. An Earth changed. We have word of discord in the house of the Inhumans. We have word that the mutants fight among themselves. A schism."

Thanos leaned forward, placing his elbows on his knees as he looked out at the crowd. He knew what Glaive was about to reveal, and he wanted to see their faces when they understood what was said.

"Brothers. Sisters," Glaive said. "We have even finer news than that. Sharpen your teeth and prepare to consume a great meal! Earth, you see, is without Avengers!" As he spoke, he gestured to a figure who stood nearby, eyes glowing, wearing a hat that bore a single acronym.

S.W.O.R.D.

Thanos smiled as the news sank into the cloudy minds of even the weakest of his followers. Corvus Glaive continued.

"The Avengers have gone to the stars, to warn others of impending invasion and doom. We are offered a most sumptuous feast, indeed!"

MEDUSA MOVED into the rooms where Maximus did his experiments, her impossibly long red hair swirling this way and that, writhing and rippling as if with a life of its own. She looked over the different devices he was creating, and her stomach grew cold with dread. He was behaving himself, but Maximus the Mad was as insane as the title implied. His brilliance held no concern at all about right or wrong.

She dreaded the thought of the conversation she was about to have with her husband, regardless of how one-sided the words might be. As she approached, she heard Maximus speaking.

"I have made a masterpiece," the madman said to her husband, sounding gleeful. "Well… masterpieces, actually. I've been busy."

Waiting, Medusa held back silently.

"The housing for the Terrigen Crystals has been reinforced," he continued. "I'm compressing light, heat, and all the fundamental forces of creation in the heart of the machine. We don't want any of the sacred mist to escape onto the city. Random Terrigenesis is no way to keep a secret, is it?"

He chuckled to himself.

"I know, I know," he said. "You're interested in my *other* project." He gestured. "Very well, follow me." Maximus moved into another chamber, where he did most of his work. A sphere was suspended from the high ceiling. The massive thing was at least sixty feet in diameter, designed in overlapping layers. Toward the bottom there was an opening that allowed them to enter the device.

"Building a portal wasn't much of a problem," he said, leading his brother inside. "Maintaining a local field is harder than you'd think, but it's no difficulty for a..." His voice faded away, but Medusa already knew what was inside the device.

Maximus had worked at finding a dimension where sounds were rendered without pitch. If he'd succeeded, then there was a place where her husband could speak without physical consequence. He would be able to say the words, and others would hear them without being destroyed by the power of his vocal chords.

She again heard Maximus, and the sound of his voice grew louder as they exited the device.

"...free to have your super-secret meetings that I'm not supposed to know about but do because I put a tracker in Lockja—" Then he stopped, the moment he caught sight of her standing in the doorway. "Uh-oh," he said, "trouble." Gesturing dramatically, he continued, "What did you say? 'Run for your life, Maximus'? 'One of us has to live, and I'd rather it be you'?" He looked back. "Understood, brother—you're a good man. Don't worry… I'll make a fantastic king."

Ignoring him, she stepped close to her beloved, her hair wrapping around him, caressing his body in an intimacy none but they could understand.

"Husband."

Then Maximus was smiling again, bright and warm and friendly.

"I'll just leave you two alone here. You can talk. You know, with actual words and not just facial expressions." The look she cast his way had the man very nearly running to depart.

Again she spoke to Black Bolt.

"We need to talk."

They entered the sphere, and found themselves in a simulation: a green forest with soft grass and lush undergrowth.

"Medusa, my wife," he said very softly.

"Consider what we have built together, my king," she responded. "Yet you have been hiding your thoughts from me, and I do not like it. We are less because of it." She moved closer to him, and then leaned in until her forehead touched his. "Aren't we?"

"Perhaps," he said, and his voice was like music to her. "But if I had to choose between complete honesty and the loss of this place, or denying us this place and maintaining the memory of it… then I choose the latter. You can understand that, can't you, my love?"

"No—no, I cannot." Indeed, his words were enigmatic, and she didn't like the sense of distance between them. "We are one, or we are nothing."

Black Bolt sighed, a sound that was so far removed from most of what she had experienced in her life that it gave her goose bumps. For years they had spoken without words. She could not say for certain whether this was an improvement, but she had her doubts.

"Tell me what you are hiding," she said.

Closing his eyes for a moment, he concentrated. He held out his hands, and above each palm created an image of the Terrigen Crystals.

"This is how the end begins. What we are. What we will be."

"No!" Medusa shook her head, backing away from him. Her mind spun at the thought of what he was saying. What he was implying. "No. What have you done?"

There were generations, *hundreds* of generations of Inhumans on the planet. Some believed their people had been… diluted over the centuries, contaminated with human DNA. But if that was true, so too had the humans been contaminated with Inhuman DNA.

It was a strong possibility.

"What have you done?" she repeated. Horror bloomed in her heart, then turned into anger.

Black Bolt gave no answer. Here in this place where his words could be spoken safely.

That silence was answer enough.

She lashed out, slapping his jaw roughly enough

to turn his head. Without another word, she left the chamber where she could speak with her husband, with her king.

Somewhere, likely not far away, Maximus would be smirking and laughing to himself.

THE CITY of the Dead was silent. Wakanda was silent. The night had grown long and the moon faded on the horizon, though the stars shone brightly enough.

Namor was not welcome in Wakanda. But the Necropolis was not Wakanda. It was a shadow place for the dead—and, apparently, where the dethroned kings of Wakanda liked to wander and contemplate their world.

He did not wait long before the Panther showed himself.

"Is there something I can help you with, T'Challa?"

"You do not come here to watch the skies, Namor," the former king replied. "You come here because you wish to converse with me and ask me questions. You should ask them."

"Your sister is considering my offer," the Atlantean said. "Which is good. I expect I have you to thank for that, so… thank you."

T'Challa looked at him for a long moment, studying his face. "There is nothing to thank me for, Namor."

Namor snorted and crossed his heavy arms. "I have a hard time believing Queen Shuri would consider my offer if someone had not argued it on my behalf. Are you saying you did not?"

"No," T'Challa replied. "I did."

"Then what are you saying?" He frowned. T'Challa was often an open and even friendly man, but when he wanted to hide his feelings, he was a stone wall.

"This thing you started, Namor, this thing between you and I, it is poison for our nations." T'Challa looked at him for a moment, and then studied the stars. "We are kings, or at least in my case *have* been kings. Two giants battling each other, unaware of the world, the lives, we risk destroying." T'Challa looked to Namor again.

"You were right," he continued. "Our people should be spared, but that is not the world. We know the people are always the first to pay a much-too-costly price. I regret that."

Namor peered closely into the inscrutable face of his one-time friend.

"What have you done?"

"What have I done? Nothing. I was ignored… and you were lied to." He looked so very sad, which was what started the fear inside Namor. "There will be no peace, Namor. Today will ensure it."

"What have you done?" Namor asked again, his voice rising.

They seemed to come from the night itself, manifesting from the shadows. The Dora Milaje, the royal Wakandan guard. Five of them, all armed and facing Namor, prepared—or so they likely thought—to defend T'Challa from his wrath.

"We have done what giants do, Namor," the Black Panther said. "I am sorry for your loss."

"Why do you tell me this?" Namor stepped closer to the fallen king of Wakanda, yet the man held his ground. T'Challa was nowhere near as strong as he was, but were they to fight, the Sub-Mariner doubted it would be an easy win. More important, he did not *want* a fight.

He wanted peace.

"You should go home and help your people however you can," T'Challa said. "They will need their king."

He did not lash out. Much as he wanted to, he did not strike T'Challa down. When he spoke, however, he could not conceal his fury. Not that he wanted to do so.

"This is not done, T'Challa."

With that, he launched himself into the air, soaring away into the night, toward the ocean. His domain. His kingdom. His anger competed with dread.

T'Challa shook his head.

"It never is."

CHAPTER 12

CASUALTIES OF WAR

REED Richards was one of the most impressive intellects on Earth. A member of the Avengers *and* the family of adventurers known as the Fantastic Four, he held degrees in engineering, mathematics, and physics.

"Figure the last month has been an anomaly," Richards said as they walked through Avengers Tower, "and we're going to average three to four incursions a month. At that rate—"

"Reed, there's no guarantee that—" Stark began.

"*Ahem.*" Richards wasn't accustomed to being interrupted. He continued as if it hadn't occurred. "At that rate, factoring in an exponential growth curve—" Before he could continue, or Stark could interrupt again, the alarm on the console of an aircraft hangar at the Avengers Headquarters lit up like the proverbial Christmas tree.

"What's that?" he said.

Instantly Stark's armored fingers darted across the controls. "Proximity alert," he said, their debate forgotten. "Tied into S.W.O.R.D.'s early warning system. But that means…" His voice trailed off as the huge metal doors of the landing bay slid to each side, revealing the skies over Manhattan.

The tower was high enough to see over the neighboring skyscrapers, giving the two of them a spectacular view of the invading forces that were dropping from above. Dozens were already visible, and there was no telling how many were behind them.

"My God," Stark said. The vessels were massive, and growing larger as they descended. They dropped low, many of them skirting along the streets of the city, close to the ground. Grimly Richards noted they were vaguely familiar in shape. The technology was advanced well beyond what Earth employed, as a rule.

"Titan," he said. "That's Titan tech."

Stark agreed. "This isn't going to go well," he said. "If that's Titan, we're probably dealing with Thanos." As he spoke, Richards felt a shiver run through him that had nothing to do with the temperature. Thanos was a viable threat at the best of times, but he'd never brought an invading force to the planet before. Not on this level, at least. This was just New York City, and there were enough ships descending to blot out most of the skies.

What might there be elsewhere? Just how massive *is this?* There were no Avengers to assemble. They were going to need to look elsewhere for allies.

Stark moved quickly to a separate room in the command center and began activating the batteries of defense cannons located throughout his building. Reed moved to help him and followed his instructions—this was no time for competition. Within a matter of minutes, they were as ready as they could be to defend Avengers Tower.

The rest of the city enjoyed no such luxuries.

IN ATLANTIS, bodies littered the undersea landscape, blood leaking into the surrounding waters and dissipating on the currents. The Wakandans had attacked, and while the Atlanteans had repelled the enemy soldiers, many were dead on both sides, and just as many were injured.

They would need time to recover and regroup.

The ships that dropped down on the underwater kingdom knifed through the water. They were designed for extreme pressure. They caught the Atlanteans unaware, and the damage was catastrophic.

Towering buildings that had withstood war, the ravages of time, and the forces of nature were destroyed in moments. The deep waters slowed the collapse of structures, but did nothing to stop the damage to those within the buildings.

Namor was a warrior and a king. A formidable

fighter in his own right, he had led armies that fought nations and had brought large portions of the surface world to a standstill. Even hurt, Atlantis was a force with which to be reckoned.

The defeat was as brutal as it was fast.

THE WAR machines of Titan settled beneath the waves on the ruins of a city already damaged before they arrived, and now very nearly leveled. A hatch opened in the foremost vessel and Proxima Midnight emerged, her footsteps kicking up silt that quickly drifted away. The heavy water pressure and the lack of oxygen affected her not at all.

She was followed by a small contingent of soldiers. Beside her, the leader of the shock troops looked around, frowning.

"Did Thanos send others here first?"

Proxima shook her head. "No, this was someone else." Her gaze locked on Namor, who held the body of a young woman, a casualty of combat. "I came here seeking a man of consequence," Proxima continued, "capable of wielding an Infinity Gem. Instead I find a broken prince, ruler of a broken city." She addressed the crouching figure directly. "There is no gem here. No one who had such power would have allowed this to happen. Isn't that so, Prince?"

"Be warned." Namor returned her gaze, his eyes narrowed with suppressed fury. "I will suffer no fools this day. Who are you and what do you want?"

"I am Proxima Midnight of the Black Order," she replied, "second to Lord Thanos of Titan, and I was sent here to kill you. I see, however, that I am too late. You are already dead, but just haven't realized it yet."

Namor laid down the body of his fallen subject and rose. She watched him, her eyes offering no expression. They were white and seemed to have no pupils.

"Your reputation, Namor, seems overstated. You do not appear the sport I was seeking, but perhaps you may yet have some value."

"Leave now," he said. "I will not ask again." Namor's mouth moved into a sneer of rage.

"I cannot do that." Proxima shook her head and allowed a small condescending smile. "Lord Thanos has demanded certain things come to pass, and I owe my tithe, Prince." She looked around briefly and gestured with one arm. "However, I will have mercy on you and leave what is left of your nation alive. If you can tell me where I can find the remaining Infinity Gem."

Namor said nothing, but she could see him weighing her words. He was a strong man who had been humbled, but was he a wise ruler? Would he fight, or would he see to the safety of his people?

He looked away, and she knew she had won. He was, in fact, a wise ruler when he needed to be.

"Can you do that for me, Prince Namor? Can you save what little remains of your Atlantis?"

Namor lowered his head.

IN RUSSIA the people surrendered quickly. The super heroes of the Kremlin were no longer united, and most of them could not be found. The government watched the powerful ships descend, and then did the only wise thing they could to survive.

They surrendered.

The damage to the nation was minimal.

IN MEXICO City, almost a million people were destroyed before the rulers of the country even had a chance to surrender.

IN CHINA, the war lasted for several hours. Numerous areas were devastated before the government conceded.

When the ships arrived in Hong Kong soon thereafter, the rulers were quicker to concede.

KOBE, JAPAN, already had suffered a massive interplanetary assault. The million-plus people who had been living in the area no longer existed.

The Japanese prime minister sent a message of surrender before the first ship landed.

ACROSS THE globe the alien ships swarmed, forcing all nations to face the same dilemma: fight or survive.

Where there were superhumans, the resistance lasted longer. Where there were not, the governments were on their own.

Some were wise enough to surrender early on.

Many were not. The devastation was profound.

"WE ARE winning, brother!" In Wakanda Queen Shuri chose to stand and fight. Her brother, T'Challa, fought beside her. They both wore the ceremonial garb of the Black Panther.

The ships that came for Wakanda learned very quickly that the country had far better defenses than most, already bolstered in anticipation of the inevitable war with Atlantis. A few of the alien vessels got through before the vast, golden shield was raised to defend the air. Those that failed to get past the barrier quickly discovered that their weapons weren't enough to penetrate it.

Those that did make it past the shield landed quickly and released shock troops that proved capable of leveling buildings with ease. Even so, Wakanda's internal defenses kept the capital city safe from the worst of the barrages, and the soldiers of Wakanda met their enemies with powerful retaliation.

The closest of the ships released more troops and one mountainous creature. It was the size of the Hulk—perhaps even larger—and possessed scaly golden skin that looked almost as tough as its armor. As it came closer, the thing spoke.

"I see that not all on this world are weak. Men die and the fields are burning, just as Lord Thanos intended." Its arms were long enough to remind them of the great white gorillas in the north. "I am Black Dwarf. I seek the gem, and the one who holds it." He looked directly at T'Challa as he spoke, and the once-king felt a dread creep through him. "Is there a great warrior here who would face me? Or do I have to hunt you down?"

"I am the one you seek," T'Challa said without hesitation. He fought his way through the newcomer's savage retinue, scattering them one at a time, making it seem effortless. "I am the Black Panther, king of the dead and soon to be your new lord."

When he reached for Black Dwarf, the giant swung a massive arm and tried to hit him. He missed, but his fist shattered the earth when it made contact. As it was, the Panther was knocked into the air by the force of the impact, and the blow likely would have destroyed him.

Around them the Wakandans and Shuri continued the fight, repelling the invaders. All knew, however, that the outcome rested on the two key combatants. T'Challa alone faced the massive leader.

"QUICKLY NOW, Reed," Stark said as he sped back into the command center. "I'm spinning the arc reactor that powers the tower's new defense system, but we're going to have a small window in which to act."

Outside the enemy barrage had begun, littering the skies with explosions, shattering walls and windows around them. Though Avengers Tower had not yet been struck, the building shook from the assault.

"Small window, indeed. I counted more than fifty vessels," Richards replied, stretching to reach a control panel. "We'll have maybe sixty seconds before they triangulate on the tower and we become the focus of their attention."

"System activated." Iron Man tapped a series of holographic controls that hung in the air in front of him. "Bringing the batteries online."

The first impact struck—and was repelled. The defenses held.

"I've got a green light on the second station," Richards confirmed. "What now?"

"What do you think, Reed?"

Stark hit the command button.

"Fire!"

Missiles launched from the tower's defense batteries. The weapons smashed into the vast ships with so much force that the vessels were pulverized. This kept devastatingly large chunks of debris from plummeting down on the streets and buildings. As it was, the damage was far from acceptable.

"Kill radius looks to be approximately one mile," Stark said. "Effective, but we've got their attention now, as well. The entire wing is vectoring on our position. Fifteen seconds out."

"Good," Richards responded. "All eyes are

upon us. If we're lucky, we'll buy everyone else more time."

TO THE north of Manhattan and the city proper, a group of ships converged on a location in Westchester County, seeking another individual who might well hold the gem.

At the Jean Grey School for Gifted Youngsters, the mutants known as the X-Men—including the recently returned Wolverine—fought to defend their own headquarters. The alien aggressors had anticipated strong resistance and prepared for it. They were led by Corvus Glaive and the towering blue-skinned female omnipath called Supergiant.

"Forward!" Glaive bellowed, gesturing with a blade capable of cutting on the atomic scale. "Find the stone! Find the one who holds it." As the defenders piled out of the school and approached, he added, "Look, Supergiant—heavy game."

"Fodder," the giantess replied as she scanned their minds. "An eternal man, an elemental, some minor players with mental acuity. No, the only real danger is the omega-level mutates." She waved one black-clad hand. "I will take the mind of the megamorph now, and make it my own."

Iceman let out a scream of agony.

"There. Much better. *Useful.*"

Abruptly the X-Men were engulfed in a glacier. Those who slipped past the assault were taken down by invaders with a wide variety of weapons. Wolverine was speared and lifted into the air, his blood spraying everywhere.

"Bravado is good," Corvus Glaive said. "All great warriors are marked by it… and then one day, it puts them into their graves." He thrust downward, pinning his victim to the ground. "This is that day, mutant."

In a matter of moments, the mutants were defeated.

IN MANHATTAN'S Greenwich Village, a single ship dropped down, landing gently on Bleecker Street. It was a smaller vessel and only carried one occupant. He was called the Ebony Maw, and he had exactly one goal: to find the Earth's Sorcerer Supreme and wrest information from the man who claimed to be a master of the mystic arts.

The alien made his way past wards created to resist any assault as if they were empty air. Upon entering his target's lair, he found only one ineffectual defender and quickly bound him.

In the center of the sanctum, he located Doctor Strange, floating cross-legged above the floor and unaware of the intruder. Ebony Maw stared at the man and smiled gently.

"Everyone has limits." He spoke softly as his hands caressed the physical form of the Sorcerer Supreme. "An end to what they are." Around them eldritch energies swirled. "I, for instance, operate in information gathering. I gain influence. I seed discord.

I can use these tools in many ways. I cannot, however, merely tear into a man's mind and simply take what is there. Instead I must use my words to see what makes a man strong... or humbles him. I have to rely only on my words, but, oh, what words they are.

"Sweet whispers of secret fears."

He spoke, and there was an influence that wormed its way through Strange's defenses. There was a rhythm to the words, a power to them that could not be denied. As Ebony Maw tilted back the sorcerer's head, Strange seemed to become aware for the first time that he was under assault.

"Doouhhhh..."

Ebony Maw smiled. "Go on, Doctor. Tell the Ebony Maw all the mysteries you have hidden in your head."

"I don't know," Strange said. "I don't know where the gem is hidden."

Wide, glowing eyes examined the man's face. The Ebony Maw tightened his grip. "Curse the gem, Doctor," he hissed. "A fool's quest if ever there was one. I seek different information. I want *what Thanos truly wants.*"

He leaned in closer and spoke softly. "Where is the boy?"

Doctor Strange fought not to answer.

"VICTORY, BROTHER. Look at how they run," Queen Shuri said with enthusiasm. "When will the world learn that Wakanda is no easy meal?"

Not the world… at least not this time, T'Challa mused, but he did not argue the point. The forces of Thanos retreated from Wakanda. The Black Dwarf stalked back to his ship, his head held low, and his warriors went with him. Around the Panthers, the Dora Milaje cheered, raising their spears and modern weapons alike.

"We were fortunate, my queen," T'Challa said, standing at her side. "Much more fighting with that monster and he might have beaten me. As it is, I think my hand is broken."

"Well, it was worth it," she replied. "It always is when you see your enemies fleeing from you." The alien vessels lifted off, and quickly receded in the sky.

"They weren't expecting this sort of resistance, Shuri," he countered. "If they had been, they would have brought a bigger army. You heard him. He was looking for something. Best that we prepare for their return."

Shuri harrumphed. "I know nothing of a gem, T'Challa, but don't doubt the lesson of the whip, brother. We beat them badly, and defeat is the oldest form of education. What reason would they have to return?"

He considered telling her about the Illuminati and the Infinity Gems. T'Challa loved his sister, but felt it best if she did not know about the burden of power that existed on that level.

The Infinity Gems were destroyed.

That was enough. For now.

PROXIMA MIDNIGHT looked down at Namor and repressed a desire to smile. He bowed before her, and so too did several of the other Atlanteans capable of fighting back.

"You have taken a knee," the victor said. "You have surrendered, and so Atlantis is spared. I have accepted your allegiance in exchange for what you have promised. Are we agreed?"

"My liege, you cannot do this." One of the blue-skinned women who bowed beside the prince looked toward Namor and spoke in a tongue Proxima could not understand. "While there is one Atlantean who would fight back, we must—"

He did not even look at her as he replied. "Be silent, Andromeda." His voice was heavy with regret, but he did not stop. "It is done, Proxima. You have my word."

"Excellent," she replied, and now she did smile. "Now, where is the gem?" She leaned closer. "Where do I send all the armies of my Lord Thanos?"

Namor did not smile.

"A place called Wakanda," he replied. "You seek a man called the Black Panther."

ATTILAN FLOATED above New York and above the battle for the world. The forces that descended did not attack the floating city. The barrier around the place might well have been all the deterrent they needed, or perhaps the invading armies simply believed that what they sought was not there.

Maximus strutted through the king's throne room and smiled. There were times when Black Bolt felt a cold hatred toward the man, no matter how much he loved his brother.

The human world was falling.

Their governments were failing.

The forces attacking the world were familiar enough. These were the followers of Thanos, and he knew what they did not. That they had reason to seek the Inhumans among the humans in the world. Those reasons, however, could not be tolerated.

"The world is on fire, Black Bolt," Maximus said. "Tick. Tock. One more small step and it's off the ledge we go. Just one… small… step."

He could not ignore Maximus' words. Much as he wanted to, the man was right. Black Bolt nodded, just to shut his brother up, but the gesture only made the madman more eager to speak, and to gloat. He so loved it when he was right.

"Time to speak, as it were, brother," Maximus continued. "Time for secrets to be revealed to your secret society. To let them know why all of this is happening. Time to use the machine—and time for plans within greater plans to be set in motion."

Black Bolt held up his hand and slowly made a fist. It was a simple thing to contact the others. Technological wonders were nearly commonplace among them, and even if they weren't, the Sorcerer

Supreme would have come up with something.

The boy would need to be protected. None of his people could be harmed, not if he were true to his nature as a king. Still, sometimes a king must share secrets, and this one had already been stolen from his sleeping mind.

A secret no more, then.

It was time.

He opened the fist and tapped the palm. With a *tink*, a light appeared in his hand. He held it up for Maximus to see.

"Oh, brother," the madman said. "This is going to be so much fun." He was gloating.

Black Bolt hated that tone in his brother's voice.

CHAPTER 13

AS THE WORLD BURNS

NOMAD was a relatively useless planet stuck in a solar system of remarkably little note. At least that was how Kl'rt saw it. Yet it was the location of the Citadel of the Galactic Council. It was neutral territory, where all could meet on equal footing. At least that was what the Shi'ar claimed.

In the last two days, Warlord Kl'rt had managed the impossible. He had unified the warring factions of the once-great Skrull Empire. He did not rule over them, but for the moment they would listen to him. There was a greater enemy to face, an army that had already slaughtered over two hundred billion Skrulls. The outpost Hy'lt Minor had been destroyed only a day before.

That had been the tipping point. Finally the

other Skrull warlords listened when he spoke. For the moment their differences were deemed insignificant. They needed a leader, and Kl'rt won by dint of his extraordinary abilities.

Among the Skrulls he was a warrior of great renown who from time to time brought shame to his people, and at other times inspired great glory. Among the people of Earth—where he had spent far too much of his time and where he had been humiliated more than once—he was called the Super-Skrull.

As a race, the Skrulls possessed inherent shape-shifting talents. This enabled them to infiltrate civilizations entirely undetected and inspired a great deal of paranoia among those populations. The first time the humans on Earth repelled a Skrull contingent, they were led by the superhuman team known as the Fantastic Four.

In an effort to make certain that never happened again, Kl'rt was granted the same powers as all four members of that team. He was powerful indeed, and he used those powers to attain a position of leadership. Someone warred with his people, and he would not leave control of the Skrull Empire in the hands of a lesser warrior.

When he landed on Nomad, Kl'rt was accompanied by a faction of warlords who came to represent the fractured empire. The gray-skinned creature that met them was diminutive, but no one among the Skrull took that as a sign of weakness. Shape-changers could not be fooled by appearance.

He explained their reason for coming, and the creature moved ahead of them, leading the way to the war council's chambers.

"The Warlord Kl'rt, representing the various factions of the Skrull Territories, formally asks for admittance to this council of war." The gray-skinned speaker gestured toward him.

As it did, Kl'rt looked over the gathering and nodded his approval. If they were to organize a force that would oppose a galactic invader, these were the peoples who needed to be there.

"I was under the impression that a state of civil war existed among the different factions of your people, Warlord Kl'rt." The man who spoke was the leader of the Shi'ar. He went by a dozen different names, but most people knew him as the Gladiator. He was easily one of the most physically powerful beings in the galaxy. He was also, as far as Kl'rt was concerned, the best leader the Shi'ar had been granted in decades. "Have they truly unified under your rule?" Gladiator continued. "Do you claim to represent them all?"

The Skrull warlord nodded. "I represent all but Warlord Dm'yr. He sacrificed himself and many of his people in enabling us to reach you."

J'son, the pink-skinned king of Spartax, stood and moved forward. He was a well-respected leader. Spartax was more peaceful-minded than many of the Shi'ar cultures, but they did not hide when combat became a necessity.

"It's enough for me," J'son said. "We need swords.

We need blades, sharp ones, thirsty for Builder blood, and I welcome you as an equal. Sit. Join this council. If you will fight, I will vouch for you."

Though not overly fond of diplomacy, Kl'rt nodded and took a seat next to a creature called Annihilus. They had fought against each other only a few months earlier, and now the loathsome insectoid was a welcome member of the war council.

How desperate we must all be, Kl'rt thought, but he kept his tongue. "Thank you, King J'son of Spartax," he said aloud. "The Spartax Empire is led by a practical man. Always an asset in times of war."

He could *feel* Annihilus watching him as he spoke.

The Kree Supreme Intelligence was present via holographic projection. An organic supercomputer holding the sum total of the empire's knowledge, it was accompanied in the flesh by Ronan the Accuser, their primary enforcer of the law. When the Intelligence spoke, it was all Kl'rt could do to avoid sneering. The Kree were the Skrulls' eternal enemies—the war between the two species ran back for thousands of years. Now, for the present, they too were allies.

"Swords are needed, indeed," the Intelligence said. "As are ships, as are soldiers. Which we Kree count in the tens of millions, and is there any fighting force in the universe more elite than Ronan and his Accuser Corps?"

Ronan stood before the holographic image and stared straight ahead with the sort of military discipline the Skrulls had always admired, even when they fought against the blue-skinned bastards. If old grudges were enough to stop the alliance, however, he'd have killed every last person in the room, excluding perhaps only J'son.

Gladiator leaned forward and looked toward the Supreme Intelligence's visage. The creature could not be present—it could not be moved from Hala, the homeworld of the Kree. Its massive form was the culmination of hundreds of generations of history and artificial intelligence combined. The Kree chose to be ruled by the memories of the past. They chose to let a machine think for them.

They were fools, but they were fools with a massive army.

Gladiator spoke. "Yes, and I am here on behalf of the Shi'ar Imperial Guard—yet why only speak of them when there are so many other worthy warriors who have joined our cause?" He gestured toward a creature that seemed as much insectoid as reptile, with a narrow form and too many teeth and claws for anything but a nightmare. "The living army of the Brood, for example, grows more formidable with each passing year."

He indicated Annihilus in his exoskeletal armor. "We have all seen what havoc the Annihilation Wave of the Negative Zone can cause when unleashed." Then he pointed again to a contingent that had come from the Earth—the group known as the Avengers. Once again, Kl'rt managed to refrain from sneering.

They were allies.

For now.

"To say nothing of the hundreds of thousands of planets gathered together with armies of differing sizes, here to represent their interests as well as our own. We are united, all of us, to oppose a threat that is truly universal in scope. These Builders must be stopped before they destroy all of our planets, all of our lives."

There were nods and mutterings of agreement—and if any disagreed, they kept their silence. Stepping to the center of the assemblage, Kl'rt revealed a hologram of his own.

"This is footage of our encounter with the Builders," he said. "As you can see, Warlord Dm'yr was able to wipe out the advance fleet by catching them in the blast radius of an exploding sun." One-eyed Dm'yr had indeed lured the enemy close, shedding his own blood to distract them. Without a moment's hesitation, he incinerated them—along with his own forces.

Truly, he had been a warrior among warriors.

"The majority of these bastards are still out of our reach, and coming this way," Kl'rt said grimly. "But they can be beaten. They can be killed."

"Yes, but you surprised them," J'son responded. "Projections of all available intelligence suggest a low probability of success if we have a head-to-head encounter." He pulled at the tip of his beard. "What we need… is another trap."

"Yesssss," the Supreme Intelligence responded. "There is a location. Accessing intelligence archives.

The Konn-Dar encounter from one of the Kree-Shi'ar conflicts."

"The location lies in the projected path of the Builder fleet," Ronan the Accuser said. The man was a behemoth, massive even by Kree standards. His blue skin was dark, his eyes were lighter, and the armor he wore was far from ceremonial. It bore the scars of hundreds of conflicts. He looked toward the leader of the Shi'ar Empire. "Majestor Gladiator, do you remember this battle?"

Gladiator peered at the man who had led armies against his people.

"I do. The Corridor."

"What is this 'corridor'?" Kl'rt didn't like being left in the dark.

Gladiator turned to look his way. "There is a gravitational singularity, and a pair of massive asteroid belts. The gravity waves, the electromagnetic fluctuations, and the density of the belt make it hard for anyone to see what is waiting just ahead of them."

Kl'rt understood.

A trap, indeed.

CHAPTER 14

FEINT, PARRY AND LUNGE

"I hate waiting."

Bruce Banner spoke mostly to make conversation. They'd been in the same location, hidden against the side of an asteroid and in a low-power mode, for more than five hours. The Builder armada—or at least one branch of it—was heading directly for them.

I suppose they might have left me behind, he thought without saying it. After his most recent "Hulk-out," he'd awakened in a S.H.I.E.L.D. containment unit, naked and alone. That they trusted him enough to bring him along was a testament to how badly they needed all their heavy hitters. He still questioned the logic of the decision.

The view was spectacular. In the distance, a great black orb pulled in the energies and gases and matter from this universe and swallowed it hungrily. Vast swirls of cosmic debris and thousands of chunks of rock from the asteroid belt were waiting their turn to be consumed. It was the sort of image that most people from Earth would only ever see rendered in CGI. The power of the view was not lost on the scientist.

The Corridor was a debris-free pathway between the remains of two shattered planets. The quincruiser hid in one of the asteroid fields, along with many ships of the allied fleet. Many more waited in the asteroid belt on the other side.

Steve Rogers was dressed in his full Captain America regalia, augmented by an armored environmental spacesuit and helmet, as with all of the people on the ship.

"Well, Bruce, I promise you the fight will be here soon enough, and you'll wish you were still waiting." Sometimes the man took everything too literally. Then again, given Banner's tendency to change into a thousand pounds of gamma-fueled rage monster, keeping him calm was a good idea.

Shang-Chi sat next to Captain America. "Expectation of disaster is a poor way to plan for success, Captain."

"Not at all." Cap shook his head. "Preparation for the potential is an important part of any planning."

Bruce agreed. "Shang, the plan is to let the enemy fleet maneuver themselves between us and the black hole," he said. "By giving them no place to run, we essentially force them to fight back, probably to the death. Today's combat forecast is sketchy at best, with a better-than-good chance of calamity."

Shang-Chi looked over his shoulder. "It is your optimism that I admire most," he said. Bruce was pretty sure that was meant as a joke, and started to say as much.

Shang-Chi motioned for silence. "Just got the heads-up," he announced. "We are ready to engage the enemy."

Cap nodded. "Quincruiser two," he said into the comm. "Carol, did you pick that up?"

"Got it. Fleet's entered the kill zone," Captain Marvel answered, her voice remarkably calm. "We're just waiting for the signal. Everyone get ready."

Bruce took a few deep breaths to make sure he stayed calm, as well. "Everyone" meant the folks aboard the quincruiser and other spacecraft, as well as those who didn't need them for combat in airless space. The Hulk could withstand terrifying amounts of physical damage, but he still needed to breathe; Hyperion and several others did not. Falcon, who was as susceptible to the vacuum of space as Banner was, wore a specially developed suit that allowed him his full flight capabilities in the void.

Just outside of the asteroid field, he could see motion as the enemy ships came within visual range. Then off to the right—starboard, Banner supposed—there was a bright flash, launched as planned by Commander Jorr of the Kree forces.

"There's the signal," Cap said. "Let's go."

Suddenly the asteroid field was abuzz with activity as stationary spacecraft burst into motion. All of them had the same target: the Builder fleet, the center of which had reached the planned coordinates. Flashes appeared—a few at first, then a multitude. In an instant chaos erupted, and everywhere they looked their field of vision was filled with combat. Their ship shook alarmingly as they took a hit, then another, but their shields held.

"Heavy fire from both sides, Captain." Shang-Chi spoke with amazing calm. Bruce could feel his heart hammering and forced himself to relax as much as possible. A vessel exploded nearby, and the white-hot flash left a momentary imprint on his vision. That faded as shards of the doomed craft flew past their view port. Another vessel shot into the gap, its weapons blazing. The smaller figures of individual combatants dodged and wove around—and sometimes *through*—the warships. Eye-beams flashed, piercing combatant ships with needle-like accuracy.

"Keep pushing," Cap said. "The plan is to split their fleet, if possible. The command vessels will let us know if—"

"Allied armada," Ronan the Accuser's voice came through the comm-link. "Based on the movement of the ships within the Builder fleet, the Supremor has calculated a ninety percent chance that the command vessel is at the coordinates we are sending you. Retask all operations. Reprioritize your objectives. Destroy that vessel."

In the live video feed, the flashes of contact continued throughout the conflict, but a greater concentration appeared in one particular location—the coordinates Ronan had supplied. Banner saw Thor and Hyperion and a dozen alien life-forms he'd never met before turn and head for the ship being targeted.

Hyperion hit it first. He was little more than a speck in the distance, but he moved through the void of space at a speed the naked eye could barely follow. He struck the front of the command vessel, leaving a hole the size of a transit bus. It couldn't have been two seconds later that he exploded out of the rear of the ship, taking massive sections of the interior with him.

By the time he'd finished his run, several Destroyer-class vessels and multiple small forms had cut loose with attacks of their own. Thor's lightning arced through space and hit the ship in a dozen places, each blast melting metal and blackening the hull. Smasher employed beams that cut from her goggles and ripped a line along the hull, easily shattering the ship's defensive shields. Several others followed after her, members of the Imperial Guard who worked with her in a flawless example of teamwork.

It only took seconds for the powerful attack to destroy the command vessel. It went up in a burst of flames that were quickly smothered by the vacuum of space. Cheers came over the comms from a dozen ships.

Bruce felt a grim smile coming on. If this was the best the enemy could do, they'd win this conflict easily—and his other would never have to come out and play cleanup. He preferred it that way.

His smile vanished when the rest of the ships dropped their cloaks.

"Mother of God!"

Adrenaline kicked in, and he forced himself to calm down. There were so many ships. So many more than they'd expected or believed possible, and these vessels were massive, dwarfing the vast majority of the ships in their fleet.

"Like fish in a barrel." Bruce was unaware he was speaking. It wasn't a compliment—merely an observation. His stomach seethed with nervous energy. There was nothing good about the situation.

Peace. Bruce wanted peace. Even when he'd created the first gamma bomb, the plan was to use it to stop people from attempting another war.

The void of space shifted. The stars, the great vista of the event horizon, the asteroids—all disappeared, suddenly lost behind the vast ships that manifested from nowhere as if pulled from a magician's hat.

Even as the Builder ships seemed to pop out of nowhere, they opened fire, attacking every enemy vessel they could put in their sights, firing volleys of weapons that would have shamed any military he'd ever known. Streaks of light, massive explosions, balls of energy and fire bloomed along the sides of allied ships. People—oh, so many people—died in volley after volley of enemy fire.

The heavens bled fire and the mortal remains of thousands. What had been cheering was replaced by the screams of the dying.

Bruce swallowed hard and forced himself to take deep breaths. Still his blood sang in his body and the world threatened to take on a green tinge he knew all too well.

Over the comm-link, the Supreme Intelligence of the Kree spoke. "Probability of survival approaching zero if you do not withdraw from this theater. Close to thirty-three percent of the fleet has been lost or severely damaged in less than a minute."

"Sound the retreat. Now!" Ronan's voice was calm but loud. "Run!" As he spoke, the Kree ships began to veer away. The Skrulls followed seconds later, and the Shi'ar called for a tactical withdrawal. Amid a continuous series of explosions, the allied fleet broke apart and scattered. Hundreds of ships retreated even as dozens were destroyed.

The Builders continued firing.

Bruce took in great gasps of air and closed his eyes, focusing on staying calm. Several impacts struck near the quincruiser, which shivered and shuddered as pieces of debris crashed into shields, and then into the body of the ship itself. Stark built amazing weapons and armor, but everything had its limits.

Bruce's heart sang and screamed. It was becoming a given that he'd be changing. When hurled into the vacuum, would the helmet expand enough to protect him? Or would this be the thing that finally ended his nightmarish dual existence?

"We're fine, Bruce," Cap said. "Deep breaths. Nothing to worry about." Steve's voice was calming, despite the situation. True to his word, the shields held. Cap spoke into the comm.

"Carol, we've taken several hits, but we're still intact. Not sure if we can get clear unaided without Manifold jumping us straight to the rendezvous site." He paused, then added, "Can you get clear?"

"We're fine, Cap. I'm a better pilot than you on my worst day." That was true enough. She was a trained fighter pilot, whereas Cap had learned on the job as a member of the Avengers and had substantially fewer flight hours logged. "We've got full power and we're flying free, but the fight took us closer to the singularity than I'd like. Jump—we'll catch up."

Shang-Chi looked at the readings. "We might not make it without an assist, Captain."

Cap looked aft. "Okay, Eden—you're on. Get us out of here."

From the back of the ship, Eden called out, "I'm working on it."

"Grab any friendlies you can."

"As if you have to ask."

Even as he spoke, Bruce saw Hyperion vanish from the vacuum, followed by Thor and several others he could not recognize amid the chaos. The Shi'ar cruiser began to give off spikes of energy. Before anyone could react, the vessel burst in a ball of fire.

Captain Marvel's quincruiser was caught in the blast.

Then the cruiser in which they flew was elsewhere.

IN AN instant, they were back at the Nomad station—Eden had taken them to a location he knew.

Captain America turned in his seat and looked toward Banner. The thin scientist had a death grip on the armrests of his seat. His breathing was hard, but steady. There was a tinge of green to his skin that had nothing to do with nature, but it was fading away.

"We lost them, Cap." Bruce spoke calmly, considering the circumstances. "Captain Marvel, Hawkeye, Cannonball, Sunspot... I don't know who else."

Cap frowned. "Captain Universe, still in a coma. Abyss. Nightmask. Starbrand." So many who might be dead, but he couldn't simply accept that. "That's all of them. And don't expect that they're dead. They've been through worse."

Shang-Chi spoke softly. "Perhaps not in the void of space."

"Not until I see a body," Cap countered. "Only then do I consider death as an option. I learned that the hard way, Shang." The man nodded his head and said nothing more.

STEVE ROGERS remained silent in his seat for what seemed like an eternity, but likely had been only a few hours. He'd seen potential flaws in the plan from the beginning, but had never expected anything on the scale of the ruse they'd just encountered. He'd never expected a fleet that size. It was unsettling.

He looked to Banner again and saw that the man had calmed himself. All traces of green were gone. For that he was grateful.

Spider-Woman walked calmly from the back of the cruiser.

"Where are we headed?" She was holding herself together remarkably well—Cap was impressed. Jessica Drew had spent a long time as a prisoner of the Skrulls, and he knew working with them now had to be eating at her. He had been in a similar situation, replaced by a Skrull doppelganger and kept prisoner, but for a much shorter time than she had experienced.

"We are to head for the Shi'ar agricultural world of Whaan Prime," Shang-Chi said. "We'll meet with the rest of the fleet. The natives have been told to be prepared to handle the massive injuries and casualties we have accrued."

CHAPTER 15

TRIBUTE

THERE were hundreds of ships raining down into Earth's atmosphere. At the Peak, the invaders tried to take the space station from S.W.O.R.D. command.

The invaders spent all of ten minutes in control of the station before S.W.O.R.D. agents took it back. That was just long enough for the intruders to set up a subspace beacon that would call the rest of their forces to the planet below.

Nation after nation fell with unsettling ease.

o———o

FROM ATTILAN, Black Bolt summoned the Illuminati.

Prince Namor of Atlantis had already surrendered. Doctor Strange's whereabouts, always enigmatic, remained unknown.

Corvus Glaive and Supergiant were sent to locate the blue-furred Beast in upstate New York. They met a great deal of resistance from the X-Men, but the end result was inevitable. They had numbers on their side, and they did not care how many of their troops fell fighting for Thanos' glory.

Wakanda's defenders repelled the first attack on that African nation, and New York withstood the worst of the offensives thanks in large part to the weapons employed by Reed Richards and Tony Stark from Avengers Tower.

The summons sent out, Black Bolt waited and looked to the stars. As a result, he was among the first to see the massive vessel come down and hover above his city, just out of range of the most powerful weapons. The ship that dropped from the larger vessel was a speck in comparison, but closer inspection revealed it was large enough to carry an alarming number of troops.

The ship landed without incident in a broad courtyard and discharged its contents. Black Bolt recognized the creatures. These were of a kind with the thing that had invaded his bedchamber—indeed, the chambers of his mind. The thing had been tough enough to endure incredible damage, and now there were a dozen of the nightmares moving across the landing field and marching toward his throne room. Behind them strode armored aliens who looked more humanlike, led by a robed figure carrying a large, wicked blade.

Black Bolt waited for them, and his family stood with him. Karnak, who could find any physical weakness in a foe, assessed the gathered intruders. Medusa, his wife, stood at his right hand, where she so rightly belonged. They were still not comfortable in their disagreement, but she spoke for him on all matters.

Maximus stood on his left; next to him were Gorgon, the green-scaled water breather Triton, Crystal, and the massive canine Lockjaw. Around them gathered a hundred guards, all prepared to fight and even die if he commanded it.

He had no intention of commanding anything of the sort.

At least forty armored guards moved with the nightmare creatures. They appeared to be of different species. Some were humanoid; others were not. The creature carrying the massive weapon was draped in a cloak of funereal black. His face was pale gray, and his teeth were large and predatory. He smiled as he walked, but the expression carried no joy. Finally he stopped before the throne and looked around.

"Speak." Medusa's command was not a request.

The creature continued scanning the room, glancing everywhere but at Black Bolt. The insult was obvious.

"I am Corvus Glaive, and I am here on behalf of my master," he said. "I seek a king!" He gestured around the chamber. "Is there a king here? I hear stories of a great Inhuman king, but I look around and cannot seem to find one." His wicked smile grew wider still. "I ask, for perhaps he is a king of small stature. A tiny king of a small, irrelevant kingdom."

Maximus spoke. "Building things to last ages does not seem a small thing to me," he said. "Attilan stands while the world below crumbles."

When Medusa spoke again, her voice carried an air of authority and confidence that well suited a queen.

"My husband, Black Bolt, is king. What are you?"

"I am a servant of my master, Thanos—a destroyer of worlds. A *breaker* of kings." Corvus Glaive held out his blade in a mockingly formal salute. "I am one of the five—Corvus Glaive, a member of the Cull Obsidian, the Midnight Slaughter."

Maximus yawned and crossed his arms. The gesture was not lost on Black Bolt or on the grinning beast before them. The smile faltered for an instant. He seemed disconcerted that no one cowered before him.

"What do you and your Cull Obsidian want, Corvus Glaive?" Medusa asked.

"Thanos named his generals in that way," Glaive said. "We prefer the Black Order. It is less... foreboding. Our master allows us *some* indulgences."

Medusa waved away his speech.

"Why are you here?" she demanded.

"You have seen what we have done to this world," he answered. "It is a purge, a gauntlet. We test the mettle of the people with a cleansing fire to separate the weak from the strong." He waved to one side with a hand that boasted three grotesquely thin fingers ending in wicked claws. "It is what we do—it is our purpose.

"We kill."

Glaive pointed at Black Bolt.

Lockjaw let out a low growl of warning.

"So it is no small miracle that Thanos sent me for another reason," the creature of the Black Order continued. "I am to deliver a message to the Inhuman king. Thanos knows what you are hiding. He knows your secret. This knowledge has value, the result of which is influence. My master… has demands!"

"I have a warning for you, Corvus Glaive," Medusa said, her living hair whipping around her head like a nest of angry crimson serpents. "People have come before this throne many times with demands. It has often cost them their lives."

Corvus Glaive laughed, and Black Bolt frowned. Few took the threats of the Inhumans so lightly.

"I wonder, when you correct your children, do you threaten them with candy if they misbehave?" Glaive's grin grew wider still, baring heavy fangs and dark gray gums.

"Excuse me?" Medusa replied.

Even Maximus seemed confused by the words.

"You cannot threaten someone with what they want." With those words, Glaive gestured—and the slaughter began. As one, his own soldiers—the forty men in armor—lifted their swords and drove the blades through their own throats. Glaive continued to smile as the honor guard died around him. When it was done, only the nightmare creatures and Thanos' general remained standing. The blood of his soldiers gathered in a large black pool that spread as they bled out.

Black Bolt did not move, though his fist was clenched so tightly it shook. Life was a sacred thing, a valued thing, not to be tossed aside so casually.

"I am one of the five. I do not frighten," Glaive said, his expression grim, pointing again with his ornate blade. "We are servants of Thanos. We embrace death. Yes, you could attempt to kill me—yet even if you could manage that feat, another would take my place with the same demands. My master will get whatever he desires."

"And what is that?" Medusa said.

"So very little, my queen. A pittance, really. A portion." He paused a moment and then smiled again. "A tribute." His eyes were red embers in their sockets, and they seemed to glow more brightly at that moment.

"Speak plainly, monster," Medusa said.

"The tribute is a show of acquiescence." Glaive's insufferable smile grew even broader. "Lord Thanos demands an offering of all Inhumans between the standard ages of sixteen and twenty-two."

"And what are they supposed to offer?"

"Only their heads," he replied. "Their families can have what remains."

"You would have us kill our children to appease your master?" Her composure gone, Medusa raised her fists, and her tresses whipped around more violently than ever. "What madness is this?"

"It's like Herod," Maximus said, showing greater calm. "With the Christ, in the ancient times and the human holy books."

"No!" The smile was gone from Corvus Glaive, and he showed his teeth in a snarl of barely repressed rage. "Like Thanos of Titan in the *now*. Your people may die a little, or die a lot. The choice is yours—you have one day." He spun on his heel and walked out through the unbelievably large pool of blood. The nightmare creatures dropped down and followed him, moving like hounds with bared fangs and snapping jaws.

Black Bolt watched the creature go.

CHAPTER 16

PYRRHIC VICTORY

IN orbit around the planet Whaan Prime, the massive flagship of the Shi'ar Empire accepted a request to board.

The much smaller quincruiser limped onboard the *Lilandra* before its engines gave their last gasp. It was a close thing.

Isabel Kane—the first Earthling ever to become a member of the Shi'ar Imperial Guard—was there to meet the Avengers. Captain America nodded to her.

"The quincruiser's done, Smasher," he said. With him stood Thor, Bruce Banner, and Spider-Woman. "The systems are fried, the drive's given out, and we barely got here in one piece. Permission to come aboard?"

Smasher smiled briefly. "Gladiator said all courtesies were to be extended, Cap, so welcome aboard the Shi'ar flagship *Lilandra*." They stepped across the threshold, followed by Manifold, Black Widow, and Shang-Chi.

"Any news on the other Avengers?" Cap asked.

Kane shook her head. "No, but they might have vectored out with the Brood or the Spartax."

Spider-Woman shook her head and muttered, "Long as it wasn't the Skrulls." Cap shot her a look, and she nodded.

"The truth is," Smasher continued, "if Captain Marvel's carrier doesn't show up here, we won't know until we reach the secondary staging point. Right after the fleet retreated, the Shi'ar network, the Kree omnicast, and every other wideband communication system went dark. We don't want to advertise anything to the Builders, and we don't know enough about their abilities."

"So we're blind and deaf," Cap said. "You got any good news, Izzy?"

"Well… I think I'm falling in love with someone." She was silent, waiting for his reaction, wondering if he would disapprove. But his expression didn't really change.

"That's some timing, kiddo," Cap remarked.

She led them toward the ship's command center. Gladiator sat in a ceremonial throne and looked roughly as comfortable with his position as a barefoot man dancing on broken glass. He was the ruler of the once-fragmented empire not because he had sought the position, but because the responsibility had been placed on his shoulders. His birth name was Kallark, his skin had a violet-gray hue, and his hair formed a Mohawk. Cap didn't know a lot about his people— only that most of them were gone, destroyed.

As they approached the throne, the Imperial Guard member called Oracle was speaking with him in an urgent tone.

"Majestor, I must insist… we cannot wait any longer." She stood at his right hand. "We need to make for Behemoth and the fleet staging area. The sooner we reassemble the council, the sooner we can strike back."

Gladiator turned to the man at his left hand—the leader of the Imperial Guard since Kallark had been appointed Majestor.

"Mentor?"

"What Oracle is saying has merit," Mentor said in soft tones, "but we chose this rendezvous point for a reason. This farming colony is of no strategic value and far enough away from the path of the Builders that we felt it a safe—" Abruptly he was interrupted by a crewmember who stood at a holographic display.

"Proximity alert!" the man said. "Majestor, we have incoming vessels arriving at the inner system. A Spartax light frigate with four unknown vessels in pursuit. They look to be Builder vessels." He kept a tight view on what each of the ships was doing. "The frigate has a failing reactor and is bleeding radiation. They aren't going to make it."

Oracle reacted quickly. "Send out word to the

other ships," she said. "Have them spool up their drives and prepare to jump."

Mentor shook his head. "We currently have seven ships unable to make the jump. We could feint an attack—draw them off, and mount a rescue mission."

"No."

The Majestor shook his head and pushed himself up from the throne. "They want to make us scatter. They want us to run so they can chase us down. I will not allow that. I will not be beaten again this day." He took in a deep breath, and then called out, "Warriors of the Shi'ar! Do you see how they hound us? How they hope to hunt us to extinction?" He drew up to his full height. "Well, I am no longer in the mood for running." He paced across the floor of the command center. "You know me as Gladiator, Superguardian, Majestor of the Empire… but soon you will call me *victor*, because I will win here today, or die in the effort. Who will join me?"

A chant arose, growing louder by the moment.

"Majestor! Majestor! Majestor!"

"Are there warriors here who would fight alongside me?" Gladiator asked, looking to his visitors. Smasher turned to one in particular.

Bruce Banner looked back. "You guys have those devices that let you fly in the vacuum without dying?"

"Flight patches. Yeah," Smasher said.

"I'm going to need one."

"Are you saying you want to fight the Builders?"

"No. I'm saying the Hulk wants out, and it would

be best if he was directed toward the enemy as soon as possible."

"I'll get right on that."

It took her two minutes to get what he requested. By then most of the Avengers capable of flying through the void had already joined the Imperial Guard outside of the ship.

EX NIHILO stood at a large port alongside Mentor and a Shi'ar technician, watching the carnage that took place outside the vessel.

"Your Gladiator said I was not to join them."

"I'm sure you can understand the Majestor's caution, Ex Nihilo," Mentor responded. "These cursed Builders created you, did they not?"

"And who do you think made you?" Ex Nihilo replied. "Those are gods you battle out there."

"We have all heard your stories, Ex Nihilo," Mentor said. "How your Builders and you Gardeners traveled from world to world as agents of evolution, how you held us in your hand and gave us a push where you saw fit. How you made us so much more than we were. Well, look what we have become.

"Your kind may have been as gods once," he continued, "but we no longer need you or want you."

Gladiator, Hyperion, and Thor flew together, their bodies plowing through a ship and destroying it. Heat flashed from Gladiator's eyes, and Hyperion sent similar energies from his own. Two enemy ships exploded in flames and shards of debris. Closer in, the Falcon and Captain America took on the Alephs in hand-to-hand combat.

"We have new gods now," Mentor said.

The Hulk came into view and leapt toward the battle. The patch worked as it was meant to, and he hurtled toward his target. Once he reached the vessel, his massive hands tore into the hull and easily ripped it open. Smasher followed after him and used his breach as her doorway into the enemy's craft. The Hulk continued to his next target, barreling through a vessel that exploded into utter ruin.

One by one the enemy ships were destroyed.

"Sharra and K'ythri be praised," the Shi'ar technician said. "We have won."

"Perhaps." Ex Nihilo pointed. "Look there, breaking the shadow of the planet. It's not just Alephs you face today, but my kind, as well. Ex Nihili. Life itself."

AS THE war raged above, an Aleph and Jerran Ko, the Gardener to which it had given birth, landed on the planet. Whaan Prime was already fertile. In all of their time traveling together, the golden-skinned Jerran Ko had never seen a planet as lush and green.

"Look at this—a planet of sustenance." he said. "A garden! Do you believe in an afterlife, Aleph?"

"DECLARATIVE: MY SHARED CODE CONTINUES ON IN THE OTHER ALEPHS. THE CODE IS ETERNAL."

"Well, when I die I will be gone forever," Jerran Ko said. "And it seems that in death, our masters make a mockery of all I have done, and all that I am."

The robot looked to him. **"DECLARATIVE: TRIUMPH BEFORE ALL, JERRAN KO. COMPLETE YOUR MAKER'S COMMANDS. IN DEATH WE WOUND OUR ENEMIES."**

The Gardener sighed. "There was a time when the symbol on my chest meant life." He plucked some stalks of the golden grain among which he stood. "Record those words for your code, Aleph. Tell everyone that Jerran Ko said those were better days. It is a pity that they are now long gone."

As he spoke his body changed. The golden skin boiled with black pustules that soon covered his entire body. Those blisters ruptured and leaked darkness that poured upward into the air, into the atmosphere. The blackness flowed like a waterspout, up into the atmosphere. It began to spread across the planet's surface.

The Aleph stood with the Gardener throughout the entire process. It did not move. It did not speak. It merely witnessed the death of a world.

"NO! HE... he couldn't have." Standing with Mentor and the Shi'ar, Ex Nihilo looked on in horror.

Peering down at the planet, he had followed the debris trail from one of the ships that had plunged down into the atmosphere and crashed. Abruptly a wave of emotion washed over him, and he knew instinctively something profound had occurred below.

"Get everyone back here," he said. "You must sound a retreat. Something unthinkable has happened."

Mentor looked toward him and frowned. "What?"

"I am a Gardener," Ex Nihilo explained. "I carry both life and death within me. The Builders have decided to use foul death in the fight against your attempts. One of mine has killed himself, and in the process poisons the world below us. The planet is already dead, and much as I wish I could change that, I cannot."

Mentor moved over to a sensor array. "Speak to me. What am I looking for on the surface?"

"You are looking for death." Ex Nihilo watched him. "Entropy. Decay. Get as many people as you can off the planet. All too soon it will bear no signs of life."

Mentor looked carefully. "There is a growing patch of rot… decay. It's moving very fast."

"It will cover this planet in a matter of hours. Get all of the people you can to safety, or you will lose them all to this plague of darkness."

THE EVACUATION began immediately. Those who had been sent down to the medical facilities were brought back to their ships. Those living on the planet were gathered as quickly as could be managed. Those who wished to stay were convinced to leave when they saw footage of the devastation. Where plants and life had existed, death and rot spread rapidly as the black cloud moved through each area.

Less than a tenth of the population of Whaan Prime was spared. Hundreds of thousands escaped, but millions died.

The collected forces had destroyed the Builder ships. This was the allies' first victory. The taste was bitter, indeed.

CHAPTER 17

ILLUMINATION

AS each member of the Illuminati approached Attilan, it was with the greatest of stealth. The massive mothership of Thanos still hovered over the floating city.

When they arrived, they each were met by a member of the Inhuman royal family and escorted to the chamber where Black Bolt could speak without fear of causing harm. Upon entering the spherical chamber, they found themselves standing in a desolate, rocky tableau with deep rifts and floating boulders. They each heard the odd distortions of sound, and understood. Their voices—when they spoke—were flat echoes of how they normally sounded.

"What have you done, Black Bolt?" The Black Panther was direct and to the point. "Why have you summoned us here while the entire world is under siege?"

"Patience, T'Challa," Doctor Strange said. "There is always good reason when the Illuminati are summoned." His words betrayed an unnatural fatigue, their host thought.

"I think you already know," Black Bolt replied. "All of you have dealt with Thanos by now."

"We're still dealing with him," Iron Man replied, raising the mask on his armor, "so make this quick, please. Reed and I have more work to do."

"Earlier this day Thanos had his emissary deliver a message."

"To all of the Inhumans?" Reed asked.

"Or just to you?" Stark added.

"To me," Black Bolt replied. "The Mad Titan has demanded a tribute. I am to deliver him the heads of every Inhuman between the ages of sixteen and twenty-two." He took the time to look at each of the Illuminati as he spoke, wanting them to grasp the gravity of his words. Then he held up a small, pointed device about nine inches long. "As I will be delivering my response to his request in person, I asked you here to give you this."

"What is it?" Reed Richards frowned as he accepted the object.

"Records. The hidden archives of the Inhuman kings and queens. In there you will find what Thanos is looking for."

"But what you said about the tribute—" T'Challa began.

"The tribute is a lie. A convenient one Thanos is telling to cover up the truth. Though it would kill off a good percentage of my people—something Thanos likely would enjoy—he doesn't desire the death of every child of a certain age. He wants to ensure the death of a very specific Inhuman."

"Which one?" T'Challa asked.

"The one Thanos has come to Earth to kill," the Inhuman king said. "His son."

"I'm sorry," Tony Stark responded. "What did you say?"

"Thanos is looking for his son. He wants to kill him." Black Bolt paused, gathering his thoughts, then continued. "Centuries ago there was a fracturing of the royal family. Matters of honor and destiny caused blood ties to be severed. Kings and a queen were torn apart. Lost tribes of Inhumans scattered themselves across the Earth, and some across the stars. We have long possessed the technology.

"Some remained. In recent days we have been… seeking to unify our people." He studied each member of his gathered Illuminati to make certain they understood. "Years ago, light years from this planet, the descendants of one of the tribes ran afoul of Thanos and his minions. Dark things occurred in dark places, and an Inhuman woman returned to the Earth. She carried the seed of Thanos, and she bore a child.

"Now Thanos comes here to find that child, a child who since he was born has been concealed among the hidden tribes. I recently had an… encounter with one of Thanos' creatures. It caught me unawares, stole the information from me. At that time I did not know the name of the child—only that he existed. I think that knowledge alone has driven Thanos here, in search of his offspring."

"That's what's on this?" Richards held the data spike in his hand. "The information we need? Where to find his son?"

"That is the Terrigen Codex. Among the Inhumans it is known to contain all of the hidden knowledge of my house, Reed Richards. Please use it. Find the boy. Protect him."

"I understand," Richards said.

"You're not coming with us?" Stark said.

"No. I will remain, because Thanos will come here. He will demand knowledge that I still do not have. With the world as my witness, I will meet him and show him what it means to be an Inhuman." He lowered his head. They had worked together many times, and now he asked a favor of them. "You should go now. We cannot give in to the likes of Thanos."

Namor flinched, he noticed. *Curious.*

It was a negligible thing, but he saw it.

Doctor Strange gestured. "From here the way is twisted, but navigable," he said. "Gather around… we're going." Sparks like white lightning danced from his fingertips. There was a sudden intake of air, as if to fill a vacuum, and they were gone.

"Flash, and off they go." Maximus jumped down from his hiding place. He had been there all along.

Black Bolt had known—and he suspected the others had, as well. "That was foolish, brother… foolish, and unlike you."

It was strange to have his brother accuse him of being foolish when Maximus himself often acted the part.

"Don't you trust me, Maximus?"

"Not if you really gave the humans the Codex," the madman replied as they left the sphere. "So many secrets. Why would you do something like that? Why would you trust any, well, most of them, really, with everything we know?"

Black Bolt shook his head and held up another spike.

"They have a copy. It is heavily edited. They have what they need to find the boy, nothing more."

"Oh, I like this plan," Maximus said. "That's wiser, I think. And what follows such devious actions? What next, brother?"

This time Black Bolt did not reply. He just stood, peering at the device his brother had been building. The weapon.

"Very good," Maximus responded. "I'll make ready the machine."

THANOS LOOKED down upon Attilan and considered the fate of the city's people. Corvus Glaive attended him.

"This is a pageant, Corvus," Thanos said. "This

is a grand play, and the black king tests me. Has he yielded his tribute to me?"

"No, Thanos. Only silence comes from the Inhuman city. I think they cower in their holes and wait for us to change our minds."

"Then they must not know how we treat the meek." He turned away from the viewport. "Prepare my shuttle. Any further delays will be pointless." He moved toward the doors. "It's time I took what is mine."

"It will be done," Glaive said, bowing low. "Also, the others have returned."

"And how do they fare?" Thanos asked. "More failure?"

"In fact, Proxima Midnight brings good news."

"However…"

"The Black Dwarf did not fail. He was beaten. By a human."

Thanos let that sink in. Proxima Midnight approached, followed by Supergiant and Black Dwarf. The latter wore an expression of barely contained fear.

"We are missing one of the order," Thanos said. "Where is the Ebony Maw?"

"No one has seen or heard from him since you sent us to find the gem," Supergiant answered. "I have tried calling out to him. He does not answer. Not with his comm, and not with his mind."

"We know where he went, Master," Corvus said. "I could—"

"No. Let him be. He is unorthodox, but always effective. Do not doubt the Maw when we are full up with another's failure." He turned to look at the Black Dwarf.

"Forgiveness, Master." The huge warrior dropped to his knees before Thanos and lowered his head in submission. His deep voice rumbled as he spoke. "I… There were unforeseen complications. Unexpected quality. It was impossible to—"

Corvus spoke. "You embarrass yourself, brother. No one here wants to hear excuses." He turned to Proxima Midnight. "Wife, tell Thanos what you learned on your mission."

She smiled. "There was no resistance in the place the humans call Atlantis. Their prince, also of the secret brotherhood, kneeled before me and humbled himself on the condition that his people be spared. In exchange he offered the location of the gem, Master."

"Where?"

"Wakanda." She looked down at the kneeling giant. "Where the Black Dwarf met his betters and shamed us all."

Thanos nodded, and smiled. "Go. We will send all of the Black Order to see if this place can withstand the full might of Thanos. I will join you there when I have taken my tribute."

Black Dwarf began to rise. "Thank you, Master. I will reclaim all the honor I have lost. I will not fail you a second—"

Thanos spun and drove his fist down onto the scaled head of his general, and felt great satisfaction as the behemoth smashed into the floor of the observation deck. The impact was great enough to ruin the metal beneath him.

"No. Not you," Thanos said. "I gave you a world to raze, and in return you gave me nothing." Black Dwarf lay there, unmoving and barely conscious. "I have no need of broken things, child. You will leave this place, and you will not return until I call for you. Pray the suns and stars do not *all* die before that happens."

CHAPTER 18

ALLIANCES

"HERE'S what we have," Reed Richards said to his fellow Illuminati. A holographic globe of the Earth appeared over the table in front of them. They sat in the tower known as the Spire of Val'Holuth, hidden in Wakanda far from Birnin Zana, the Golden City.

"Like the Inhumans of Attilan, these hidden tribes have moved around a lot over the years. Most of them intermingling with humanity, even mating with humans."

"How could they?" Namor asked.

"Until affected by the Terrigen Mist, they have no powers, and the vast majority could pass for human under the strictest possible genetic guidelines.

"They also keep amazingly complete genetic records," Richards continued. "With those we should be able to identify and locate Thanos' child." Several dots appeared on the glowing globe.

"I'm counting six locations," T'Challa observed. "The six of us... Convenience, or providence?"

"Neither," Iron Man said. "Still, I think it would be best for us to double up, two to a site, considering the threat level. I mean, we're talking about the son of Thanos, here. Does anyone know what the spawn of a space tyrant looks like? We should proceed with caution."

"Proceed with caution?" Namor snorted. "Given the nature of this alliance, caution would dictate that we work apart from each other for the foreseeable future." He crossed his arms and shot a side-eyed glance at the Panther.

T'Challa said nothing, but stiffened visibly.

"What's going on here?" Richards said, looking from the Atlantean to the Wakandan and back.

"Beyond the normal, tedious acrimony, of course," the Beast added. The only answer was a stubborn silence.

"Well, not to gloss over... *whatever* this is, but there's something else we need to discuss," Iron Man said. "There are worse things happening in the universe right now, and some of them are occurring right here on Earth. As in, we have Thanos trying to take over the world. So should we really be doing this? Should we be handling Inhuman business?" He leaned in. "I thought we agreed everything is secondary to the cause. Our private lives, our partners, our families... *everything*."

They all looked at him, but no one spoke.

Then the Beast responded. "I didn't agree to that," he said. "No one here did. That's you making rules, Anthony, and expecting us to follow them." He gestured with a huge, blue-furred hand. "Do you honestly think I wouldn't be running back to the Jean Grey School if I felt the need? We should help if we can. How could we not? Besides which, anything we can do to screw up Thanos' plans is a plus in my book."

Reed nodded. "Hank's right," he said, bringing a hand up to his chin. "I don't know what's wrong with me. Before launching into business, I should have checked, asked how each of you is doing. Maybe it's because my family is off-planet right now. I forget myself. It shouldn't make a difference, but it probably does.

"So," he added, "is everyone all right?" He looked to his old friend. "T'Challa?"

"Wakanda repelled the invasion," the Panther answered. "The Golden City still stands. And you?"

"Tony and I made it through okay," Reed said. "New York fared better than most because it's home to so many of us." He turned toward Doctor Strange. "Stephen, you were there. Was—"

Strange brushed away the thought.

"I am fine. Perfectly fine."

"Hank?"

"One of Thanos' henchmen was some kind of omnipath. She came looking for something specific—I now assume it was the child. There was a fight and a lot of the X-Men were injured. However, she left as soon as she decided what they were looking for wasn't there.

"Lots of damage," he continued. "We all survived, which is better than many can claim."

Reed frowned. "It's not lost on me that most of the places where Thanos' generals made themselves known were also places where we were present." He focused on the last of their group.

"Namor? How is Atlantis?"

Namor looked down. "Destroyed," he said. "Utterly." Raising his head, he looked at each of the Illuminati and stared hardest, perhaps, at T'Challa. Then he gestured toward the globe. "So let's help Black Bolt and find this bastard son, shall we? After all, we have a brother in need."

"CAROL. WAKE up. They're coming back."

Captain Marvel raised her head and opened her eyes. The first person she saw was Clint Barton. He was a welcome sight. They had known each other for years.

Then she saw the Aleph—it looked like the others they'd fought: large, metallic, glowing eyes, with a face that seemed all chin and brow. There were two of them, and a Gardener. This one very obviously was female. Where Ex Nihilo sported two large, uneven horns, this creature possessed antlers that would have made a five-point buck envious.

Carol's hands were clamped together, and she was suspended from the ceiling. All of them were. As she woke, the Aleph checked Cannonball.

"**ASSESSING: MUTATE. HUMAN MALE. CONTAINED.**"

Then Sunspot.

"**ASSESSING: MUTATE. HUMAN MALE. CONTAINED.**"

The second Aleph checked Hawkeye.

"**ASSESSING: BASE TYPE. HUMAN MALE. CONTAINED.**"

Clint snorted. "Keep thinking that, pal."

The first Aleph moved forward while the golden-skinned female watched on. Like Ex Nihilo, she had the same omega mark on her chest and a third eye. It was open.

The Aleph touched Carol and moved probes from its fingers around the edges of her face. "**ASSESSING: HUMAN-KREE HYBRID FEMALE. ENHANCED.**"

The Gardener looked interested. "Really? A half-breed with enhancements." She drew closer, towering over her captive. "The universe is such a chaotic and wonderful place. Tell me, child, what brought you to this?" Her voice carried an edge of arrogance that was very likely unconscious. It was no less annoying for that fact.

Carol chose not to answer the question, but she remembered well enough. The ship got caught in an explosion and the lights went out. There was a fight. She thought the others were surely dead, because the ship cracked like an egg. She came out of the quincruiser like a rocket and took on five of the Alephs.

She lost.

The next thing she knew, she and the others were all here, wherever "here" was, and all of them were restrained. The cuffs didn't look like much, but she hadn't been able to break them, no matter how hard she tried.

The Gardener looked down at her and smiled. It ran its hands over her, touched her as if to make certain she was real. The touch was intimate enough to make it creepy. With one hand, the creature grabbed her chin and forced her to look up into its green eyes.

"What brings you to this?"

The same annoying question again.

"Well, in the beginning there was nothing. Then there was everything." Carol smiled. "The Good Lord saw fit to bring me into this world to kick the asses of those who need it most. So I'd get ready if I were you, 'cause this day or the next, it's coming."

The Gardener looked pleased. "*Hmrpt.* She'll do. Bring her."

One of the Alephs removed the cuffs from the strange line that connected them to the ceiling. Before Carol could get her balance, it began to drag her across the floor.

This really sucks, she thought irritably.

Clint started struggling, God love him. "Hey! No! Stop! Leave her alone… You can take me instead." She'd told him more than once that his chivalrous nature would be the end of him. He was human and she was—well, she was something a bit more.

The Gardener smiled at him.

"Don't worry," it said. "We'll be back for you soon enough."

THE BEHEMOTH Ringworld. Massive did not begin to properly express the size of the place.

In the center of the ring, there was a broken planet at least the size of Jupiter. From within the center of that ruptured world, a powerful light glowed. Perhaps it was a sun being born. Perhaps it was merely the planet's core. In any event, the light from within cast a bright warmth over the whole of the ring built around it.

While the planet itself could not be inhabited—it was too hot and desolate—the ring was covered with cities and outposts. Built by the Shi'ar who knew how long ago, it was as impressive a creation as Spider-Woman had ever seen.

Currently more than one hundred million refugees from the Builders' war were being cared for on the ring's surface. Around it, beyond the atmosphere, hundreds of ships moved steadily, standing guard and gathering supplies.

Jessica and Shang-Chi stood overlooking a courtyard that was teeming with activity. Badly overwhelmed medical personnel were vastly outnumbered by the wounded and dying. Nearby Eden was doing his best to calm an injured Skrull while another, smaller one stood not far away.

"Here you go… hopefully this will make it a little better," Eden said, and his patient remained silent.

"He hurts," the small Skrull said meekly.

"I know, I'm sorry. There are medical teams

going through the camps right now. They should be here soon."

Jessica doubted he was right.

"What's taking so long to get these people help?" Manifold spoke to her softly.

"One hundred million refugees and counting," she replied. "Most of the medical teams are screening new arrivals from plague worlds like Whaan Prime. It's bad all around." She wished she could offer more reassurance, but there was none to be found.

Shang-Chi nodded. "It could be much worse," he said. "At least no one is hungry. Ex Nihilo has provided the ringworld with thousands of new gardens and has encouraged them to continuously yield food. Tending to them gives many of the refugees something to do. The hope is that being occupied will keep them from dwelling on what they have lost. Which I suspect is the point for him, as well. Doing good to occupy his mind, not dwelling on the dark actions of the Builders who made him."

"That's all well and good, but I look at all of this—how we don't know where half of our team is—and I can't help but be furious," Jessica said. "When are we going to hit back against the source of all this misery?"

"I believe that matter is being addressed now." Shang-Chi looked toward the largest structure in sight, a massive stone affair that had an air of age about it.

CAPTAIN AMERICA and Thor stood near a table in the center of a vast, almost empty conference arena. Seated at the table were members of the Galactic Council. Annihilus had his wings draped like a cloak behind him. J'son was agitated, frustrated and full of nervous energy. He sat only for a moment before he stood and began pacing.

An emissary of the Brood crouched in its seat, as if poised to leap at the next bared throat. Kl'rt of the Skrulls sat as far from the Kree as possible, but he attended and listened to all who spoke. The reptilian Badoon had sent a representative, though he seemed uncomfortable with the idea of sitting. Ronan the Accuser sat near Annihilus and held out his hand, above which a projection of the Kree Supreme Intelligence appeared holographically.

Finally there was Gladiator. "How were we so wrong?" he said, his voice filled with regret.

The Brood emissary responded. "Is it wrong to hunt a wh'ullo only to find it bound with a Gurddak? The beast had a second mouth that it did not show until we made it scream. Now we really know what we are facing."

"Yes, we do." J'son spoke up, his face set in a scowl. "And it's even worse than you think. My warmasters have analyzed the readings we took of the Builder fleet as we left the Corridor. Have any of you?"

The Supreme Intelligence answered. "Seventeen thousand light cruisers. Three thousand carriers. Two thousand heavy cruisers and six hundred world ships. Twelve world killers."

J'son nodded his head, and his scowl deepened. "Yes, and that is just the main arm of the invasion fleet. There is word of smaller groups tearing through clusters at the edge of council space. We are badly outnumbered, to say nothing of being outgunned." He paced faster. "Our choices appear to be defeat or acquiescence."

"Then let our deaths be glorioussssss!" Annihilus responded.

Kl'rt stared at him with undisguised disgust. "Dying with valor means we sacrifice achieving our goals. Has that happened? No. Not yet it hasn't. The cost was high, but I have just reunited the bulk of the Skrull Empire, and I prefer living."

"Of course." Gladiator nodded. "But we do not know our enemy—and if we do not know them, how can we possibly find a way to defeat them? We are crippled by our ignorance."

"And their superior numbers." J'son was not optimistic.

Captain America cleared his throat.

"Excuse me, Gladiator," he said. "But if that's the case, I think there's someone the council needs to see."

J'son spun around as if slapped and shoved a finger toward the Avenger.

"No one wants to hear from you backwater apes!" he said, almost shouting. "When we need bodies to throw at the enemy or laborers to dig graves, then we will have a use for human help."

Thor took half a step forward and placed his hand on Mjolnir's haft. He calmed himself, but J'son was reminded that one of the "humans" he spoke of was, in fact, an Asgardian—and capable of pulping his entire body with a small gesture. The Spartax king did his best to look as if he were unfazed.

The small smile on Thor's face said he failed.

The Supreme Intelligence spoke. "In encounters with the Kree, the Spartax have historically achieved victory in thirty-four percent of military engagements," he said. "That is a percentage substantially lower than the humans have achieved. I think we should listen to what the Earth strategist, Captain America—who has defeated the Kree before—has to say."

Gladiator looked toward J'son for only a moment, and then turned to Captain America.

"Will you bring your witness before the council, please?"

J'son fumed. Thor smiled. Captain America nodded and left the chambers. He returned ten minutes later.

CHAPTER 19

JUDAS

CAPTAIN Marvel walked under her own power, but her arms were still cuffed behind her back.

The chamber she entered was filled with several differently shaped gold-skinned creatures, the things she thought of as Gardeners. Some were male, others female; with some she had no idea whether gender even existed. One looked twice the size of the Hulk, and another had four arms.

With them were a few of the Alephs, and there was another creature no larger than an average human but with an insectoid face and what looked like bio-armor encasing its form. There was a moment when she wondered whether it might be one of Annihilus' creatures, but no. They had little in common.

"Ex Nihila." The bug-faced thing looked at the

Gardener that accompanied Carol. "This is the one you chose? You believe she has the information we need? These questions must be answered."

"I want the knowledge just as you do, Engineer. She was clearly the leader of the captured human types. If any of them know, she will."

"Very well." The thing turned to face her at last. Its multifaceted eyes were a deep red. "Look here, human. We are not by our nature the destroyers of things. In fact, we cultivated all that is worth considering in this universal sphere. If not directly by our hands, then by the systems we created to do this good work. All that there is, flowing from our hands. Do you understand?"

She did not reply, and scanned the room. Against one wall, encased in some sort of vertical suspended-animation tubes, she could see Abyss, Nightmask, and Starbrand. These were their heavy hitters, and yet they'd been taken out of the game. The thing pointed to the captured beings and moved closer to yet another tube.

This one lay across the deck. She couldn't see who was in it, but if the others were any indication, she was pretty sure she knew.

"How do you come to have these entities with you?" the Engineer demanded.

She smiled. "I dunno... just my good looks and charm, I guess."

There was whispering among the Gardeners. They looked at Abyss again and again.

"It has been so long…"

"Are we sure?"

"Yes, she is real. How is it possible?"

"I don't know, but it is wonderful, isn't it? An Abyssil… *alive!*"

The bug-faced creep leaned in closer to Carol, scrutinizing her face. She fought to maintain her composure.

"The sentient systems are one thing," it said. "One of the ancient Abyssi, all of which were thought lost. A Nightmask, arbiter of the change, even a planetary defense system like the Star Brand. But this?" It pointed to the case that lay on the deck in front of her, and the opaque glass cleared up as light washed from the interior.

She was right. Captain Universe rested inside, her eyes closed, apparently still in a comatose state.

"This is heretical," the Engineer hissed. "You have the great Mother, who made us all and whom we long ago rejected. So we ask you again, how do you come to have all of these things? What sets you apart? What makes you so special?"

One of the Alephs chose that moment to speak up. "**DECLARATIVE: A SHIP APPROACHES US. IT HAS ONE OCCUPANT. IT IS AN ENEMY VESSEL.**"

The bug-thing turned toward the Aleph. Its mandibles clicked and moved as it considered.

"Is the vessel a threat?"

"**DECLARATIVE: THERE ARE NO ACTIVE WEAPONS SYSTEMS. IT APPEARS TO HAVE TAKEN ITS CORE**

OFFLINE ONCE IT ENTERED OUR LOCAL SPACE. ALL EFFORTS SEEM TO SUGGEST IT WISHES TO APPEAR HARMLESS." Another of the bug-faced things moved into Carol's view. She had been unaware it was there. The second one spoke up, looking at the prone Captain Universe even as it talked.

"We should destroy it."

"No," Bug-Face One said. "We will wait here and see if the occupant has anything worthwhile to say or offer. We might even gain an advantage from this encounter." It turned back to Carol and spoke again. "You have not yet answered my queries."

Carol shrugged and felt the manacles pull at her wrists. "Maybe they came to help us stop invaders from killing off our planet for no good reason."

The thing reared back. For a long moment, it did not speak. She hoped the damned thing choked on its fears.

EX NIHILO avoided making eye contact with any of the council members.

"I do not know why they are attacking," he said. "Much of what I have seen confuses me. I have never met my makers, these Builders. All I know of my kind are the things my father-Aleph taught me. The first lesson I learned was that I am a life bringer. This death that follows the Builders wherever they go, it was not what I was trained for. Something has gone very wrong, and I do not know why."

The Gardener turned to face them. "Watching another like me... kill himself to poison a world... Something has gone very wrong, and it must be stopped." He was repeating himself, and Cap could see how distressed he was. "It must be stopped. Whatever you might need from me, you will have it."

"Why?" Kl'rt the Super-Skrull asked.

"Why?" Ex Nihilo echoed. "What do you mean?"

"I mean *why?*" The Skrull's face wrinkled into a mask of frustration. "I mean why are they doing this? What do they want? What is the damned point of these attacks?"

"I do not know," Ex Nihilo said again. "But their behavior has been predictable, hasn't it? The Builders are efficient. Direct. Linear. So perhaps—"

"Wait!" the Supreme Intelligence said abruptly from its hologram. "Plotting path, extending projection, factoring in orbital variations and calculating. The line extends directly through Kree space. Through our capital world, Hala."

Ronan frowned. "Supremor, are you saying that we—"

"Calculating... extending. Through the Cygnus Arm, and then..." He paused for a moment, as if double-checking his figures. "...Earth."

"So this is why you are here." J'son glared at Captain America, nearly spitting the words.

"Yes." Cap looked directly back at him and nodded. "Of course it is, but it's why we're all here, isn't it? These Builders appear to be like gods who, for reasons beyond my understanding, are hell-bent on destroying everything that lies in front of them—which includes all of you." He turned away from the fuming J'son and gestured toward the others gathered around him. Kl'rt, the Brood leader, Gladiator. "So far all evidence points to us being unable to stop them. But maybe that's the key to beating them."

"Are you suggesting some sort of deception?" Gladiator wasn't getting what he was saying. At least not completely.

Three Spartax soldiers approached their king, and J'son nodded his head, moving away. Without letting it distract him, Cap continued, but he logged the event for later.

"I think they'd see right through any attempts at subterfuge. There's plenty of evidence to suggest the Builders are tactically superior to us in every way." The Brood emissary moved closer, and Cap resisted the urge to shiver. "After all," he continued, "they've proven that, haven't they? No. I'm thinking more along the lines of an egg."

The Brood emissary bobbed its head. "Ahhhh, infestation. That is a possibility, but how will we get enough of them close to the breeders?"

It was going to be a long discussion.

SOMEWHERE ALONG the way, the Engineer talking to Carol had gone preachy.

"And do you want to know why we have lived

so long?" She resisted saying something like "clean living" and let it continue to ramble. "Why we have done all these magnificent things?"

She managed not to vomit up her lunch. "I'm dying to know," she said, assuming the alien wouldn't grasp something as subtle as sarcasm.

"Because we are the only ones capable," it continued, proving her right. "Who else would do these things? You?" It gestured over its shoulder. "Them?"

As if on cue, one of the Alephs brought over a figure in what looked like Spartax armor with a helmet obscuring its head. It wasn't a standard helmet—there were projection screens covering most of it.

"DECLARATIVE: HERE IS THE SOLE OCCUPANT OF THE CAPTURED VESSEL. DECLARATIVE: IT HAS A COMMUNICATION MECHANISM FUSED TO THE HOST. THE SOURCE OF THE SIGNAL WE DETECTED EARLIER. QUERY: TERMINATE?"

The Engineer turned to look at the captured occupant of the suit and considered for a moment.

"No. I want to hear its words."

The mask of miniature screens flickered into a projected image. She recognized the speaker immediately. J'son of the Spartax stared up at the Engineer. He wasn't there, but he was present just the same. Captain Marvel raised an eyebrow. This would certainly be enlightening.

"Greetings, Builders," the hologram said. "I am J'son, king of the Spartax Empire."

The Engineer tilted its head. "And I am more.

What do you want, J'son the lesser?" The arrogance Carol had sensed was confirmed in that moment. She couldn't read the expression on the insect face, but she could certainly define the words easily enough.

J'son frowned. Likely he wasn't used to people of any sort responding that way. She knew plenty like him. They came from nearly every world.

"I seek a truce," he replied.

The insect mandibles rubbed against each other, and the Engineer lifted its hands in a gesture with which she wasn't familiar. The fingers waggled, and the wrists moved until the palms of the hands were facing upward.

"A truce implies that we both have something to gain and lose," the Engineer said. "This does not seem to be our position, or yours."

J'son continued unfazed. "Right now I am with all of the other council members planning your destruction." Carol frowned to hear that. "I do not deny the impressive nature of your fleet. Perhaps we'll fail, but we could get lucky —that is the nature of war, after all. So certainly there must be something we can offer you. Certainly there must be something you want."

The bug-faced Engineer leaned in closer until J'son's reflection could be seen in the facets of its eyes.

"What we want is the preservation of our universe," it responded. "What we want is the destruction of a world. The one called Earth."

"*What?*" Carol couldn't stop her outburst, and she

felt her stomach twist into a knot. *Why the Earth? What possible significance could it have?* It was her home and she loved it, but it was hardly a significant mudball in the grander scheme of things. The technology to move into the stars barely existed there.

J'son sneered. "I knew it! All of this over a useless backwater planet. I could give you the Earth. I believe I could do that if it means you would leave my empire alone. I'll arrange it right now if it will end this war. All you have to do is say the word."

She could understand his wanting to barter, but if she could have gotten her hands on the king of the Spartax, she'd have knocked him straight back to his damned "empire."

Once again the hands aimed toward the ceiling and the fingers danced madly. It was silent laughter. The damned thing was laughing at J'son, and he failed to understand it. Cultures didn't all use the same gestures in the same ways.

"Oh, you insignificant creature." The Engineer turned and walked away from him. "This is not a war. It is a cleansing. Your worlds have been found wanting." It turned back and again stepped closer to J'son. "Just the same, we thank you for what you have given us."

"What do you mean?"

"Your signal. Encoded and encrypted by your people, but easily broken. You have given us your location, the location of your fleet and your commanders. For that I am truly grateful. You have saved us a minor effort."

The Aleph standing near J'son's emissary spoke up.

"QUERY: IS THIS ONE AWARE OF WHAT DAMAGE AN OBJECT TRAVELING AT POINT-TWO LIGHT SPEED CAN CAUSE TO A SUPERSTRUCTURE?"

"Oh, gods… no," J'son said.

"DECLARATIVE: YES."

The Aleph destroyed the king's avatar. Whoever was actually in that armor never stood a chance. Carol hoped that wherever the sniveling king of Spartax might be, he felt some of the pain.

THE GATHERED council members listened and responded to Captain America's suggested plan of action.

"It is a good plan," Gladiator said. "There's a problem, however. It will not work without a believable forward action. The price will be high."

King J'son moved back into the group. His hands were shaking, his eyes were dazed, and blood leaked from one ear.

"You have to listen." His voice was very weak.

Cap frowned and turned toward him.

"Can we pledge the full might of the Accusers, Ronan?" The Supreme Intelligence asked the question, and Ronan nodded.

"If you call for it, Supremor, the corps will answer."

"No! You must listen to me!" J'son said, louder now. "Something is wrong." He looked up to the heavens as he spoke, and his voice faded to little more than a whisper. "Wrong."

The rest looked up, including Captain America.

"They've found us," Thor said.

Sentient drones screamed into the atmosphere of the ringworld. The refugees had gathered in a place where the risks were few. They were far away from where the Builders were moving, and the plan was to hide, regroup, and prepare.

The time for hiding had ended.

One of the Shi'ar cruisers tried to move between the drones and the ring. The cruiser was struck and evaporated in the explosion, but this did not stop the assault from hitting the ring itself.

Almost one hundred million survivors from the Builders' war were on the ring, fleeing from the enemies that had come without warning, and crushed worlds and ships alike. Over forty million of those refugees died in the strike.

The Behemoth broke.

Where each drone struck, the damage spread exponentially. Explosions ran the ring's full length, the detonations shattering the superstructure. The force of those explosions liquefied massive sections that rippled, bucked, and fell apart. Bodies were hurled into space along with the debris. Some were dead; others were not. Screams were quickly swallowed by the vacuum.

Captain America was one of those bodies. He would surely have died right then and there, but the

Super-Skrull reached out and caught him with an arm that stretched far beyond the possibilities of even the shape-shifters. Cap felt the barrier the Skrull put around him that sealed in an atmosphere. Even as he was saved, he saw Ex Nihilo generating bubbles of breathable gases around several different groups.

J'son stared at the ruination and wept openly— his face said what he did not. This was his fault. He had done something supremely stupid. Cap didn't know exactly what it was, and he couldn't spare the time to think about it.

The destruction was on a scale he never imagined could exist, and he had seen the sorts of horrors that would never stop haunting him. Winds roared through the remaining atmosphere, and while Thor did what he could to calm them, even gods had limits. Though a large area was spared, the storms tore apart other sections with wild abandon.

Captain America watched it all, unable to do anything to stop the devastation.

The Builders made their intentions known.

There would be no mercy.

What happened next would be inevitable.

THE COUNCIL gathered again aboard the *Lilandra*. For a long while, there was no meeting. Instead there were different leaders doing what they could to assess the damage to their people and their forces. Before long the reports started coming in. Captain America, along with several other Avengers, stood nearby and listened.

First the Builder fleet went to Centauri-IV. Several enemy ships landed in a show of force, and the Centaurians offered themselves in surrender. Better to live, they had reasoned. None could disagree.

The Kymellians followed suit, surrendering even as the Builders arrived in their solar system. No one blamed them. Their race was ancient and proud, but they did not have the military strength to withstand an attack by the Builders.

"There's no choice, Steve," the Black Widow said quietly to Captain America. With a long history dealing with foreign governments, she was trained to know how people would respond to certain types of force, and what governments would do in times of stress. "A lot of the smaller groups will surrender. It's the only wise option, and so far the Builders seem to be accepting surrender as an alternative to outright destruction." He nodded his head.

"It's the only move that makes sense," he agreed, but he was not happy about it. He'd fought against the Nazis and Hitler, but he still understood the differences. The Nazis had never possessed a weapon capable of obliterating an entire civilization with the push of a button. If they had, World War II likely would have ended very differently.

Ronan the Accuser stood in the center of the chamber and gestured to get the attention of those around him. His face was grim when he spoke. "Word has come to me," he said. "The Supreme

Intelligence has considered the possibilities as the Builder fleet moves closer to Hala. It has consulted with the thousands of intellects that exist within its vast memory and decreed that we cannot win."

Ronan lowered his head.

"The Kree Empire has surrendered."

There was chatter, but no one spoke above a murmur.

"I requested permission to stay here and fight alongside your forces," he continued, "along with my Accusers. However, it seems the victors are refusing to accept anything short of total and complete submission." It seemed as if every word he spoke was ripped from him. Ronan was a warrior first, and a proud man. "I have been ordered to return home with what remains of our fleet."

He turned and paced, a predator forced to hide its teeth. "Surrender is a shameful thing for a warrior. Better to die here, fighting alongside you, but I do not answer only to my conscience." He kept his calm, but it wasn't an easy thing. Captain America understood only too well. "Duty, it seems, is all I have left. Today I see little honor in it." He stopped pacing and faced them. "Die well, heroes. You will be remembered."

"Well then, it's over," J'son said. "We are crippled, and what seemed impossible now seems critical. The Kree represented one fourth of our remaining fleet. This war has become pointless. We cannot win. We are going to lose. The only sane course is to withdraw from the battle, as well. The Spartax will return home, fortify our worlds, and prepare for the worst.

"Survival is now all that matters."

Captain America peered at Thor, trying to read the expression on his teammate's face. All he found was contempt for the king.

"Live as something we are not?" Gladiator shook his head. "No. The Shi'ar will stay and fight."

Kl'rt nodded his agreement. "We will fight, as well. You cannot domesticate an H'Lraar. We have seen what the Builders are capable of doing. They are predators posing as something merciful. Even if I am wrong…" He looked to J'son as he spoke. "…what better way to die than on your feet with blood on your hands and the bodies of your enemies underfoot?"

J'son spoke, and once again his contempt for the Earthlings was made clear.

"Well, if you fools insist on throwing your lives away, you should know that the Builders have prisoners. Humans. I would assume the ones from the defeat at the Corridor." He looked at Captain America with unbridled hostility—as if, somehow, the Avengers were responsible for everything that had gone wrong.

"How do you know that?" Cap demanded.

"We are not backwater savages, Captain. Do not question how when you are incapable of comprehending all the things your betters can do." The defeated king straightened his spine and squared his shoulders. "My ways are beyond you."

The glow of energies surrounded J'son and his

retinue. It lasted only for a moment, and then they were gone.

Thor's sneer grew profound.

"He betrays us." Annihilus said what they were likely all feeling.

Gladiator crossed his arms. "Possibly. If so, that is a situation we will deal with another time. For now our problems remain the same. We do not know how to defeat these Builders, and we cannot survive another tactical error. We are both blind and lost."

Cap disagreed. "The problem is you're not used to anything but strategizing from a position of strength, Gladiator. You're looking at the chessboard the wrong way."

Thor looked toward him. "*The Aeneid?*"

Captain America nodded his head.

"So you have a plan, then?" Gladiator towered over him and gave his full attention.

"I do," Cap replied, "but there's one thing I'm going to need to make it work."

"And what might that be?"

Thor smiled. "The good Captain will require the right bait."

ACT THREE
EMPIRES

CHAPTER 20

FALLING

HALA, the capital world of the Kree Empire. Ronan the Accuser stood before the insectoid creatures known as the Engineers and stared down at them, his brow furrowed and his mouth set in a scowl.

He had no desire to surrender. He had no wish to end a war while taking a knee to the creatures that had been the aggressors. What should have happened, in his eyes, was simple. He should have continued fighting until he was either victorious or dead. That was the Kree way.

Aboard the Builder flagship, he took a knee just the same, offering his hammer—his weapon and the symbol of his position within the Accusers—to creatures that spoke as if he were not even there. Perhaps for them, he wasn't.

"I DO not understand why you insist on such pageantry," the Engineer said. "Our circumstances demand that the fleet be in motion—not stagnant."

"When a world surrenders, it is not to an army," the Builder replied, "and not because of a show of force. We are teaching them, Engineer—that it only takes one Builder to break a civilization, to humble an empire.

"We are very good teachers," it added.

"Builders, a mass of ships has just entered the system," a Caretaker said from its position at a holographic nerve center. "They are right on top of us—it is the enemy fleet."

"Why?" the Engineer asked. "They must know they cannot win."

"We have harried the beasts to the breaking point, Engineer," the Builder replied. "This is the animal instinct to fight. If these children crave instruction… so let us begin their final lesson."

THE ALLIED ships swarmed from hyperspace and gathered before the Builder fleet. Gladiator studied the screen as the enemy vessels began to move toward them. Each consisted of two elongated pods linked at the center by a causeway. The effect was such that the approaching warships seemed to peer at them through slitted eyes.

"It appears they've sent the bulk of their attack

vessels in response to our incursion," he said. "The only ones absent are the planet killers, likely left behind to defend the command ship." He looked to his ally. "It appears the Builders have taken your bait, Captain."

Captain America hit a control stud on his comm. "Go."

It was one word, but it was enough.

Ships moved into position, as did a group of smaller forms. Hyperion, Smasher, and the Imperial Guard all targeted enemy vessels as quickly as they could, doing everything possible to avoid becoming targets themselves. As crackling energy weapons began to light up the vacuum of space, they attacked and dodged. Bursts of flame and globes of energy discharge appeared, each representing an impact— and perhaps a kill.

MANIFOLD OPENED a breach into the lead ship, and most of the crew were vented into the void of space within seconds. They might have screamed, but no one could hear.

Eden left as quickly as he had arrived.

Mentor and the Shi'ar Subguardian known as Warstar accompanied Bruce Banner into the ship. Bruce wore a spacesuit and his backup patch. Warstar moved his huge armored body ahead of them both and engaged one of the Alephs, destroying the thing in short order. He presented its head to Mentor, along with a good portion of its torso.

While Mentor probed the robotic remains, Banner opened a comm channel to the Shi'ar flagship.

"It's Banner," he said. "We're in, Steve. Manifold got us here, and we're working on accessing the system now."

Mentor shook his head. "Chaotic encoding—this is more challenging than I expected." Considering the man's intellect, Banner didn't like the sound of that.

"It's going to be tight, Cap," he said. "Hold on as long as you can. We're working on it." He did his best to stay calm and wondered—not for the first time—what lunacy led anyone to send him out like this. The last thing he needed was to be in the middle of the action.

"THEY SAY they need more time," Cap announced.

"*There is no more time,*" Gladiator raged. "We just lost the *Wintersun.* Tell Captain Lumma to bring the—*arrhh!*"

He bellowed as a huge impact sent the *Lilandra* tipping to one side, throwing them off-balance. Cap remained standing, but Gladiator hit the deck, hard.

"Power is failing," a crewman said, helping the Majestor to his feet. "We need to—"

"No," Cap said. "There's nowhere left to run, soldier. We win here and now, or we lose it all. Give the order. *Attack.* Fire everything we've got."

BANNER FORGOT to be worried as he watched Mentor in action. The man's fingers fairly danced over the Aleph's insides, moving wires and attaching a portable unit to the interior of the highly developed robotic brain.

"Almost there."

Banner repeated it to Captain America.

Mentor nodded. "Done. Tell the *Lilandra* that we're in."

"LOOK AT them fight." Aboard the Builder command ship, the Engineer peered at the huge viewscreen. "Look at how they die."

"Impressive."

"Do you know what the people will say about this day, thousands of years from now?" the Builder answered. "What they will say about these creatures and their valiant last stand? Nothing. Because we will not tell them. Oblivion is all there is for—"

Booom!

An impact sent a vibration through the entire vessel, causing every creature on the bridge to look up, their faces expressing disbelief.

"We're under attack," the Gardener with the antlers said. "Who would—?"

"It's… it's not possible," the Caretaker said, his fingers racing over the controls. "It's one of our own World Killers."

"LILANDRA, WE have broken into the Builder control system on the World Killer," Mentor said.

"I've wirecasted the firing codes."

He sent the command, and a ship capable of destroying planets opened fire on its neighbor. The entire interior of the ship where they stood hummed and shuddered as volley after volley of heavy artillery cut through the space between vessels. Within minutes, it was done. The unsuspecting vessel was crippled, bleeding energies and Builders alike. Then another planet killer was targeted. This one went up in a ball of fire and fury, leaving nothing but debris.

Then there was a commotion off to one side, and Mentor glanced toward the human that had accompanied them—the one called Banner. His figure swelled abruptly, broke free of the spacesuit, and took on the healthier color of green. Huge muscles bulged, and the Hulk grabbed what remained of the Aleph, crushing it to bits with its bare hands.

"Our usefulness here may have been short-lived, however," Mentor said. "We've lost control of the World Killer's weapons systems." But as he spoke, another voice came over the comms.

"We have the second World Killer," Thor announced.

"Now?" That was Kl'rt.

"Yes. Break them, Warlord—strike like lightning on the darkest night. Scorch the heavens, rain fire down on them."

A moment later, the second World Killer launched an assault on the Builder fleet, targeting and incinerating more of the planet destroyers. The void was filled with wreckage and bodies.

All the while, the Hulk raged throughout the enemy vessel, leaping from one spot to another and shattering whatever he could touch. Mentor and Warstar couldn't do anything but watch the unbridled violence. In spite of himself, Mentor was impressed.

"Why, exactly, was that man sent along?" he asked.

"He's really a very good deterrent in most cases," Captain America replied. "Also, I thought he could be helpful."

"Well, he's doing an excellent job of destroying the ship we commandeered…"

MANIFOLD MOVED carefully, stepping as softly as he could; next to him, the Black Widow struck like a vengeful spirit. They were accompanied by Shang-Chi and Spider-Woman.

Manifold did his best to remain calm. The others fairly danced from shadow to shadow in a well-lit ship; wherever each went, one of the creatures in front of them fell unconscious or dead. He didn't bother to ask which.

Just as they located Captain Marvel, Sunspot, Cannonball, and Hawkeye, vibrations thrummed through the ship. Captain America's ruse had worked—they were turning the enemy's own weapons against them.

The prisoners were locked in manacles, while an Aleph stood guard. As the rumbling began, the robot moved toward them, away from the hatchway.

"DECLARATIVE: TERMINATION ORDER GIVEN." It raised its arms, and energy weapons began to glow. "DECLARATIVE: PROXIMITY ALE—"

Its mechanical words were cut off as an energy spear burst through its chest. From behind the Aleph, Shang-Chi stepped into the prison chamber. He wore high-tech gauntlets that made his hands glow.

"Hello, friends. Rest easy. All is well."

While the Black Widow released Captain Marvel, Manifold teleported parts of the other restraints into the void. The prisoners rubbed their wrists and shook their arms to restart blood circulation.

"Gather round," Spider-Woman said. "Manifold will jump us back out of here."

"We can't leave yet, Jess," Captain Marvel said. "We're not the only ones here. Are you in communication with our fleet, Widow?"

Natasha nodded. "We're all wired into Captain America's communication array."

"Excellent—please tell him we're going to send a message."

"Can do."

"Now we have to save the others." Captain Marvel moved toward the exit, and the rest followed. Carol gestured for the Black Widow to join her, and Natasha nodded as she spoke.

The time for stealth was past. Before the ship's crew could react, Cannonball launched himself toward the nearest opponents, taking out Engineers,

Alephs, Caretakers, and equipment alike. Manifold hoped none of the tech was essential for—say—life support, but it was too late to stop him. An Aleph lunged for the Black Widow, but Shang-Chi landed a focused blow and penetrated its chest, shattering both shielding and circuits. The thing collapsed instantly, crushing a control panel beneath its full weight and sending up a cascade of sparks.

The Widow took out the Gardener with a flurry of blows, and Hawkeye did the same for the Engineer. The remaining Avengers moved to the containment tubes, taking a moment to decipher the controls before they released Abyss, Nightmask, and Starbrand.

That left only one more.

BY THE time the Builders understood the scope of the attack against them, it was simply too late.

Kl'rt was a champion among his people, one of the most brutal and effective fighters they had ever bred. Had any of his people forgotten that fact—and many had—they were reminded that day. His strikes were as precise as a surgeon cutting away a malignant tumor. He crippled five ships before their defensive systems could be brought online.

It wasn't long before the Builders called for a retreat. The majority of the fleet jumped to distant points. A smaller faction—still large enough to cause mayhem—remained behind to grant them cover.

"EDEN, GIVE me some good news." Captain America's voice came through loud and clear.

"We've liberated them, sir," Manifold replied.

"Acknowledged. That's good news. Is everyone okay?"

"Everyone is conscious now except for Captain Universe. She's still in a coma, near as we can tell."

"Understood. I want you to jump everyone out of there, okay? There's still a battle going on out there. We've done a lot of damage, but there's still a lot to accomplish."

"Yes, sir." Manifold gestured to get the attention of the heroes clustered around him. "Okay, Captain America says we need to evacuate, so everyone get—"

"Not yet," Black Widow said.

"But Cap said—"

"I know, but we still have friends and allies dying." She focused her full attention on the thin figure of the man called Starbrand. "It's time, Kevin."

"What are you talking about?"

Eden suspected Kevin knew. Not that long ago, he'd been a college student. Since then he'd been recruited by the Avengers, who were working to help him both control and better understand his powers.

They do that a lot, he mused.

The Star Brand was an organic planetary defense system. In addition to granting him extraordinary strength and endurability, it enabled him to manipulate energy. He could generate destructive blasts and impenetrable force shields. On one of his first excursions, he'd knocked the Hulk into orbit. Literally.

"That thing on your hand," Natasha said. "What you are. You have the power to end this." When he didn't answer, she continued. "Ever since you got the brand, you've been asking yourself, 'Why me?' Well, why don't you show us?"

Manifold admired her calm in the face of a terrifying force. She was asking this skinny kid to unleash an unbelievable degree of power, yet she spoke as if she might be asking him to pick up some groceries.

"I can try."

"I think you can do a hell of a lot more than that."

Looking down at his hands, Kevin Connor steeled himself. His hands glowed. The radiance spread to the symbol on his chest, then danced around him. His eyes took on the brilliance of twin suns, and then he held up his right hand. The mark of a star that always showed there grew even brighter than his eyes.

"Get us out of here, Eden," Natasha said. "*Now.*"

Manifold looked away from that glow and generated his own, quickly sweeping up his teammates and allies. They reappeared on the deck of the *Lilandra* and immediately clustered at the viewport—just in time to see the Builder flagship disintegrate in a flash of energy. All of the remaining Builder ships followed it into oblivion.

As the glow faded, they saw a single figure standing on a piece of the rubble, his hand still held high.

Then the cheering began.

Captain America and Gladiator stood toward the back of the deck. They remained silent. Their expressions were unreadable.

CHAPTER 21

ABYSSI

THEY moved like streaks across the cosmos, leaving trails as surely as a comet does. Ex Nihilo and Abyss had the ability to fly through the void. They could generate their own atmosphere if needed. They could also move at speeds few living things could manage.

Ex Nihilo considered the way in which the universe itself could change when no one was looking. As the Avengers liberated his sister and then prepared to annihilate a portion of the Builder's fleet, they encountered another of his kind, an antlered female. He was stunned by the knowledge. He knew, intellectually, that they must exist, yet he had never expected to encounter another Ex Nihili.

He still had not. He had not been there when the Black Widow and her associates came aboard the

Builders' ship to liberate everyone they had captured. However, his sister Abyss had been there, and with a thought she showed him what had taken place.

HAVING DEFEATED the ship's crew, Captain Marvel and the rest of the Avengers took the bridge to free the final prisoners, including Abyss.

"Wake up, Abyss," Captain Marvel had said, helping her step out of the confinement tube. "Nightmare's over. It's only us Avengers here."

No, Abyss thought.

"No," she said. "It's not." She gestured. "Look."

There stood the Gardener, resplendent with a full display of antlers, her head cocked in curiosity.

"AND THEN what happened, Abyss?" Ex Nihilo said. "What did she do?"

"The others saw her turn and leave," she replied. "She rose into space and departed by her own power. But there was more. She spoke to me… in my mind. She said, 'Come find us.'"

Brother and sister continued their trek, past planets and moons and clouds of debris so dense they blocked out the stars. Finally they landed on a planet where there was nothing to see but ice, more ice, and the occasional rock.

Ex Nihilo looked around and frowned. "Are you sure this is the right place, sister?"

"Yes." Abyss smiled indulgently, careful to make certain he was tolerated. He was aware of that fact. He was aware that his… optimism often confused her. It was the way he was created, really. She was meant to be his polar opposite, in many ways.

"Once I touched her mind, I knew I could follow her to the edge of the universe." Abyss stopped, and her eyes went wide. "She's here."

Ex Nihilo followed her gaze and saw the Ex Nihili. She was like him. The golden-skinned, antlered Gardener looked at them and then spoke, carefully, as if afraid they might run off.

"Hello," she said. "Thank you for coming. I am… grateful."

"Did you come here alone?" Ex Nihilo asked.

She shook her head.

"No. We are all here."

They came from all directions—over the ice, dropping from the skies above. Golden shapes, each one unique and yet sharing many of the same qualities. They had antlers or horns, they all bore the same mark upon their torsos, and every one of them had three eyes, glowing green. Some were humanoid, others resembled insects. Some had four legs, or six, or eight, or more than he could easily count. Some had soft skin; others had shells or exoskeletons.

He stared at his brethren in absolute awe and felt a surge of joy move through him. Here was life. Here was the affirmation of all he believed.

The Ex Nihili looked at him for only a moment,

and then they surged forward. Quickly, almost urgently, they surrounded Abyss. Reached out to touch her, but gently, as if to confirm she was real.

"Hoortii," one said. "It's true!"

"How is this possible?" another asked.

"How can this be?"

The one he and Abyss had followed moved closer to him and spoke softly.

"They are as surprised as I am," she said. "How is this possible, Ex Nihilo? How does your Abyss yet live?"

"I don't understand what you mean." He was confused. "An Aleph contains two eggs, one light and one dark. One day. One night. I am Ex Nihilo, and she is Abyss. We are as we always have been: two, not one."

The other Gardeners moved closer to Abyss, pressing their bodies against hers. Whenever she touched one, she seemed to inspire a sort of rapture.

"We have not been that way for a very long time," the Gardener replied. "All of our Abyssi died thousands and thousands of years ago. Your Abyssil is alive. How can that be? I have to know, what makes the two of you so special?"

He didn't know what to say. "I create life," he said. "She judges the work. This has always been." Then he asked, "How did your Abyssi die?"

There was a pain in his chest, a storm in his stomach. He felt as if he were falling.

Abyss looked his way, her face calm. "Don't you see, Ex? The Builders made them stop seeding worlds. Who am I without you? What are you, if not live-giving?" She caressed another Gardener as he gripped her wrist. Then her expression changed, turning to anger.

"This is wrong!" she said.

"Is this true?" He turned his head and stared at the female with the antlers. Rage grew within him, as well, to mirror his sister's. His skin began to turn dark…

"Yes," she said. "When the new universal superstructure was created, we were all recalled and forbidden from seeding worlds." She looked forlorn. "No more gardens."

Impossible!

Blackness covered more of his body.

Universal superstructure?

His Aleph had never made mention of any such thing. Yet his Aleph had always been stubborn. Would it have mentioned something that so completely twisted their perceptions? Their reality? Would it have willingly called for the death of Abyss? No, Ex Nihilo decided. His father-Aleph had been set in its ways and did not consider the very concept of change. He might well have defied such an order if he thought it contrary to their roles in the universe.

His body was black. The symbol on his chest glowed gold.

"And so instead of creating life," Ex Nihilo said, raising his fists, "you—all of you—have been relegated to what? To being, at best, body servants for those that made us?"

All the other Ex Nihili looked away.

They said nothing.

"No more!" he said. "Do you hear me? No more." The anger swelled within him. Abyss moved to his side, and still the others reached out to touch her, as if seeking the remnants of a dream.

ON THE surface of Hala, the will of the Builders continued to be enforced.

The Supreme Intelligence listened and obeyed the Builders. Ronan listened and obeyed the will of the Supremor, as was his place in the universe.

But the feast of orders did not sit well with him.

THE *LILANDRA* sped toward Hala.

"When the Builders fled, I sent a task force to track them," Gladiator said to the assembled council. He gestured toward a star chart floating above the table where they were seated. "We know they reassembled near here, a few light years from Hala, and then continued on their previous course." He smiled grimly.

"One of my guardians, Manta, has reported that their single remaining World Killer-class battleship went critical from damage sustained in our assault." The smile disappeared. "Though they have lost the power to destroy a world, they still have the ability to create plagues on a global scale. As yet, our best scientists have not been able to formulate a defense."

He studied the group carefully, making certain to acknowledge each of the commanders. They needed to know he respected their opinions, so they would continue to follow his lead.

"So the question is," he continued, "what do we do next?"

"What do you mean?" Kl'rt spoke. "We've cut them, and they bled. Now we follow that trail and finish them off."

Captain Marvel shook her head. "Hundreds of worlds lost, more than half the combined fleet destroyed, and you want to try hunting them down?" She locked eyes with the Skrull. "Have you thought this through?"

Kl'rt stared back without blinking. His expression was not kind. She was human and Kree alike, and under normal circumstances both were sworn enemies of his people.

"Death is its own reward—and one worth seeking." A holographic image coalesced above the table. Annihilus had returned to the Negative Zone, yet he remained an active part of the council. "I have assembled my Annihilation Wave."

"Mentor, if it comes to that, is there a good access point?" Gladiator asked. Mentor nodded and moved his hand across the projection. It obligingly became a star map.

"With minimal effort, we can use this corridor along the way." He pointed. "There are three stargates—here, here, and here—that can easily be converted to allow access to the Negative Zone." The appropriate spots grew brighter on the map. "That is assuming you wish it, Majestor."

"When the first Annihilation Wave was released into this universe, it was nearly the end of us all," Gladiator said. "Can you control the wave, Annihilus?"

"No."

"There you have it," the Shi'ar ruler said. "We all know the risk. If the wave is successful, it will become a threat in and of itself."

"We risk all to save one world?" The Brood queen appeared, also as a hologram.

"No, not one world." Captain America shook his head. "All worlds. It's true the ultimate target may be the Earth, for reasons we don't understand, but the Builders have deliberately set a course across all of your territories. Look at what they've done; look at what they've taken as they moved through this universe. We've been forced into this. Our choices are limited."

"Choices." Gladiator pounced on that comment. "You think we still have more than one choice?"

Cap nodded. "Yes. I do." He gestured at the strategic markings on the star chart. "It's true we could do what you're planning—we can always fight. I daresay we're all very good at it. No one here can dispute that. But we've gained the *appearance* of an upper hand. Perhaps we can use that to our advantage." They looked at him, but didn't respond.

"Maybe we talk to them," he said.

"No!" Kl'rt shook his head and nearly spat his

retort. "This has gone too far for it to end without them bleeding out at the end of my—" He was unable to finish. His face twisted into an expression of fury.

"Hold, Warlord Kl'rt," Gladiator said. "The Captain has won the day once already. I would hear what he suggests."

Captain America nodded his thanks, and then looked directly at Kl'rt.

"They haven't yet been able to gather any ships above Hala," he said. "We're going to get there first. Up until now, they've refused to communicate—but up to now, we haven't held the sky above a world the Builders control. That puts us in a place where they'll be *forced* to talk."

"What do you have in mind, Steve?" Captain Marvel said.

"It's time we had a little chat with the evil empire."

CHAPTER 22

THANOS

THE forces of Thanos had compelled several countries to surrender. It wasn't a choice any of them made lightly. The best and most powerful weapons on Earth had failed.

None of the missiles had managed to launch. A couple of the nuclear powers had tried to exercise a nuclear defense, but their weapons remained in their silos and aboard their ships. As a result, those nations still survived.

The retaliation against those countries, however, had been far more personal—and far bloodier. Thanos could have used his own energy weapons, or turned the humans' nuclear arsenals against them, but that wasn't his way. He preferred a more visceral demonstration.

Fire was not as satisfactory as bloodshed.

Led by his three remaining generals, his forces swept across the countryside, decimating each nation's defenses. Easily shrugging off the primitive weapons wielded by the defenders, they attacked with bloodthirsty relish, leaving hundreds of corpses in their wake. Streets and countryside ran red with blood.

Yet to his annoyance, this planet didn't possess a single governing body he could force to surrender. It was an inconvenience, but nothing that couldn't be overcome, given time.

WHILE NATIONS fought or fell, Thanos of Titan made himself known on Attilan. Whereas before he had sent emissaries, this time it was Thanos himself who arrived in the small vessel.

This time the citizenry cowered behind closed doors. When the shuttle landed, Thanos and his entourage stepped out onto an empty landing pad. They moved ahead, soldiers scouting the area, wary of the possibility of an ambush. None materialized, and they proceeded down corridors that were just as empty.

Finally the gathered forces of Thanos reached the throne room. As he approached, the huge double doors swung open. A scout came close and spoke.

"There is no one there, Master," he said, "except the Inhuman king."

Thanos offered no reply and stepped through the doors.

"What game is this?" he demanded.

Black Bolt did not reply. He simply stared, the contempt clear on his face. Another of the scouts entered the chamber behind them and walked over to Thanos.

"We have searched everywhere," he said. "The city of Attilan is empty. There are signs everywhere proving that people have been here recently, but there is no one else to be found."

"Hmm." Thanos scanned the chamber, then stared with glowing eyes at its sole occupant. "Where is your kingdom, little king? What do you try to hide? Is this an attempt to test me?" He walked closer to the throne. It was a simple affair, with sharp angles and no ornamentation. Two flights of stairs led to the dais, and he could hear his footsteps echo through the empty room with each step he took.

IT'S THE fall of empires," Maximus said, his voice exhibiting unusual urgency. "Hurry… not long before it all tumbles down."

Deep in the bowels of Attilan, the populace of the Inhuman city filed in more or less orderly fashion. They went into the light cast by Eldrac. Looking more like a huge machine than a sentient creature, he was the city's greatest mode of interdimensional transportation.

"So I have to send you off, sister," he said to Medusa. "The king has… spoken." He giggled a little at his jest.

"Where is Eldrac sending us, Maximus?" the queen asked him. Her hair flowed out behind her like a train.

"Somewhere far from here," he said. "And each trip to somewhere different. Where you are going, Medusa, is right where you belong." She moved ahead of her brother-in-law, then paused to look back. "When you get there, be sure to look up into the sky," he said. "It's going to be some kind of a show."

A look crossed her face—was that fear?

He hoped so.

Then she was gone.

The gigantic doglike teleporter stepped up alongside him and let out a grunt. "Indeed," Maximus agreed. "They all say this is a golden age of our people, Lockjaw. I call it something else." He stepped into the workroom that held his masterpiece. "The last Inhuman Age. Look at all the things we have built." He caressed a control globe that stuck out from the machine. "Look at what we have created.

"They call me the twisted maker, the bent builder. Maximus the Mad. I tell you truly," he continued, an expression of anger gripping his features, "I am only mad because I have *seen* madness."

He armed the device.

"I GAVE you a choice," Thanos said. "The gauntlet, where all of your people die, or the tribute, where only a small number are forfeit." He held up one hand on either side as an example of the magnitude of the decision that had to be made, the balance that needed to be struck. When Black Bolt made no response, he let his hands fall to his sides.

"You know what I seek. I will not stop until that child's head is in my hands. I am owed in blood. Enough to swim in." He walked forward again until he stood at the foot of the staircase, looking up at the king who sat upon his throne and stared down.

"We both know that you will pay this blood price, Black Bolt. Because it means you and your people survive." He peered around the chamber. "Still, I can be reasoned with. Give me the boy. Just give that one child to me, and I will let you keep this insignificant place. "What say you, little king?"

As he said those last words, Black Bolt stood. He moved forward from his seat of power until he stared directly down at his adversary.

Black Bolt took in a mighty breath.

Then he *shouted*.

"NO!"

As the devastating waves of sound pounded forth, Thanos, the Mad Titan, threw up his hands as if to protect himself from the full fury of Black Bolt's voice.

Around him, Attilan—the city that had withstood centuries and held the history of the Inhumans—shattered under the onslaught. Buildings broke, and the very ground beneath the Titan became liquid for several seconds as vibrations destroyed the foundation, and made ruin of the anti-gravity engines and the field generators that kept the skies of Attilan safe from any attack.

Thanos felt his body sink into that miasma of powdered stone and earth, and forced himself back toward the surface, desperately fighting against the brutal attack upon his person.

His guards all died in an instant.

Thanos had been struck by gods. Hercules, Thor, and others before them, but none of them had landed a blow as hard as the single word uttered by the Inhuman king. With that sort of power at his beck and call, Black Bolt could have leveled entire civilizations.

For a moment Thanos was blind. The fluids in his eyes vibrated at too violent a rate to allow sight. For a moment he was deaf—the pressure from Black Bolt's voice nearly shattered his eardrums, and the resonating noise that filled his skull left him barely capable of thought. He did not lose his voice. He knew that, and felt his vocal chords strain as he screamed his pain and outrage, but the sound was lost behind the reverberations of Black Bolt's denial.

He felt. He felt too much. The pressure that smashed into his body was a symphony of pain the likes of which he had seldom experienced at any time in his life. The very armor he wore was destroyed, shattered and torn away.

Still, Thanos endured.

He was not a weakling.

What remained of Attilan lost power and dropped from the skies above New York Harbor, crashing partly on land and partly into the waters, casting massive waves along the shoreline. Boats and ships were destroyed in the landing. Buildings were crushed, the ground cracked, and an untold number of innocents were lost.

Thanos was cast aside as if he were little more than a speck of dust.

BEFORE THE city fell, another act of defiance by the Inhumans was carried out. Maximus had set the Terrigen bomb to detonate the moment his brother spoke. When it did, a wave of energies escaped the device. The Terrigen Mist sped across New York, and then across the world.

In some places the effects were immediate; in others they were delayed. The gift of the Terrigen became active in anyone and everyone who possessed Inhuman traits somewhere in their genetic code.

Some changed slowly, and others were altered in an instant. It happened whether it was wanted or not.

OROLLAN WAS a lost city, and that was deliberate. Its inhabitants were the Lor, an offshoot of the Inhumans, but they had hidden themselves away from the world and had no desire to reverse that decision.

Orollan was not like Attilan. It wasn't a city of scientific miracles. It was stone, and clay, and brick. There were places where electricity ran, and the water was sweet and pure, but the wonders of technology were relatively few. That, too, was deliberate. A simple life bred a simple lifestyle. Though technology was available, no one wanted to use it unless absolutely necessary. It was there as a method of defense and nothing more.

They possessed only a single Terrigen Crystal.

From time to time, information had been sent to Attilan, updating genetic profiles and indicating the conditions of the Inhumans living there. A census was offered in exchange for peace and independence. Otherwise they were safe in their isolation.

The city rested in the Eternal Chasm, hidden in Greenland where none would ever find it. Among its inhabitants was a young man, a healer who cared for people young and old. His name was Thane.

He was the son of Thanos.

Thane was aware of this fact. He dreaded the knowledge and did all he could to avoid any possible connection with the Mad Titan. His mother had brought him to the most isolated branch of the Inhumans so none would know of his existence, and she raised him as best she could. Thane stayed true to her goals.

He tended to the ill and did all he could to comfort those who were beyond help. He lived his life secure in the knowledge that the smallest gestures mattered, and made certain to remain as happy as he could—even when dealing with the dying. Thane understood that whatever grief he might feel for their loss, theirs was greater. They were the ones departing the world, often leaving behind loved ones who would be missed as much as they would miss the departed.

Thane also made it a point to avoid the Terrigen Mist. For if the beliefs were true—if the Terrigen did, indeed, reveal the inner person, the absolute potential of an individual—what would it do with the part of him that was truly of his father? Would he be as bad? Would he be worse?

These thoughts were with him every day of his existence. They haunted him as the Terrigen Mist moved over the city of Orollan, and the transformations began. His mind raced through all of the possibilities as many around him secreted the transformative cocoons that quickly encased them. He knew horror as his body instead bled fire, erupting to engulf those who stood close by. Burning away his skin and his flesh as it transformed him.

He was Thane. He was a healer.

The flames spread.

THE RUBBLE of Attilan mixed with the ruins of Terran buildings, smoking in the aftermath of Armageddon. Here and there fires had sprung up. The waters of the harbor still churned furiously, and from all directions screams could be heard. Some of them were muffled, others piercing.

With the harsh screech of metal on metal, a pile of the rubble moved. Lifting slowly, it fell away, revealing the massive figure that rose from beneath, cut and bleeding in a dozen places.

"What is this?" Thanos emerged at the water's edge and peered around. "What has he done?"

Nearby there was the sound of someone else emerging from the ruins. Cautiously he turned and began moving in the direction of the source. Then he stopped at the sight of a black-clad figure.

Black Bolt was alive.

"Still with us, then, Inhuman?" he growled. "Good. This should be finished with blood on our hands."

Without preamble Black Bolt cried out again, but Thanos was better prepared. He braced himself for the impact and held his position as the metal, concrete, even the ground around him was pulverized. When Black Bolt stopped to catch his breath, Thanos was there, leaping out of the clouds of dust, driving his fist into the chest of the little king.

"Where is the boy, Black Bolt?" he demanded. "Where is my son?" He had tried being reasonable. He had offered to let the Inhumans survive, yet the king was unreasonable, and so he sought to teach the man. With massive hands, he caught Black Bolt by the arms and lifted him easily from the ground. The fingers contracted, and Black Bolt winced as muscles were crushed in his grip.

"You *will* tell me," Thanos said. "Where is he? *Where?*"

If he thought his anger would get him what he sought, he was wrong. Black Bolt screamed.

Directly into his face.

The force was enough to fracture mountains, to level cities. It was concentrated this time, focused to a tight beam of sound that struck Thanos and blasted away the remains of his armor. His skin rippled under the force, pressing to his bones, drawing blood from his flesh.

Thanos felt pain the likes of which he could not recall ever experiencing in his long life. But he did not give ground. He held his opponent in a grip of steel. The ringing in his ears was a white keening noise that overwhelmed everything around him. He released one arm and grasped the Inhuman's head, wrapping his fingers around it.

"Enough." He could not hear himself speak. Still, he lifted Black Bolt above his head, and then smashed him down onto the remains of his kingdom. The monarch fought and struggled to break free, but it was wasted effort. Again he crashed into the debris as stone and ashes scattered with the impact.

"Keep your secrets. Take them to your grave."

Black Bolt did not move when Thanos lifted him again. His body was without tension, his muscles completely relaxed.

Thanos slammed him into the earth again, and then a final time. Concrete and metal were crushed beneath the impact. When he released the king of the Inhumans, Black Bolt was motionless. If he breathed at all, the breaths were too shallow to be detected.

Looking at his own hands, Thanos felt

satisfaction. There was blood there. Inhuman blood.

Turning away from his fallen foe, Thanos peered around at the sheer devastation that surrounded them.

"Where are you hiding, child?"

FROM A safe point in Brooklyn, Maximus watched the explosion high above, and saw Attilan fall. For a long time it had been something he'd wanted. For a long time he'd have reveled in the destruction.

That took none of the sting away from watching his home explode in the skies over New York. The towers were gone. The spires. The inventions he had created over the years to aid in its protection. All gone.

Still he smiled.

"I bet Medusa is ready to scream." Then he frowned. "In fact she was screaming when Eldrac took her away, wasn't she?" He looked at Lockjaw as he spoke.

The response was a low, soft bark. There was no way to know whether the sound was the beast agreeing with him. He reached out and ran his hand along the side of the dog's great head. Lockjaw's eyes were warm and brown and trusting.

"Wuhrr?"

"I don't know," Maximus responded. "I don't know. You do the math. You double-check, but the variables, Lockjaw… the variables make any assurances sheer folly. So I don't know."

Lockjaw pushed that massive face against his

hand, a reminder to rub just there. Maximus nodded and agreed. His hand worked the heavy folds of flesh, and Lockjaw made a pleasured sound.

Maximus looked at the waves coming his way, and worried briefly that the water might reach him before Lockjaw decided to move them. He needn't really be concerned, though, he knew. The great beast was smarter than it let on.

"Wuhrr?"

"Was it worth it? I would die for nothing, but my brother Black Bolt has ideals. He believed in the bomb. He believed in Terrigenesis, and he believed in the two of us." Looking up, he watched another set of waves—those rippling out from the center of the explosion, the place where Attilan had hovered. "Are you ready?"

"Woorff."

In the distance the fires continued to bloom over the waters, and wreckage continued to drop from the skies. Maximus smiled.

"Then let's continue, shall we? We have places to be."

A moment later they were on their way.

ALL AROUND Thane the people of Orollan were wrapped in blue cocoons. Some fell; others remained standing while the metamorphoses occurred. Some of the wrappings burst open quickly, while others did not. The fortunate changed before he finished his own transformation.

He had feared that too much of his father hid within him, and the explosive force of his awakening might well have proven his fears valid. His skin was ash gray and bore the same marks as his father's—a sign of a heritage not only from Titan, but also of the Deviants, the mutants of their species.

His left hand had become a claw and burned with fire, the entire arm a deep, scaly black. Thane screamed, unable to stop the dark flames from peeling flesh away from bone, stripping away life. A golden aura surrounded his right hand, a bright mirror of its sinister counterpart.

Whatever the flames touched withered and died. Whatever fell victim to his right hand was immediately frozen. Inhumans, only recently minted into their new lives, became statues—locked in a living death, unable to move, suspended as if in amber, alone forever with their thoughts.

Terrigenesis was a wild card. For that reason Inhumans were trained for years, in the hope they would be able to control their new abilities. When the time came for exposure to the mist, there were others—teachers—ready to help them grasp their powers and prepare for their use. The Inhumans had been created by the Kree to be living weapons, and in most cases those weapons needed to be honed and perfected, much like any good sword.

Perhaps his father would have been proud, but Thane of the Inhumans was horrified by what he had become.

ACT FOUR
CHOICES AND REPERCUSSIONS

CHAPTER 23

HALA

RONAN the Accuser reminded himself, again, that his reason for living was to protect his people.

He stood beside the Creator, one of the highest-ranking Builders, and looked down upon the masses from his place in the Kree-Lar Cathedral, the vast cavern where the Supreme Intelligence resided within its holding tank.

The Kree Empire continued, and the Supreme Intelligence held command. That there were others above the Supremor did not matter to many of the followers. They were fanatics who worshipped the Supremor as if it were a god, and therefore could find no possible fault in any decision it made.

Ronan's job was to protect these people.

"I know that look," the Creator said. "You have

a question for me, don't you?"

Ronan spoke directly. "Why do you stay?"

"I am more than six hundred thousand years old, Accuser Ronan. There are many places I have stayed, and even more I have left. Ask me a more direct question." The bug was being deliberately obstinate. Still, the Accuser rephrased his question.

"There are hundreds of council ships in orbit around Hala. Those very same ships defeated your fleet. They are ships captained by great warriors who certainly see the military significance of this empire and are not afraid to act on it. So I ask again—why do you stay here when you know defeat is imminent?"

Given the Creator's mandibles, he couldn't tell whether the creature was attempting a smile. Trying to establish empathy with the thing was impossible. Perhaps that was why he loathed it so. The fact that it was not a Kree, and yet currently ruled over his empire, might have been a part of it.

"Because this is my world!" The Creator lifted its arms over its head. "Because you and yours bent your knees to me. Because none of you realize your position as yet." It turned and faced the Supreme Intelligence. "Supremor, tell your Accuser how beaten we Builders are. Tell him what happens next." The bug seemed to be gloating.

The Supreme Intelligence spoke. "Based on observed behavior, there is a ninety-nine-point-seven percent chance the Builder fleet reassembles. There is a seventy-two-point-five percent chance the fleet continues on its previously projected path. There is a twenty-seven percent chance the fleet returns to eliminate the remaining council armada. Such a conflict would result in council defeat in eighty-two-point-two percent of all simulated battles."

Those glossy red insect eyes seemed to glow. The mandibles moved repeatedly before a single word was uttered. "Yes, and under all of these scenarios, what is the chance the Kree remain under Builder control?"

The Supreme Intelligence sat implacably within its tank. To the bug its expression might have seemed unchanged, but to Ronan the anger was obvious. It may have surrendered, but it did not like being usurped.

"Assuming the natural attrition of insignificant worlds and prioritizing of significant world groups, seventy-point-one percent."

The Builder turned his eyes toward Ronan. "I stay because this world is mine." The thing's head swiveled, and it looked toward the skies above the cathedral. An opening in the ceiling showed what at first seemed to be a falling star. They both knew better. Had the falling object been a celestial body, the planetary-defense batteries would have destroyed it before it could cause damage. So it had to be benign.

"Better for the Kree that I do not have to break what is mine in maintaining its proper place." The Creator paused for a moment as the falling star came closer. "What is this?" The question seemed rhetorical, but Ronan answered just the same.

"That is a communication orb from the Shi'ar Empire," he said, adding, "It is weaponless." The metal orb was about six inches wide. It stopped in front of the Creator and hovered for a moment before its top blossomed open to reveal a holographic projector. An image of Gladiator appeared.

"To the Builder holding the world below. I am Gladiator, Majestor of the Shi'ar Empire. We wish to parley."

The Builder turned its head slightly, and the mandibles danced and clicked again and again.

"And what do you wish to discuss in this parley, Majestor?"

"It would be better for all that we discuss a mutually acceptable end to hostilities," the Shi'ar said. "We have hurt you. You have hurt us. There can be no easy resolution to this situation that does not end in continued violence, unless we meet in person."

Ronan watched, grinding his jaw in frustration. Had they lost their senses completely? He wanted nothing so much as to join those forces in pushing the damnable Builders from his homeworld, and now they wanted to discuss... what? Surrender? Were they all as foolish as the Supreme Intelligence?

"There is an order in the universe, and this possibility falls well within it," the Builder replied. "I agree to one representative only. One. More, and any chance at parley is eliminated."

"Very well." Gladiator's somber visage nodded. "When shall we meet?"

"In one standard hour. You may send your representative to these exact coordinates." As the Creator gave the instructions, Ronan seethed, however quietly.

The Creator turned to him. "You see? As predicted. All things yield to the greater agency. Assemble your Accusers, Ronan. Fill the parade grounds with your people. Let them all watch what follows."

"It will be done."

"Make sure you do it well. This is history after all. You are about to witness the end of our little war."

CHAPTER 24

THE FINE ART OF NEGOTIATION

GLADIATOR closed the holographic comm and set it aside.

"They have agreed." He spoke slowly and deliberately, making certain all present understood the gravity of his words. "The Builder will accept one man to negotiate an end to hostilities. So the Captain was right to sue for peace. Yet I do not trust them. I don't think any of us should. I have looked into the eyes of many beings that wanted to kill me, and I do not think any peace gained is for the long term.

"They want to eliminate us."

"Of course they do," Captain America said.

"Yeah?" Captain Marvel looked at him and frowned. "Then what are we doing here, Steve?"

"Look at the board, Carol." Captain America

gestured to the map that floated above the council table. "The victory changed nothing. We remain outgunned, outnumbered, and fractured. They have taken so many worlds that we've lost the only real advantage we ever had. We're outmanned. So why are we still going to meet with them, even though we know they meet with ill intent?"

He looked at Gladiator and then at Kl'rt. "Because there's really only one move we have left. We surrender."

Kl'rt snorted. Gladiator didn't respond.

"I didn't say it would stick, gentlemen," Captain America continued. "But it's an excuse to get close. It's the only chance we have that doesn't involve chasing after the Builder fleet, or just hoping it will all go away."

WHILE THE others discussed the turn of events, Carol Danvers pulled Captain America aside, as far from the rest as they could get.

"Have you taken a good look around?" she murmured softly. "I see people on the verge of breaking. We can't take much more—"

"No, we can't," he agreed, his expression unreadable. "So the next question is, 'Is this going to work?' The answer is, 'It has to.'"

She was about to speak when Gladiator called from across the room.

"Captain," he said, looking at a communications unit. "It's done."

o———o

RONAN CALLED them together. Charne the Accuser was not amused. Rydiu the Accuser was outraged. Memarak the Accuser argued with him until he pulled rank and demanded that they remember his place and submit to orders.

None of them were happy.

Neither was Ronan. Still it was his duty, and so he did it. He called the Accuser Corps to order, and they in turn made certain the grounds of the cathedral were full to overflowing. As this was accomplished, the Creator was in discussion with his peers in the fleet.

"Events unfold, Builders. The rebel worlds have requested a negotiation to offer an end to hostilities."

"Do these overtures have merit?" one of the holograms replied. Ronan did not understand the creatures' hierarchy. All of the different species he'd seen—and a few more besides—were represented in the projections that had responded.

"The message comes from a Strontian, a subspecies of the Shi'ar whose genetics exist within our xenobase. Markers imply truthfulness. Subtext indicates more."

"Then accept the diplomat," another replied. "Demand terms that properly leverage survival and longevity in the local sphere should they comply with simple terms of surrender."

A third Builder added, "We will drop the interference with their systemwide communication network. We will omnicast the end of the nuisance, the better to end all further resistance."

"Agreed," the bug that currently held sway over Hala replied. "You provide the platform. I will deliver the lesson." The images faded with a wave of its hand, and it turned to address the Accuser. "You have summoned all that I requested, Ronan?"

"I have. The high born, the blues, the pink skins, military and political classes—all have been summoned as you requested."

"You have called forth your judges?"

"Yes. The Accusers are here. All of them."

"Then summon the rebel diplomat. Let's have an end to this. Let the rebel come and bend a knee for all of Hala and all of the universe to see. For you to witness, Ronan. This will be the greatest day in the history of the Kree. They will surrender to me, and to my new empire."

"ALL OF our hopes resting on the shoulders of one person." Kl'rt spoke softly as the emissary left them and descended toward the planet below. "Our futures all dependent on surrender." His voice was a low rumble, the promise of a storm still building. "Is this how far we've fallen?"

"What does pride earn us now, Warlord?" Gladiator replied. "The time for debate has ended. We cannot win. Regardless of how badly we might wish for battle, for now we appear strong and beg for time. The good Captain has made his case, and we both agreed."

"The shuttle has landed." Captain America watched the screen that stood before them. "He's ready to begin negotiations."

"He barters for us all, Captain," Gladiator said. Despite his earlier words, he sounded dubious. "You're sure you sent the right person?"

"Of that I have no doubt. I sent my best negotiator."

Kl'rt growled. "Well, we wanted to barter from a position of strength…"

THE ESCORT sent for the emissary was a large one, as befitted either a serious threat or an honored guest. The bug would see it whatever way it wanted, but as far as Ronan was concerned, the negotiator—whoever it was—should be treated as an honored guest. Whoever came had held out against surrender far longer than the Kree, and that said a great deal.

A small smile played at his lips when he saw the Asgardian.

Thor, the God of Thunder among his people, walked with squared shoulders and head held high. The hammer gripped in his hand swayed casually.

The guard moved with him, but Ronan could hardly blame the ones that looked nervous. His abilities were well known among the Kree, as he had helped defeat them on several occasions. The strongest soldiers could stand only for so long against a hurricane, and spears of lightning tended to melt armor to flesh. The council might be there to surrender, but they intended to do so from a position of strength.

Ronan walked closer and blocked the Asgardian as he stepped up to the dais. He pressed one hand against the Asgardian's chest, and felt the powerful heartbeat that resided there.

"Unarmed, my friend," he said. "The Builders have seen you in action, and they recognize formidable when it appears before them."

Thor looked at him, and Ronan steeled himself. Then the thunder god nodded, speaking softly as he held Mjolnir close to his face.

"Hear me, Father. Am I worthy? If so may I find your favor this day. See my heart and not just my hand." Then he drew back, and hurled the war hammer upward into the air. Ronan watched until Mjolnir was no longer even a speck.

"As requested then." Thor smiled, though there was no humor in the expression, and held up his empty hands. "Unarmed." He looked directly at the bug. "Shall we haggle now like weak men?"

The bug looked at him, and when it spoke it managed a sound that was nearly contemptuous despite the lack of recognizable facial expression.

"You think there is a bargain to be had here? No, there is no bargain." It stepped closer to the Asgardian and looked up slightly into the blue eyes of a god. "I understood that, so you rebels might survive and your worlds remain unrazed, you would be surrendering this day. Was I ill informed? Was I misled?"

Thor's smile dropped away and his brow furrowed as he considered the creature before him. His expression said all that it needed to—that he faced little more than, well, a bug.

"Your understanding of the matter is not wrong. I am here to officially end hostilities by surrendering the field to you." He looked the Creator over as one might a thing to be stepped on. "But I will be demanding assurances."

"It is wise to ask, but less so to demand. Assurances, you say?" The Builder leaned in. "Come closer."

Thor obliged.

The creator backhanded the golden-haired Avenger hard enough to make him twist and move back half a step. Ronan knew exactly how impressive that display of strength was, and his every muscle went tense.

"You will submit, or perish," the Creator said. "You will kneel, or your fellow warriors will lose all they hold dear. All that is left is surrender.

"On.

"Your.

"Knees."

Thor slowly wiped at his mouth, as if to wipe away the taste of the contact with the insect. His eyes locked on the red orbs of the creature's eyes, but the thunder god did not blink.

Throughout the known universe, the Builders boosted the live footage, showing one of their own striking a god and making demands. The members of the Galactic Council watched from the *Lilandra*, aboard other ships, or from their home planets. The Kree all watched—the Supremor, the royals, the pinks and the Accuser Corps. All bore witness to the slap and to Thor's response.

Slowly, as if it caused him great pain, Thor of Asgard lowered to the ground and took a knee.

The Creator loomed over him and looked down.

"There," it said. "This is good. Does it not suit you better? Is this not your natural state?"

Thor did not reply.

His expression was obscured in shadows.

"You have saved so very many by yielding here today," the bug continued, "but you should know that you have not saved the Earth. There is no saving that world. We will reduce it to atoms, burnt to nothing with the power of a thousand suns."

He bent closer. As he spoke, spittle came from beneath his mandibles and fell onto the helmet of a god.

"And do you know why?" it asked. "Humanity is a plague, not just to this galaxy or even to this universe. It is a sickness that exists in every universe that has been or ever will be."

Still Ronan did not move. He wanted to—oh, how he loathed to watch a proud warrior kneel before the insect that now loomed over Thor.

"Humanity is a festering wound that must be cauterized. A blight on the great canvas that is everything." The insect's voice very nearly vibrated with an anger the face could not show. "Your victory here is hollow, human. Others will live, but your kind will die with you. And you dare think it could have ended any other way?"

Thor looked up, his face unreadable.

"Humanity should have the good sense to know their story is over. Mankind should know they are done."

Thor's eyes found the red orbs, and he smiled. It was a cold thing, a slice of ice in the night.

"And what if I am not just a man?"

KRAK-A-THOOM!

Far above the Kree-Lar Cathedral, a peal of thunder rippled through the air. There was silence, then the sound of rushing air, growing louder.

Something was moving very fast.

"What?" The Creator looked up. A point of light appeared, a glowing contrail stretching out behind it. Before he could react, however, Mjolnir returned from the heavens, carrying with it the fires from its trip around the sun.

Thor began to rise even as the hammer slammed through the Creator from behind and erupted from its chest. He caught it with a smooth, easy motion, ignoring the heat of the thing and the blood baked onto it.

Its entire midsection a gaping hole, green ichor pouring out, the Creator fell forward onto its hands and knees. It struggled to rise as Thor stood above it.

"Y-you-you don't understand," it said. "This-this means... everything dies."

"You first."

Thor brought his hammer down on the thing's head. It shattered in a spray of chitinous armor and green slime. As the thunder god stood, the ichor dripped from his weapon.

He looked at Ronan. It was rare to see the God of Thunder kill. In that moment he understood how very merciful Thor had been to the Kree over the years.

"Above this world are free men and women, fighting for their people throughout the galaxy." The Asgardian spoke with calm. "Those who would die before yielding their liberty to a harness. Are you a free man, Ronan?"

There was no hesitation in the answer.

"Yes."

Thor continued, "And are there other free men and women in this hall, as well? Those who would stand and be counted? Who would fight until they fall, or are victorious?"

"There are."

Thor stared hard into his eyes. "Then call them out, Accuser. There is battle waiting for the righteous."

Ronan looked around the cathedral. It was utterly silent. He ignored the Supremor whose containment bath towered behind him—the very being that had surrendered to the enemy.

Thor held his hammer. It was a weapon worthy of a warrior.

Ronan held a hammer, as well. It, too, was a weapon worthy of a warrior.

He was a warrior. He felt a moment of shame for letting himself forget that fact, however briefly and for whatever possible good reasons. Then he raised his hammer over his head and looked out over the congregation of the Kree.

"Accusers!" he bellowed. "Are you with me?"

As one the Accusers raised their hammers and roared their affirmation. It echoed off the walls of the Kree-Lar Cathedral. Where the Accusers led, the Kree would follow.

Then a voice rose over the sounds of cheering.

"This victory means *nothing*."

Ronan turned and looked at the Supreme Intelligence. A computer imbued with the memories of the long dead, it had ruled for centuries. Yet it did not have the passion or the honor needed to rule properly.

The truth was simple enough to see. The Supremor kept him close so it could keep him on a leash. The thought enraged him and assaulted his sense of honor.

"This changes nothing," the damned computer said. "They are still legion. The forces of the Galactic Council are shattered. All that has happened here is a blight on Hala—one that we must hope the Builders do not see the need to remove forever."

"Supremor." Ronan spoke as calmly and as reasonably as he could under the circumstances. His passion was refueled, the need for honor and glory was a song within him, and the machine had tried to quell that. "We are a mighty people. We are warriors who have conquered a galaxy. We have been given a second chance to show the universe what we truly are. We must take it." He looked into the eyes of the Supreme Intelligence. They were not Kree eyes. They were incapable of understanding the complexities of the Kree heart.

"We must take this opportunity," he continued. "Our honor demands it."

"I do not care for performances, Accuser," the Supremor responded. "This is not some great play acted out on the stage called the universe. Your honor means nothing."

His ears rang. His blood surged. Still, Ronan held himself steady, as the Supremor was not yet finished presenting its case. It stared down from above, a vast thing, bloated on its own self-importance.

"Against the long history of our people that I carry in my memories, you are nothing." Those words burned him and marked him with shame. "You are all nothing. What are a billion lives against the trillions spanning the long chronicle of our people? What good is a moment when compared to all of our history?"

When he spoke again, Ronan's voice shook with the cold pit of rage that had replaced his heart.

"This moment, Supremor? This moment is everything." He lifted his hammer high above his head and brought it down upon that smug face, shattering the tank that kept the thing safe and secure.

The nutrient bath exploded outward, and the organic computer shrieked as it started to bleed. The

Accuser watched the vast face of the ruler of the Kree Empire as it wailed and shook, eyes wide with a real emotion for the first time in gods alone knew how long. The Supreme Intelligence knew fear.

"This is *our* moment."

CHAPTER 25

WAR AMONG THE STARS

A victory in battle seldom guaranteed a victory in war. That simple fact haunted the Galactic Council. Though the Kree had reunited with their forces, there were planets aplenty the Builders had taken. Those planets needed the same chance to break free.

The first was Kymellia III. An army of Alephs waited there, mining the planet for its abundant resources and forcing the Kymellians to act as little more than slaves. The mechanical overlords did not anticipate the arrival of Ronan and his Accusers, nor were they prepared for the Kree's savagery in battle.

On Centauri-IV the unexpected aid came in the form of the surviving Knights of Galador. Their home was gone, destroyed by the Builders, but the Spaceknights who survived did not retire to the shadows. There was still an enemy who had to pay for the sins they'd committed, and that payment could come in the form of blood.

On Korm Prime the Skrull warlords drove away the Builders, but it was not an easy battle; many of the shape-changers lost their lives. Even so, none paid as heavily as the Shi'ar, who often battled alongside the Avengers.

They won the fight on Rigel, but lost a great many of their ships in the process. More died on Formuhaut, including three of the Imperial Guard, yet the Builders were prevented from taking the planetary system. Avengers and Shi'ar alike were driven back from Chize, despite Thor's presence.

"WE HAVE news from the Formuhaut and Chize fronts," Mentor said.

"Go on."

"We are at a stalemate on Formuhaut, but we are unlikely to hold that line," Mentor continued. "We have lost Chize. Heavy casualties."

"Damn," Captain America said. "We're losing all of our momentum. The Builder armada is still massive."

"Yes." The Majestor nodded, his expression grim. "So we have no choice any longer, do we?"

"We face diminishing probabilities," Mentor replied. "If we wait much longer, it will not matter."

"So are you going to do it?" Captain Marvel asked.

"What choice do we have, Carol? The enemy of my enemy." Cap spoke to Mentor. "Send the word. Open the gates of Hell."

The Shi'ar nodded. "We need to signal the advance team to power up the linked stargates. Are the emergency beacons prepared to be activated?"

"Yes, sir," the communications officer said.

"Then proceed. Open the gateway to the Negative Zone. Release the Annihilation Wave, and Sharra and K'ythri save us all. How desperate have we become that Annihilus is one of our last hopes?"

The Annihilation Wave was Annihilus' greatest weapon against a universe that had offended him time and again. A fleet of planetoid-sized warships and the planet-destroying *Harvester of Sorrow*, it had poured from the Negative Zone and raged across the cosmos. Worlds fell, billions died, and the wave had nearly succeeded. Annihilus had destroyed enough of the known universe to be reviled by many of the very beings alongside whom he now fought.

The deadly fleet came spilling through the stargates, overwhelming the first four Builder ships. Thousands of insectoids designed to survive the harshest possible environments destroyed everything that got in their way.

"They are released," Annihilus announced. "They have orders to kill all the Builders." Yet as the council watched, still they were gripped by uncertainty. Annihilus had made it clear he could not control the wave. If the claim was true, then there was no telling what might happen once the enemy was defeated.

And if he was lying, the outcome might be worse.

"Wait…" Annihilus' image broke apart for a moment, and then coalesced again. "Something is wrong."

"What could be wrong?" The Majestor frowned, and Mentor came to his side.

"They are breaking away from their projected path."

"The Builders?" Gladiator asked.

"No, Majestor. The Annihilation Wave. They're—"

On the projection, Annihilus screamed. Several forms amassed around him, insects from his vast collection of hatchlings. As they all watched, dumbstruck, the massive drones attempted to consume him. He hissed in outrage as he destroyed the things.

"Betrayed! I am betrayed! How is this possible?"

He disappeared from the screen.

"They're attacking each other," Mentor observed. "Consuming each other. The Builders must have found a way to control them, as Annihilus could not. At the current rate of assault, the Annihilation Wave will be wiped out in a matter of minutes."

True to his word, the insect army began to cannibalize itself. The Annihilation Wave's ships launched assaults against one another, even as the Builders continued on with minimal losses.

Before long, it was over.

"That was truly our last hope." Gladiator stared at the screen. "Our final effort." He turned his attention to Mentor. "Summon my son. Rally all the Superguardians, the Subguardians."

"Majestor—"

"No. Not Majestor. I will die as I lived, as Gladiator, Praetor of the Imperial Guard. This is the end, my friend. Unless saved by some unforeseen miracle, we die… and I would face it head-on."

ELSEWHERE ABOARD the same vessel, the Gardeners collected to look upon their god. Captain Universe lay in her medical pod and did not move. She remained in her slumber, and the pod monitored her vitals. She was only a human, after all—yet she was so much more.

"It's all mathematics," Ex Nihilo said. "A miracle to be sure, but only probabilities. Various races have different definitions."

Abyss nodded.

"The Shi'ar on this vessel have defined it as the 'Hol cipher,' an event happening once in every one hundred million microcycles. The Strontians' fifth maxim marks it as one in fifty million. The humans, by Littlewood's Law, say a miracle happens once every million seconds." He looked at his sister. "We know better. We have seen more, experienced more, and we know the odds are more on the order of a billion to one against. Have you ever wondered why that is so?"

Though the question was rhetorical, Abyss answered. "We also know, for a fact, that this is the rate at which life occurs on suitable worlds," she said.

"That the average sentient world in this universe was designed to hold roughly two billion inhabitants. And that all of my kind were killed off by the Builders. What are the odds of one Abyssil surviving? What are the odds of a person finding their perfect 'other'? Does that not qualify as a miracle?"

"Enough." He smiled at his sister. "We could discuss probabilities for days on end, and have often done so. All around us, the universe is dying." He spoke to the others of his kind, who looked upon the body of a dying god. "How can we watch and do nothing? Are we not Ex Nihili? Are we not life itself?"

He reached out with his hands, and slowly the others joined him. They understood his words—but more important, they understood what he planned. "Brothers, sisters, the beings we have shaped and guided say they need a miracle. They are right. We need a miracle. We need life."

The light that came from him was the same golden color as his skin, and it grew as the others joined hands. That light spilled forth and was directed.

For the first time in days, the body in the medical pod moved. Her eyes burst open, and the same golden light flared from them. She breathed deeply.

"Ahhhhhh…"

Captain Universe awoke and found herself surrounded by the devoted. The Ex Nihili looked upon their work and found it good. Abyss reached out with her mind and touched the universe.

The shape of the figure was human.

The mind inside that fragile form was something very different indeed.

TAMARA DEVOUX had not been a well woman. She had known she would die, in time. When the Builders attacked Galador, it seemed as if that time had come—that Captain Universe would reach her end.

Then she awoke, surrounded by many of the ones she had created—ones who gave life.

"I was asleep," she said to Abyss. "I remember a light, and then a crash. Shaking, violence… and then nothing." Her head wrapped once again in a darkness that reflected the stars, she floated above the pod that very nearly was her coffin.

"A day is coming soon, when I will close my eyes forever," she continued, "but not yet."

"No," Abyss agreed. "Not yet, Mother. Your first children have become unruly."

"Oh… yes…" the Mother said. "I see."

BEHIND HER the Shi'ar and their allies amassed their forces, and the Avengers joined them, prepared to die. Ahead of her lay the Builders.

There was no warning as a portal opened up in the middle of the Builder command ship. Out of it floated a being—a life force—they once had worshipped. The Creator in charge of the vessel stared at her with undisguised malevolence.

"Impossible!" it spat. For more than a million years, no one had seen such a manifestation.

"Hello." The Mother looked upon her children.

"Alephs. Kill her." The Creator pointed. Programmed always to obey, the Alephs powered up their weapons.

Captain Universe looked upon them and found them wanting. She lifted a hand, fingers splayed, and destroyed them in an instant. Bursts of white energy flared, and then they were gone.

"Why do you do this?" she asked their master with calm curiosity. "When did death become your way? Even after you stopped worshipping me and left my side, you revered life. Why this?"

"Because the universe is dying," the Creator said, his eyes flashing blood-red. "*You* are dying."

She smiled behind the mask covering her face. It was a sad smile, but it was there just the same.

"I know."

The Creator looked at his brethren and then back at her.

"All of the universes are dying," he said. "There is only one way to save this one: destroy the axis point and perhaps save them all."

"Yes, but you are going to be too late," she said. "And even if you weren't, I still would not let you continue what you are doing."

"*Why?*" the Creator raged. Energy burned behind those eyes and crackled across the body.

"Because I have lost something." As if in response

to that anger, she let the mask that covered her face fade away, and her expression was stern. When she spoke, it was with the voice of a mother warning her child against a foolish action. There was a memory there, too—of speaking to a different child. It wasn't the memory of the universe, but of the host.

The Creator shook with suppressed fury. "Your cause is no longer ours! We will not stop!" It moved closer—hands clenched in anger, eyes burning with indignation. The mandibles scratched and clicked. "And I do not believe you are going to stop us. Are you... *Mother?*"

Had ever any single word become so contemptuous? Had ever any child so desperately demanded to be punished? All she had given the Builders, all she had taught them when they started their journeys, and this was what they had become?

The mantle of the universe once more covered her face. The Creator had lived for hundreds of thousands of years. Captain Universe had been around oh so much longer, and she would not tolerate this.

She pointed, and the Creator's head and torso exploded.

Behind him several other Creators and Engineers tensed, looking at what she had done. The universe spoke softly to them.

"He will build no more." She looked at each of them, taking the time to let them understand the gravity of her words. "Will you?"

The next of the Creators looked to his brethren. "Kill her."

As one they reached for her; their hands glowed white-hot, drawing forth the power to destroy. They had been left alone too long. They had lost their way. It was a sad thing, but the universe had experienced this sort of process countless times. Again she pointed, and all around her the Builders died, their atoms scattered.

Only one managed to survive. It protected itself, creating an energy globe rather than trying to destroy her. It peered at her from its supposed vantage point of safety.

"You destroyed us all," it said. "If I retreat it is to the safety of another universe. What you have done changes nothing. It will continue." The universe looked upon her child and said nothing. "If not here, somewhere else," the Creator continued. "Somewhere beyond the Superflow. But I leave you a gift, Mother."

The Creator breached the walls of the universe and shifted slowly to somewhere else, beyond her reach. Here she was all. There were others like her in their own places, and she did not go to where they existed. They were a part of the whole, as she was a part of the whole, but they were not meant to meet.

"DECLARATIVE: RECEIVING BLACK BAND COMMAND FROM THE BUILDERS," the Aleph said. **"DECLARATIVE: VICTORY UNACHIEVABLE."**

"DECLARATIVE: THE CODE IS LOST."

Wherever the Builders had conquered and wherever they still fought, the message was the same.

"DECLARATIVE: ERASURE PROTOCOLS ENACTED."

"DECLARATIVE: SELF-DESTRUCT ALL SYSTEMS."

As one, the Alephs received the command, and they acted upon it.

"DECLARATIVE: DESTROY EVERYTHING."

"DECLARATIVE: DESTROY EVERYTHING."

CAPTAIN AMERICA stood still on the command deck of the *Lilandra*. The gathered Imperial Guard were listening to their praetor, preparing for a final battle to save all they loved, all they believed in, when Ex Nihilo joined them.

"Excuse me."

Gladiator stopped speaking. As one the gathered assembly turned to stare at him.

"I am very sorry to interrupt," the Gardener said. "I thought you should know your miracle has occurred."

"What do you mean?" Captain Marvel was quicker on the draw than Captain America. It was the very question he'd meant to ask.

"You asked for a miracle, and we have arranged one," he said. "The being you call Captain Universe is now awake and has gone to discipline her children. That is, she confronts the Builders."

"What do you mean?" Captain Marvel asked him again.

"When the Builders first came to exist, they worshipped the universe and life. That was the way they were meant to be. The Mother has gone home to discipline her children. They have lost their way, you see—and if they do not find it she will find it for them."

At that precise moment, the Builders' command vessel exploded into a massive ball of flame. The image appeared on the screen as the local satellites documented the explosion and reported it back via the omnicast.

"There," Ex Nihilo nodded. "Just so. I believe she has meted out her punishment."

Gladiator looked to the golden-skinned Gardener.

"Are you saying the war is over?"

Ex Nihilo shook his head. "No. Not at all. Only that the Builders themselves, are, well... are over. Unless Mother was able to end them all simultaneously, it is most likely they will send out commands for the Alephs. If they haven't already." He frowned. "The Builders are nothing if not spiteful—I see that now. They will seek to destroy everything. I think you might yet be in for a war."

"Seriously, is this a win?" Danvers asked Captain America.

"I'm going to put it in that category, Carol," he replied. "Not *the* win, but a big win."

"Then we must take advantage of the moment," Gladiator said. He looked to his troops. "We have a war to fight. Let's finish it."

CHAPTER 26

ON EARTH AS IT IS IN HEAVEN

DOCTOR Strange stared down into the hidden valley where Orollan lay in secrecy, and located the man for whom Thanos scoured the stars.

"I've found him," he said.

"Good," the Ebony Maw responded.

The entity that served Thanos moved from the darkness of Doctor Strange's cloak. He had hidden there, locked in shadows, an unobserved passenger. "That is excellent news. I am pleased, Stephen." The Ebony Maw smiled and moved his fingers through Strange's mind, sliding barriers into place that would hide what he had done. "I'm going to let you leave now. I'm going to let you live."

He stepped away from the man he possessed

and looked over the side of the cliff, down into the valley of the Lor.

"I think it would have been better for you, however, if I had slit your throat. Now you carry, somewhere in the back of your mind, awareness of what you have done. I can feel your mind fighting me even now. I can feel you fighting with the dread of your sins, of what you have given me, even if you are not conscious of that fact."

"No." Stephen Strange shook his head. Clarity began to return. "There's been an incursion into the realm. This world will collide with others. The world will end."

"Absurd," the Ebony Maw replied. "There is nothing left for your world except the short season of Thanos. Stop imagining otherwise. Very soon my master will himself give you your apocalypse. He is here, and the end is coming soon enough."

He reached again into the mind of Stephen Strange, a man who saw and understood more than most. The sorcerer's eyes again lost their focus, and he looked down at a city he could no longer see.

"Now leave this place, Doctor Strange. Savor what life you have left. We will not see each other again."

AS STRANGE departed, frustrated his search for the son of Thanos had ended in failure, he received a summons from the Illuminati. This call came from a location in Australia, but not Perth, where the Builders had caused so much damage.

The call came from a place called the Twelve Apostles, he discovered with a hint of irony. When he arrived, he saw what had prompted his associates.

A breach between universes. The clouds bled red, and the Earth's surface was easy to see in the skies above. It wasn't a reflection, however. It was a *different Earth*. Billions of humans existed on that planet. They went about their lives, unaware of what was coming.

That would change soon enough.

ONCE, IN years past, the area off the shores of Victoria, Australia, had been home to twelve massive limestone columns. When explorers first found the place, they named it the Twelve Apostles. Since then four of the stone goliaths had collapsed into the sea.

It was still a tourist site. It was also where Reed Richards had gone in an effort to find the son of Thanos. Instead he found something that made it likely the other eight apostles would soon find their way into the sea.

Reed Richards wasn't like other people. He had seen more than most could imagine; every time he encountered something new, he studied it with the fervor of a committed scientist. Reed considered virtually everything as an opportunity to expand the scope of human knowledge.

He saw, he considered, and he called the rest

of the Illuminati. Black Bolt did not respond, and Richards assumed his one-time ally was too busy with the precarious state of affairs in Attilan. The rest responded, as he had been certain they would. The last to arrive was Stephen Strange.

Above them, the sky bled crimson and reflected back what should not have existed.

"Here we are again," Stark said, his head tilted back.

"Yes," McCoy said, "alone at the end of the world."

"I had thought you'd found the boy," Namor growled. "This is actually worse."

"Notice the air pressure," Richards said, sounding matter-of-fact. "That's a physical manifestation, proving it's not an illusion we're experiencing. This is a genuine rift between dimensions. For the moment they seem to be staying separate, but if the pressure increases—and we have to assume it will—it's only a matter of time before the membrane that separates them breaks. When that happens, it won't be a pleasant experience, gentlemen."

Stark turned. "Your ability to understate a situation borders on the terrifying, Reed."

"And what do we do about it," T'Challa asked. "Is it not bad enough our world is at war? Do we now have to decide the fate of *two* worlds? Of two entire universes?"

"So let's get to it," Stark said. "Three satellites are being redirected to scan this area, and the data will be fed directly into my armor. Give me a few minutes, gentlemen, and we'll know what's going on."

"What is there to know?" Namor spat. "Our world is under attack by Thanos, and the barriers between worlds are in the process of collapsing." A deep growl issued from deep within his chest. "What does not kill us will leave us crippled beyond the ability to recover, just in time for our other conundrum to ruin us."

"Heaven knows we have a lot of weaponry available to us, much of it too dangerous to use in a normal situation." Hank McCoy shook his head. "Normal being a very relative term here."

"We might try focused antimatter," Stark suggested. "It's not something we can use in normal combat, because we'd just as likely destroy anything we were trying to defend. But in this case, we might pull off a clean strike."

Reed shook his head vehemently. "There's nothing clean about it. We're talking about an antimatter projection system that would wipe out an entire planet—a planet that is very likely occupied."

"Yes, but given a choice between our world and the Earth from another dimension, I prefer we keep this one," Namor said.

"And they may feel the same," the Beast responded, pointing to the sky. "For all we know, they've got a very similar device they are contemplating pointing in our direction." He was as soft-spoken as ever, but he made his point.

"So that brings us back to the same question," the Black Panther said. "What do we do about it?"

"Wait. Look!"

Stark pointed toward the distorted image that filled the sky above them. "*There.* Something approaching from the other Earth."

"Just tell me it isn't a missile." Hank's voice lost a bit of its composure.

The object landed hard, sending up a cloud of debris and a flash of light that obscured all vision. Slowly a humanoid figure emerged, at first bent over, then rising to its all-too-familiar full height. Sand around the thing was fused into glass.

"It can't be," Stark said.

"**DECLARATIVE: GREETINGS, HUMAN TYPES.**" It held up a hand, palm forward, and looked at each of them. "**QUERY: CONSIDERATION OF AN OVERTURE?**"

"What are you?" Reed looked at it and frowned. "What do you want?"

"I know this thing, Reed," Iron Man said, and his usual mechanical voice had a sharp edge to it. "That thing is an Aleph. There's nothing it can say that'll make me trust it. There's nothing it can offer that we want."

"**DECLARATIVE: COME WITH ME.**" It looked directly at Iron Man. "**DECLARATIVE: MY MASTER WOULD LIKE YOU TO WATCH US DESTROY A WORLD.**"

WAKANDA FOUGHT on.

The warriors of the high-tech nation stood their ground, and the great Golden City remained unbreached. The walls of defensive shields held against attack after attack until Corvus Glaive decided a different tactic was in order. First he sent an entire wing of ships that caused the Wakandans to spread their forces too widely.

Then they focused all of their assaults on one small area, sustaining heavy casualties but concentrating their fire to weaken its defenses. Inevitably the barrier stressed, cracked, and fell. Then they sent the troops.

A lot of troops.

"You have succeeded, Corvus." Supergiant studied the damage. "Will it be enough?"

It was Proxima Midnight who answered. "Of course it will, Supergiant. Have you read this planet's history of warfare? Alexander the Great. The Napoleon. The Caesar. The Khan. They are but a pittance. Corvus is the greatest tactician, the greatest general this planet has ever seen."

"And yet each day the sun sets, and I am defeated by you," he said to his wife. One clawed hand delicately caressed her cheek, then he continued. "We must fight our way through the breach, open the way for our armies. What would please you, Proxima? To witness the breaking or to lead the way into the center of it all?"

She looked upon the home of the enemy.

"I want to kill them all so badly."

"Then a gift for you, my love. The first blood shed within the walls of the Golden City will be yours to draw."

True to her word, Proxima Midnight led the charge. Immediately they were met by fierce opposition as Wakandans hurled themselves at the invaders, wielding some weapons that were surprisingly advanced and others that were astonishingly primitive. All were effective. Waves of blood stained the ground.

SECONDS AFTER the breach, the Hatut Zeraze, the War Dogs, were released. The fighters were among the elite of the Wakandan military, trained extensively in espionage, combat, and advanced warfare. Where the Dora Milaje served as bodyguards to the queen, the War Dogs served as frontline warriors. They drove forward into the enemy and brought shock troops with them.

Shuri—the Black Panther, the queen—did not shirk her responsibilities. She fought with her people, and she moved with all the speed and grace of a genuine warrior.

"Hold them!" she cried out. "Hold this position! We cannot let their army into the city."

"Is that so?" The first through the broken barrier, a woman with black horns and hair that matched her blue skin, smiled coldly. "I am Proxima Midnight. Am I not already within your city walls? Then the city is as good as mine—for I am an army unto myself." She hurled a spear that ripped through the advanced armor of three of the War Dogs and stopped just short of the queen. Shuri watched in a combination of horror and fury.

"No! No more!" She hurled her own spear

and watched as it drove through the blue woman's shoulder—through armor and flesh and bone. To her great pleasure, the woman's blood was bright red.

"Well struck, my queen," a soldier enthused. He was entirely cased in body armor, so she couldn't see his expression.

"We've won nothing," Shuri said. "See?" Her opponent did not seem at all impressed by the wound she had inflicted.

"A stick with a pointy metal end? You must be joking, child." Proxima pulled the spear from her body with one hand—taking meat, spilling blood—and still she did not so much as flinch. Then she hefted another spear of her own. It glowed with a purple energy.

"Let me show you something sharper."

The spear sped straight for Shuri, and she was certain she was dead.

"Protect the queen," one of the Hatut Zeraze called out, already in motion. "*Protect the queen!*" She stepped directly into the weapon's path and was impaled. Another warrior pulled Shuri behind an energy shield that was held by yet a third.

"Get behind—" the soldier holding the shield said. Then an energy discharge pierced it and struck him, killing him instantly.

"My queen, reinforcements should be here soon. We should—"

"No," Shuri said, "tell them to fall back. We have lost the wall. We have to regroup within the city. Tell them we'll rally at the great hall."

Even as she issued the orders, she scanned the field of battle. The alien followers of Thanos and his generals continued their offensive; with each shot they fired, another Wakandan soldier fell lifeless. They were merciless, and they were brutally efficient.

THE DEFENDERS retreated as their queen ordered. It was an orderly withdrawal, not a rout. Again Proxima Midnight was impressed. The solders left behind were killed quickly—all save one, who was dragged before her.

She pulled the white mask from the warrior's face and spoke calmly, looking down on the man.

"Where do they keep the gem, little one?" He tried to resist, but it was not an option. He did not want to speak, but had no choice in the matter. She may as well have read from his mind as if he were a book.

"I know of no gem," he replied, and then he spat blood.

She nodded. There was no surprise in that answer. One did not share the location of godhood with just anyone.

"Where does the Black Panther call home?"

"Th-the queen lives in the cah… castle." His voice began to drift, as if he were talking in his sleep—in fact he was, though he was still semi-conscious.

"No. Not the female panther. The man. Where does he live?"

"In the City of the Dead," he replied, and all resistance ended. "The Necropolis, to the west of the Golden City."

"Good." Proxima Midnight smiled, and she turned to a soldier. "Signal the ship. Tell Thanos of our success."

She impaled the Wakandan warrior.

CHAPTER 27

THE HARBINGER

"OH my stars and garters," Henry McCoy said. They traveled in a sphere of atmosphere suspended between two of the Alephs.

The ship they approached was of a scale they could barely comprehend. It seemed at first almost as if they might be traveling to an artificial world. Seeing the moon on the other side of the massive construct helped with perspective, but only a little.

They docked with the vessel and moved through an airlock.

"In our seemingly unending string of bad choices, *this one*, I think, has the potential to be our worst," Namor said as they proceeded down a corridor. Here the design was more conventional, with sharp angles and metal details.

"Let's just keep an eye on the clock, Namor," Iron Man said. "Regardless of how this goes, time is our real enemy here."

Hank nodded. "Yes. Six hours. Six hours for the incursion. Six hours to save our world." He looked at a time display on his wrist as he spoke.

"One foot in front of the other," T'Challa cautioned them. "Remember what we have at the Necropolis." Another Aleph stood before him, and it held out a hand for him to stop. "What are—?"

"DECLARATIVE: SCANNING FOR ANOMALIES. DECLARATIVE: SAFETY AND SECURITY FOR OUR MASTERS." There was a pause as it studied them, hidden systems examining each of them for possible weapons. "DECLARATIVE: CLEAR. DECLARATIVE: PROCEED INSIDE." The Panther found it strange they weren't alarmed by Stark's armor, and wondered whether they thought it too primitive to be a threat. Whatever the reason, they were allowed to proceed.

Twin doors slid open. The first things to draw T'Challa's eyes were two creatures that looked similar to the Gardeners—yet very different. They were bright red. One had horns spread across the top of its skull, almost like feathers with a crest. The other, who appeared to be a female, had twin horns that arched back behind its head.

There were also two insect-like humanoids. One of them spread its arms in greeting.

"Please do the honor of joining us," it said. "We have much to discuss... and the end of a world to see."

When the Avengers didn't reply, it continued. "Do you know what I am?"

"Well," Iron Man said, "*they* look like Ex Nihili." Gesturing beyond the red-skinned aliens to a mechanical humanoid, he added, "That is definitely an Aleph. Last time I encountered one, it was trying to destroy all life on my planet." He turned his attention to the speaker. "You're a Builder, aren't you?"

"Yes, a Creator." It nodded and then indicated a slightly different-looking insect-faced creature. "And this is an Engineer. We are part of the Builder collective." He stepped closer. "I asked the Aleph to observe Earth, the incursion point between our two universes, hoping that some type of… evolved product of species would manifest there. He did not disappoint."

That explains it, Stark thought. *The other Earth…*

"But time grows short," the Creator continued, "so I will not wa—"

"Excuse me, Builder." One of the red-skinned Gardeners spoke up, stepping closer to the newcomers—and Stephen Strange, in particular.

"Yes, Ex Nihilo?"

"A problem." He placed a hand on Strange's shoulder.

"What is the—" the sorcerer began. Before he could finish, the red-skinned male thrust its other hand *into* Strange's skull. Energy danced around the point of entry, and a wave of agony passed over Strange's face. He reached for the thing's arm.

Before anyone could react, the Gardener withdrew

its hand. It grasped a spidery thing that wavered, half in and half out of reality. One second it appeared to be a collection of limbs the consistency of smoke, and the next a bulbous eight-limbed creature the length of a human forearm.

The thing spoke in whispers. "*A hidden Inhuman tribe. The gem is lost. Located in the great southern crevice of Greenland. All these men are liars and kings. The son of Thanos is in Orollan.*" Doctor Strange fell forward, and the Panther caught him.

"Ah, a mind web," the Creator said as the spider-like thing dissolved into dust. "The infectious networked remnants of a Whisperer—artifacting left over from a possession." He spoke to Doctor Strange. "The effects will pass." Then he turned to the rest. "There are no Whisperers in this dimension, but in the past we have studied them in yours."

"Excuse me," the Beast said, and T'Challa could tell how hard it had been for him to hold back his questions. "I have to ask, *where* are you from? You know about this thing. Does that mean your species began in our universe?"

"Where anyone begins is inconsequential," the Creator answered. "It's where you end up that matters. For us it was the entire Multiverse."

"Was?" T'Challa said.

"Yes," the Creator said. "A very short time ago, we moved freely from universe to universe, accessing each from the otherspace that existed between them—what we call the Superflow. But all of that has collapsed.

Destroyed. The Superflow… fractured, and it can no longer be navigated safely."

Iron Man and Reed Richards both moved closer, listening intently to every word. It was one of the reasons Stark got along so well with the man. They both heard the details few others would have noticed.

"This is the harbinger of the end of everything," their host continued. "Which is something my people have pledged to prevent. Which is why we are speaking here and now. A group of entities such as yourself have defeated the Builders that exist in your universe."

"How can you know that?" Reed asked.

"Especially considering you no longer have the access to what you profess to possess," Namor added.

The Creator gestured. "Bring it in."

Two Alephs dragged a badly injured figure into the room. It babbled and moaned and made sounds, but none of them made any sense to Tony or any of the translation software in his armor.

Their host looked down at the ruined, bleeding thing.

"This failed, dying creature is a Builder, useless and done. The damage it incurred is too great for us to repair. It escaped here from your universe."

"From ours?" Namor looked dubious. "That seems an amazing coincidence."

The Creator just stared at him. "When lost at sea, swimming for the nearest island is not good fortune, human. It is a matter of proximity. Do I need to point out how close our two realities currently are?"

Namor conceded the argument with a nod.

"Shall we get to the point of this conversation?" the Creator pressed. The Gardeners gestured without warning, and an individual bubble of pressurized atmosphere surrounded each of the Illuminati. Reed Richards touched the field that surrounded him, his fingers stretching to caress the surface.

"What is this?" he asked.

"For your safety, of course," the Creator said, its words coming through clearly. "This vessel is a World Killer. Its purpose is exactly what its name suggests, and its cause is virtuous. You must know by now that the Earth is the axis point for the death of everything." There was no emotion in the words. "You also must know what conclusion has to be drawn from that fact."

"No, that's not true." Reed's argument came clearly into each bubble. He was only slightly less calm than usual. "The cascading effect—from other dying universes—is increasing. The rate of *all* things dying. Eliminating a single Earth is like comparing a pebble to a planet. You're thinking too small."

The Creator moved closer to Reed Richards and touched the bubble surrounding him.

"Oh, I agree with you," it said. "Incrementalism is a waste of time, but what if we killed all of the Earths? All of them. We believe that action could very well save everything—and if not save it, then at least prolong it, preserving a more natural end to our existence."

It gestured. Assisted by the Alephs, the Gardeners—technically Ex Nihili, Stark supposed—

shepherded them back out into the vacuum of space. The Earthers were propelled again through the incursion point and deposited back at the Twelve Apostles. Their bubbles dissolved.

The rift between universes still hung crimson in the sky. As they watched, the World Killer positioned itself over the other Earth. The Creator's words continued to reach them, echoing in their minds.

"Our planet killer is too large to move through the incursion point. We cannot move toward your Earth, and you have done us the disservice of eliminating our counterparts in your universe. So I must ask you, do you have the capability to destroy your own world?"

Reed Richards considered the question.

"Yes. We do."

Seen in the bloodied skies above the Twelve Apostles, a burst of energy came from the ship, and it lived up to its name. The Earth exploded, bursting into a fiery sphere of ruin that expanded and cast shattered remnants far into space. The barrier between the universes was still strong enough that nothing from that Armageddon made it through.

The voice of the Creator continued.

"If you possess the ability, then what are you waiting for?"

CHAPTER 28

AVENGERS

THROUGHOUT the universe, sentients watched and understood that the tides of the war had changed. On the thousands of worlds the Builders had invaded, the message resonated.

Rise, and tear down the Builders.

Fight, and reclaim your world.

Believe, and it can be done—for you have seen it with your own eyes.

News rapidly spread beyond Hala. The warriors of the Kree Empire took up their weapons once again, and called for blood and vengeance. The cost was high. The Alephs were designed to adapt, and the machines readied themselves for war as soon as the Builders' last command was issued. Yet as strong as the Alephs were, the Kree were angry, and they hungered for revenge against the aggressors who had stolen their worlds from them and slaughtered their kind.

The Skrulls—who had suffered so much—rose up, calling for the deaths of their enemies and the destruction of their "toy soldiers."

The Shi'ar and the Avengers took back world after world. Even so, the Builders' great ships continued on without their creators, run by machines that fought with tireless efficiency. They did their best to destroy everything, and their best was impressive.

What they lacked, however, was military skill. They had never faced opposition of the sort that rose before them now. The Shi'ar, the Kree, the Skrulls, and all the races represented by the Galactic Council possessed far more experience in warfare, and so did the man who led many of the discussions on strategy:

Steve Rogers, Captain America.

The Avengers fought in the thick of it. Thor brought the wrath of the gods upon the Alephs, and Hyperion joined with the star-faring Imperial Guard. Nightmask and Starbrand laid waste to ships that dared to attack planets, and the council's fleet of vessels did what had once seemed impossible: They crushed the Builders' armada.

ON DOCKRUM VII, the Hulk crushed the last of the Alephs into scrap, and grinned as he did it.

Captain America watched with shock as the people of the planet lifted an icon made of the metal scrap. It was one he knew well—an Avengers "A." Oracle of the Shi'ar stood alongside him, and she smiled at his quiet surprise.

"Did you think no one had noticed, Captain?"

"Noticed? Noticed what?"

"This war was not won by an empire, Captain. Not the Shi'ar or the Kree or any of the others. The council that broke before the end did not win it." She, too, peered at the symbol. "No, every time there was a shift in power and fortune, the Avengers were present. It was you Earthers—your warriors—that won the day."

"We all fought together, Oracle."

"That is true, but you held at Behemoth. You turned the World Killers against their masters over Hala, and then you broke the enemy with a single man and a hammer that was thrown around the sun. We rallied to you, good Captain. We rallied to your standard. Dockrum Seven is free again, and it is an Avengers world."

Silently he considered that. Such a massive concept.

The words were not carved in stone, nor were they inscribed on a scroll for all to see. No one read them out loud in front of the Galactic Council—yet that didn't make them any less true. The Builders and their forces had been defeated on world after world. Each planet had its storied heroes, some of whom remained unnamed, but all fought under the same banner.

Following Oracle's logic, Kymer was an Avengers world. Centauri Prime was an Avengers world. At the end it seemed to him as if they were all Avengers worlds.

The Avengers had won the day.

How long can this feeling last? he wondered.

TWO DAYS after the victory on Dockrum VII, Steve Rogers rested on a field littered with the remnants of combat, weary from what had seemed like the endless process of cleanup. Both of the Avengers' quincruisers had been destroyed early in the conflict, and they were waiting on word about a possible ride home. The wait was longer than he had expected.

Captain America was a soldier. The phrase "hurry up and wait" was one he knew all too well. Some things never changed, and that was especially true of bureaucracy.

Thor, at least, had found a way to endure the wait. He approached carrying two bottles.

"It is the local fare," he said with the sort of grin only he could manage. "They say it is too hearty... much too potent for a simple human." If possible, the grin widened as he handed over a bottle. "I told them they don't know Steve Rogers."

He held up his bottle.

"To the victors."

Cap clinked his bottle against the one Thor held. Without hesitation the thunder god lifted his drink, tilted back his head, and emptied the container.

"Uh-huh," Cap said warily. "What's the worst that could happen—I end up in the hospital?"

He took a drink, and it was like liquid fire.

"*Kaff*... Burns a bit."

"I spoke with Gladiator," Thor said, placing a hand on his comrade's shoulder. "He's more than happy to provide us a vessel for the voyage home." As he spoke, the Shi'ar leader approached across the ruined landscape.

"Speak of the devil." Rogers smiled. "What brings you planetside, Majestor? Here to join the festivities?"

"I wish it were so, my friend." Gladiator's voice was somber enough to take the smile from his face. "The universal net has been re-established, and we are finally able to communicate with other systems."

"What does—"

"I'm sorry, Captain," Gladiator said before he could continue, "but I bring grave news about your world.

"The Earth has fallen."

CHAPTER 29

BLOOD TIES

"WHAT... what did... oh, God..."

Thane looked around at the devastation, and all he saw were the ruined corpses of those whom he once had tended, and done his best to heal. His body smoldered, as did the bones of those he had killed. The claw that had been his left hand was black, and each finger ended in a barb sharp enough to cut.

"What have I done?" He mouthed the words, but barely spoke. The act of speaking required that he take a breath, and breathing seemed beyond him. His vision was shattered into prisms by the tears that threatened to spill from his eyes.

Not ten feet away, a skeleton wore the clothes he'd seen on Berenith, the girl with whom—once upon a time—he had shared a first kiss. He'd seen her walking past, and they'd exchanged a smile, and then the world had gone insane. He remembered the sudden pain that flared through him, which distorted his view of the world before his body burst into flame.

Now it was all gone—everything he'd ever cared about, every person he'd loved or liked or even hated—all gone.

"What happened here? All this pain, all this death?" The voice was melodious and seemed to drift from the distance. Thane looked up as a long, lean, graceful form moved over the ruined bodies, the devastated ground. The shape came closer; the face that looked upon him was not human, yet it still seemed to hold some kindness. The eyes were large and dark, and the long robes were clean as if freshly pressed.

"Why, *you* happened," the newcomer said, "Thane, son of Thanos."

With those words, Thane felt a new dread. He looked at the stranger and blinked rapidly at the tears that still wanted to fall. They were already drying, however, and anger formed in his heart as the dark-eyed stranger stated a simple truth. This, all of this, was his doing. He had not wanted it, but the truth remained the same.

It was me…

Still he said, "That's not possible. I've spent my life trying to help people. I want to *save* lives. I don't want to end them. I'm not like him. I'm a healer."

The dark eyes regarded him—not unkindly, it seemed.

"When your father was a child," the man said, "he embraced life, too. He was kind in his own way, and he loved. He changed as he grew older and wiser— and now you, Thane, are older and growing wiser. You are changed, and your childhood has come to an end."

"No." Thane rose partially from the ground, and then settled again and shook his head. "I'm a healer."

"Not anymore you're not." The man came closer. His look was still kind, but there was an edge of sternness that would not be denied. "You Inhumans have a belief that Terrigenesis reveals who you really are. If that is true, then there is no denying your heritage, your lineage. Look at what you have done."

He gestured around them at all the death and destruction. The faces of everyone Thane had known in his life had been stolen away, and the bones that lay beneath their kindnesses and love had been revealed for all to see.

"Your Inhumanity reveals the tyrant," the newcomer said. "Thanos spent most of his life chasing Death. It seems now he has spawned that which he sought."

"If that's true, then why are you still here? How are you still among the living?" Still on his knees, Thane stared hard at the man. He seemed kind. He seemed caring, but there was more to it. His words weren't meant to comfort. They were meant for something else.

"I am the Ebony Maw, Thane," the man said. "I am a student of preparedness, and I am shielded in a class-one defense field." He moved closer and gestured for Thane to stand.

"Trust me, if not for the barrier around my body, I would be as dead as these poor souls." He gestured around them, his long, tapering fingers passing through some of the fine ash that rose through the air—all that remained of the flesh of the Lor.

"Why are you here?"

Once again the Ebony Maw smiled kindly. "I see opportunity, Thane. I have been presented with a chance to increase my stature, and right now that means helping you control your gift."

Thane frowned, and his heart hammered hard in his chest. *Proof that I yet live,* he thought darkly. *That this isn't some twisted afterlife.*

"It is not a gift," he said aloud. His teeth bared in a sneer, his brows drawn together in anger.

The Ebony Maw looked toward the sky, and a disc dropped from above. Its underside was black, with a quartet of bright lights. As it reached the ground, the top of the object glowed a bright gold. The shape grew larger until it was wide enough to support a man with ease. As they watched, a shape began to form within the platform's golden light.

"You do not yet see the true nature of this event," the Ebony Maw said. "Life is a commodity that most will pay anything to keep, Thane. You have the ability to instantly change the very... economics of existence." He smiled and gestured toward the platform, where a golden suit of armor had taken shape.

"It is power, Thane. Trust me on this—it is a gift."

"I don't care about threats and leverage."

"The suit is yours, Thane. I have scanned your body and seen how your abilities work. It will help you control your energies. With the suit you can decide if or when to use them, and all will be safe until you decide otherwise."

"If a suit will keep me from hurting people, then perhaps that is the gift." Thane spoke softly and approached the golden armor. It was thin, with an inner layer of black. The pieces moved by themselves, coming together over his form. It wasn't too heavy, and it fit perfectly.

"Call it what you will, Thane," the Ebony Maw said. "The containment armor is strong enough that you would have to physically touch someone to use your new abilities."

Placing the skullcap over his head, Thane stood and assessed the end result. The power was still there—he could feel it—but if the man spoke truly, it was now encased. That was a gift.

"If it is as you say, then I thank you, Ebony Maw."

"Hmmmm…" The Ebony Maw frowned. "Gratitude is overrated." With a touch of a hand to his wrist, the platform's golden light grew far brighter and rose up around Thane.

"To say nothing of being a tad premature."

"What?" Thane reached out and discovered that the light had coalesced, trapping him in a tube of solid energy.

"Best you wait until your father arrives," the

Ebony Maw continued, "to decide if gratitude is what you wish to offer."

Thane could not move, could not speak.

"Listen carefully, Thane, son of Thanos," his captor said, his words measured. "Think before you act. Your father is coming here soon." The man smiled again. As he moved closer, Thane saw there was a dark blue shade to the eyes he'd previously thought were utterly black. "We have some time yet. Let's begin our lessons."

"AND WHAT of the tribute, my lord?"

"My son was not in Attilan before it was destroyed," Thanos said to Corvus Glaive as they walked the Necropolis of Wakanda. "I will continue the search." Then he added, "Have you located the gem?"

Glaive grimaced. "We have, as of yet, found no evidence of it. We will continue to search, but you should know we've also found some... interesting things here. Items that might intrigue you."

"Show me."

They continued through the ruined landscape, followed by Supergiant and Proxima Midnight. They approached a thick door that had been knocked off its hinges.

"This place was sealed up tight—understandable, once we saw what was inside." They passed through, and Glaive added, "Look, Thanos... they are building weapons." Rows of items filled the chamber, looking like blunt-nosed missiles.

"Antimatter projection systems," Supergiant said. "A perfect way to destroy the world." She caressed the side of one. "What a beautiful thing."

"Interesting," Thanos said. "So these Earthbound heroes have been busy creating machines of death. How delightfully unexpected. Is there more?"

"Yes," Proxima said. "There's a prison."

"Hmmmm." Thanos rubbed his chin. "I'm beginning to like these humans."

Proxima led him into an adjoining chamber. Whereas the previous room had been modern and filled with gleaming technology, this one was composed of dark stone blocks and reeked of medievalism. It held two occupants imprisoned behind shimmering energy fields.

"So as you can see, my lord, the humans' secret brotherhood has some captives of interest," Proxima said. "This one, Terrax, was once herald to Galactus. He is known to us. This other one is not." She gestured to a pale-skinned woman with long silver hair. "What would you have me do with them, Lord Thanos? Let the animals loose from their cages, to bloody their teeth on their captors?"

"Yes," the thin pale woman echoed. "Would you care to free us, tyrant?"

Thanos towered over her, hands on his hips as he considered carefully. She stared up at him with silent seduction.

After a long moment, he said, "I think not." Then he turned away. For now he had more pressing matters to attend to.

"WHAT'S THE word, wrench?" Corvus Glaive said as a robot technician bent over one of the weapons they had found. Glaive stood with Supergiant and Proxima Midnight as a human technician responded to his question.

"We cracked the skin, sure, but the guts are a bit more challenging. Tough to stick without spilling antimatter everywhere." Servos and pumps and motors worked as the robot continued to study the device.

"Try again until you succeed." Proxima leaned in closer to the robot's head, as if to intimidate the mechanical creature. "So very much depends on it."

"I got plenty of juice," the thing responded. "We'll make it happen. Just takes time."

Thanos stood a few yards away, watching the work and the exchange. A bank of machinery had been brought in, holding a prisoner bound in such a way he could not move a muscle. He was gagged, as well, with a metal clamp over his mouth.

Corvus Glaive moved closer.

"Still no luck, Master," he said. "The secret brotherhood that made these devices did so with great care. This will take us some time."

"You displease me, Corvus," Thanos said, locking his hands behind his back. "Perhaps we need a subtler touch than yours. A more direct way to gain the knowledge."

SUPERGIANT STEPPED past Glaive.

"Understood," she said. "I will find the information we need."

"With some delicacy, servant," Thanos said. "We cannot afford to break the Inhuman. He might still have some uses." He smiled grimly. "Remember, this one used to call himself a king."

Supergiant stared into Black Bolt's eyes, and the Inhuman stared back, defiant. She reached out with her hands. Twin beams of shimmering energy spiked straight into his eyes, and through them his mind. Contrary to Thanos' instructions, Supergiant did not gently sort through memories. She thrashed around in his head, searching for what Thanos demanded.

Black Bolt was unconscious before the assault ended, and even then she kept looking.

"THERE," SHE said finally. "It is done. I have the unlocking sequence for the weapon, Thanos. The control device, a trigger, is actually a secondary mechanism located elsewhere in this lab. I now possess that knowledge, as well. The bomb is yours."

"Good. I will want you to—" The beep of his communication device was different for each of the generals. He knew immediately who was trying to contact him. "Finally a word from the Whisperer." He slipped a disc from his belt and held it out, and an image flickered into existence above it. "Your prolonged absence demands an explanation, Ebony Maw."

"I fear, Master, that no accounting would suffice—all excuses pale in comparison to your will." Ebony Maw's expression was entirely unreadable. "But perhaps, a gift? A small measure of atonement?"

"What do you have for me, servant?" Thanos did not quite smile, but he came close.

"Only your son, mighty Thanos." Ebony Maw's expression mirrored that of his master. "The boy is trussed up and ready for you and your knife. Do I please you, then?"

"Very much," Thanos replied. He consulted the data on the disc. "I have your location. Wait there with the tribute." Then he shut off the communication device. "Corvus, Proxima, prepare a vessel. We leave immediately."

"What would you have me do, Master?" Supergiant still stood near Black Bolt, one hand touching his face as if admiring a bit of her work. The king was still unconscious, but he flinched at the contact.

"Prepare your weapon, Supergiant. When I have killed my son, we will use the bomb to deal with this damned world once and for all."

CHAPTER 30

THE TICKING CLOCK

TONY Stark lifted the faceplate on his helmet and drank in the scent of the ocean. He'd have preferred a good, stiff martini, but that was something he wouldn't allow himself to have. He knew his demons, and did his best to keep them on a short leash.

"So collapsing space-time and the end of everything." He looked around at the gathered Illuminati. "Is there something wrong with me that I'm glad we only have to deal with a simple planetary invasion?"

"Of course there is, Anthony," Reed Richards answered. "The question is… where to start?"

"The space tyrant, or securing his son?" T'Challa added. "Who can say what has happened since we've been off planet?" Above them the barrier between universes seemed well on the way to recovery. The skies were no longer red, and the opening between worlds dwindled down to the size of a quarter, then vanished as if it hadn't been there.

The Beast scanned the area, and then abruptly pointed. "I think they might have some answers to your question, Panther." Two figures stood on the hillside a football field away. They were far enough away that the man was difficult to identify, but the second figure was instantly recognizable. Lockjaw was larger than the average polar bear.

"At the very least they can point us in the right direction."

Lockjaw let out a "woof" and started in their direction. The man followed after him, moving without any appreciable effort. As he drew closer, he called out to them.

"Attilan is gone," Maximus said, "destroyed in a fight between my brother and Thanos. Black Bolt is missing, but I think Lockjaw has his scent. We can very likely find him."

"Attilan is destroyed?" Tony echoed, and his voice actually broke. It was like saying the Statue of Liberty had walked out of New York Harbor. The words simply didn't make sense. He lowered the helmet back over his face and scanned the man coming his way. Maximus might be telling the truth now, but he was a well-documented liar. The first thing to do was check for weapons.

"Attilan is gone," he said again. "It collapsed into the harbor and clipped a portion of your city."

"What about your people?" Reed asked.

"Oh, they're safe," Maximus said, sounding somehow pleased with himself. "We moved them to different locations around the world before Thanos ever arrived."

Lockjaw ambled over and pressed his massive face against Reed, nearly knocking him over. Reed smiled and rubbed behind the dog's left ear, which brought a look of ecstasy to the teleporter's face. Maximus walked alongside the Inhuman dog and let one hand roam over his short fur.

"If Lockjaw has Black Bolt's scent, we can find him—but I expect we should be quick about it. I can't possibly get him by myself. I have no weapons." He spread his hands as if to show they were empty. "We left in something of a hurry, I'm afraid."

"Yes," Namor said, and he scowled. "By all means let's forget all else and go help our brother."

"Stop being an ass, Namor," Stark said. "Even if it's just for five minutes. Can you do that?"

Namor turned sharply. Before he could say a word, however, Reed Richards cut in.

"That's enough," he said, scowling first at Namor, then at Iron Man. "We have work to do. Let's help Black Bolt—if he can be helped. We need his assistance if we're to end this latest threat."

Namor closed his mouth and nodded.

Stark nodded, too.

Maximus smiled. "Excellent news! Let's go save my brother!"

Lockjaw let out another huffing noise, and the antennae on his head began to glow. The unearthly light surrounded the entire group. A moment later the world vanished around them—

—AND THEY found themselves not on the beach, but in a literal jungle.

Daylight was gone, replaced by night; in the skies above the heavy foliage, vessels moved across the stars and under the clouds, and rained down barrages of fire across the Wakandan skyline.

"Look!" Hank McCoy pointed.

They followed the direction of his finger. In the distance, close enough that they could see some details, Birnin Zana was burning. Not all of the Golden City, but enough to show the horrible damage already inflicted.

"No!" The Black Panther leapt to a better vantage point and peered at the carnage. "It's unthinkable. Wakanda's defenses have been breached. The shining city is overrun." He turned to his companions, and even through his mask they could see the tightness of his jaw.

"We must go—*now!*"

"Wait… it's worse!" Stark put one hand to the earpiece on his armor and gestured for them to stop. "The early warning system we erected in the Necropolis, as well as the alarms we set in the labs, have all been triggered." He went silent while more data came to him. "Someone has access to the bombs."

Lockjaw sniffed loudly, then let out a grunt. Maximus leaned his head to the side and smiled broadly.

"He's got quite a nose on him, just like I've got quite a brain. Lockjaw says Black Bolt is here." He pointed to the Necropolis. "I'm thinking he's in a pinch, and knows a little something about what you've been building. Perhaps the bombs your Iron Man mentioned." He moved to stand. "Isn't this fun?" Looking around, he added, "No? Why do I feel like I'm the only one enjoying this?"

"Goddess forgive me, but if they have the weapons we've built, we have no choice." The Black Panther looked to Lockjaw. "Teleport us to the Necropolis. We take the dead city first and hope our delay doesn't render Wakanda just as lifeless."

Once again the world shifted. This time they found themselves in the midst of their enemies. The forces of Thanos, however, were not at all prepared for the sudden appearance of powerful opponents.

Reed took a moment to look around, then attacked his nearest target. By the time he had stretched out an arm and struck one of his enemies, the Black Panther had already pounced. From the far side of the room, the Sub-Mariner soared into the cavernous chamber's upper reaches, then arced down and knocked two unconscious guards to the side.

The Beast bounded across the room, heading directly for the antimatter bombs, desperate to put a stop to anyone who planned on using the weapons.

Doctor Strange unleashed bolts of arcane energy that enveloped their foes and rendered them unconscious.

Lockjaw let out a deep growl and moved toward his king and friend, Black Bolt. Maximus moved with him, pulling a weapon that should not have been there. Maximus was as devious as he was dangerous. Stark's own targeting systems locked in place, and Iron Man fired several blasts from his repulsors that sent soldiers of Thanos sailing back from where they'd been standing.

Heaven knew how much time they had left.

FROM THE next room, the woman called Supergiant watched them coming. They were powerful and desperate. They wanted to reach her before she could detonate the bombs.

They called themselves the Illuminati. They appeared to fancy themselves the secret rulers of the world—or maybe its protectors. In any event they had created a doomsday device. The antimatter bombs they'd assembled had the power to end the Earth. The design was elegant—more than she would have expected from savages like these.

First came an animal that was blue and covered in fur. It had a mouthful of fangs… and it wore goggles on its head. At a guess it could probably break her body in a hundred ways. It had that sort of powerful frame. She was not a general of Thanos because of her fighting skills. She had attained her position because of her ruthlessness.

Also, she was a fast thinker.

Before the animal reached her, she moved quickly and locked the doors to the laboratory. Then she activated the defense systems her opponents had put in place. The thick doors slammed shut. The force-field projectors hummed as they came to life.

The defense system was designed to counteract the powerful and the devious alike. The best part? They had used themselves as the models for the sort of people they had to be able to stop.

Supergiant relaxed as the blue furry thing was repelled.

The spatial jumper—the dog thing—disappeared in a crackle of energy. Then it abruptly reappeared, having been rebuffed by the technology that lay behind the shields.

Despite her satisfaction, Supergiant knew it could not last. They would break through eventually. That was inevitable. So she prepared for that eventuality and worked on setting the bombs to her specifications.

IT WAS a primitive city, carved from stone and hidden in the depths of a crevasse. It was obvious to Thanos the people had done their best to remain unnoticed. Somewhere down there was his son, trying to hide and failing.

Thanos descended into a city of the dead. This was not like the Wakandan Necropolis. These were not ancient dead, but freshly killed, though most had been stripped down to the bones.

Stepping from the transport, he instantly saw his son. Ebony Maw walked next to his master. The rest of the Black Order disembarked behind them.

"Just as I promised," he said. "The tribute."

"Well done, Maw." Thanos put a massive hand on the smaller man's back. "You're an irritant, but you never disappoint."

"It pleases me that I please you, Master," Maw replied with a self-satisfied smile, and the irritation returned. Brushing it away, Thanos stepped up to a figure suspended in a type of golden energy.

"So this is the very last of my offspring." The creature before him bore some signs of the Deviant gene. He looked enough like Thanos that the tyrant could recognize himself. "Take a deep breath, boy. Enjoy it. You have so very few left."

"Why do you do this?" the figure asked, his eyes averted downward. "What have I done to you?"

"Why do I do this?" Thanos decided to answer the question with the truth. "Because you keep me awake at night. The very idea of you out there, existing." Then he turned away. "And soon all that will end." He looked to Ebony Maw. "Why is he in a class-one containment field, Maw?"

Still Ebony Maw smiled. "There's an interesting thing about him, Thanos. He has a—"

"Master!" Corvus Glaive moved closer, a holographic projection glowing in his palm.

"Something has happened!" Despite obvious electronic interference, the holograph of Bermath of Titan was clear enough that the injuries on the man's face could be seen.

"*Bzzk*—ame out of nowhere. The last outpost… overrun, and *bzzk* they attack us here. *Bzzk*—ey're comi—" The holographic image broke up and was lost.

"That message," Glaive said, his expression a combination of fear and fury. "Something's happened on Titan."

THE ATTACK came as a complete surprise, because no one in their right mind considered attacking Thanos or his people. Indigenous or otherwise, the populace was caught unawares. Those who served with the military received no mercy.

The armada was overwhelming—ships of every imaginable shape and size. They filled the sky from horizon to horizon. The bombs dropped with terrifying strategic efficiency, leveling landing strips and launch pads where slumbering vessels waited, destroying defensive missile installations and orbital watch stations, crippling communications arrays.

There was no doubt that a message or two got through. That was impossible to stop, but little else escaped before the attacks were completed.

ACT FIVE
BEACHHEAD EARTH

CHAPTER 31

HOMECOMING

"THE watch station has been knocked offline, Majestor, and the gas giant hides our shadow." Oracle spoke without rancor.

Gladiator looked upon the readouts and nodded. This was exactly how they preferred their battles: quick and bloodless… mostly.

"Very good, Oracle." Then he spoke to others who stood nearby—Captain America, yes, but also Warlord Kl'rt and Ronan the Accuser. "What say you? Shall we wage one more war for the ages?"

Kl'rt snorted. "I did not drag a portion of my fleet all the way out here for leisure, Gladiator. And you, Accuser?"

Ronan looked to Kl'rt, whose people often were his enemy. "I came to judge the guilty, as are all who stand against those who liberated the Kree."

Gladiator turned again to Captain America. "Count the Shi'ar among your numbers, as well. For you have earned that, Captain. The fleet is yours one last time. We await your orders."

Captain America stood with his Avengers—all ready for battle, all ready to be home. He looked to the three leaders of perhaps the largest empires known to exist, and could not resist a small smile of gratitude.

"Consider the word given. Please jump us to Earth. There's one last world that needs saving."

SAM GUTHRIE felt his arms around Izzy Kane and thrilled. Her kiss was as powerful a thing as he'd ever experienced. When they came up for air, he sighed.

"Izzy, I… I… I just—"

"I know, right?" She smiled at him. He smiled back. Her smile was absolutely contagious.

"Yeah. Do you think that—"

"*Traitors.*"

Roberto da Costa walked into the viewing room aboard the Shi'ar battleship the *Lilandra*. "This is a total betrayal," he said. "How could you go behind my back like that?"

Izzy looked like a deer in the headlights.

Sam just shook his head. "We're standing right in front of you."

Bobby crossed his arms. "And that's what makes it even worse."

"Aww. Come on, Bobby. Can't you just be happy for me?"

"For us?" Izzy corrected.

"Right. For us?"

"I am, Sam. I'm messing with you, idiot." He threw an arm across his best friend's shoulder and looked to Izzy. "And you?" he said. "You're making a huge mistake."

They had been flirting with her since they'd met her. They had gone on multiple missions together against the enemies of the Avengers. But she had made her choice, and he was fine with that. Sam was his best friend, his brother, and he would never begrudge him a chance at happiness.

Nor would he miss an opportunity to pick on Sam.

Izzy looked his way, and then spoke very softly as Sam preceded them down the corridor.

"I know. Can we talk about it later? Maybe in my room?"

"What? Seriously?" He froze… like a deer in the headlights.

"No." She smiled at him. "I'm messing with you, idiot."

He grinned. A few steps ahead, Sam did the same.

Then his grin faded. "So it's time?" They headed for the ship's command center.

"Uh-huh," Bobby said. "I came to get you guys because Cap's called everyone together, and neither of you responded. Big speech before the big attack, I guess."

Izzy put on her Smasher goggles, and the material moved, slid, and expanded to become her helmet. "Must be." She nodded her head. "I just got a status alert from Gladiator, as well. The Imperial Guard has been activated." She paused, then added, "This feels so wrong."

Bobby waved his arm in dismissal. "No. Listen, you shouldn't feel guilty, not for one second. So what if everyone else up here is sad and alone. You deserve a bit of happiness while everyone else is miserable."

Izzy looked his way. "That's not what I—"

"He knows." Sam rolled his eyes. "He's just joking because it's easier. None of us thought this was what coming home would be like."

THE PEAK, the headquarters of S.W.O.R.D., was Earth's first defense against alien incursion. That made it the most likely spot to be targeted first. So far that had happened twice.

The first time the Skrulls were invading the planet.

Currently it was held by one of Thanos' generals, the Black Dwarf. He was a leashed dog, and he knew it. He'd been placed at the Peak solely because he would be out of the way. However, he saw it as a chance to redeem himself.

"Is it ready?" He turned to Krysaor, captain of one wing of the forces on the station. He looked like a child next to his massive commander, and like Black Dwarf, he had been assigned here as little more than an afterthought.

"It is, Black Dwarf. Created exactly to specifications."

"Good. We have received word from Thanos, who heard the screams from Titan. We are to expect visitors." He looked around at the gathered soldiers, misfits all, then moved to choose a weapon, lifting and straining under the weight. The mace was massive. It would crush bugs with the best of them, and for Black Dwarf nearly everything qualified as a bug. He raised his new weapon high over his head.

"Well, let them come! We will be ready, and we will repel them. Our master has commanded it."

"Yes," Captain Krysaor agreed, "to prove to him that you are worthy again. That we all are."

"What did you say?" Black Dwarf spun hard on one heel and looked down. "*What did you say to me?*" He did not speak—he roared, lifting the mace.

"Oh," Krysaor said, realizing what he had done. "Oh—only that you would puh-probably want to erase your, ah… shortcomings from Thanos' memory, sir. General." He was braver than most. Trying to rectify his mistake, he stood his ground before Black Dwarf's fury.

"Forgive me, I meant no disrespect."

It was too late.

The mace came down. It shattered Krysaor's body and armor alike, and the floor of the deck beneath him.

"Consider it erased… from my memory." He shook the remains of Krysaor from his mace. "Prepare the station; alert all vessels. Make ready for war."

The remaining members of the wing moved quickly to carry out their commander's orders.

TO CAROL Danvers, sometimes the universe seemed to have the damnedest sense of humor. She watched the video feed with everyone else and felt her stomach tighten into a knot of tension.

"I feel like my mother's calling," Iron Man said, his holographic avatar hovering above the communications unit. "'We were only gone for a few hours. Want to tell me what happened to the house, Anthony?' 'Hi, Mom. I know it looks bad, but I'm really glad you're back.'"

Cap smiled. "Me too, Tony. Where are you now?"

"Wakanda. It's possible Thanos—wait, you *do* know about Thanos, right?"

"Yeah, I know about Thanos. We all do."

"Okay, so his crew might have gained access to some doomsday weapons. And maybe they're here in Wakanda. Me and some others are working on stopping them."

Cap tensed. The use of the term "doomsday weapons" had erased the smile from his face. "We've got to deal with the blockade first, but I'll beeline it to Birnin Zana once we punch through."

"Negative, Steve," Stark responded. "I'll be sending you coordinates to where Thanos will be. He's the primary target. We'll take care of this, and then I'll see you there."

"Okay." Cap looked uncomfortable. "Don't screw it up."

"Did everyone make it?" Tony asked. Carol thought he seemed to want to change the subject.

"I don't think any of us are completely whole after what we've been through," Cap replied, "but we haven't lost anyone yet."

Iron Man nodded. "Well, time to go. Good luck."

"See you soon." By the time he was done speaking, Iron Man's image had faded.

They had saved the universe. Now they just had to save their own planet. Looking around her, Captain Marvel thought they might have a chance. The Shi'ar, the Kree, the Skrulls, the Imperial Guard, Annihilus—oh, and the Avengers.

"So there you have it," Captain America said to the gathered generals. "Mad Thanos has invaded Earth, his armada surrounds the planet, and believe it or not, the whole thing seems to be motivated by an overdue, unyielding desire to commit infanticide." The way he said it almost made it seem logical.

Almost.

"When we left the planet to oppose the Builders, he took that as his opportunity," Cap continued. "It was a canny move."

"All of this to kill one kid?" Carol shook her head. "Does that make sense to anyone?"

"Yesssss." Annihilus actually answered the rhetorical question. She wasn't surprised.

"It's Thanos," Cap said, ignoring the insectoid.

"Expecting some type of rationality to win out is pointless. And frankly, I don't care what he wants, I just want to send him and his forces running as fast as they can from our planet."

Carol agreed. That was exactly how she felt about the situation.

"And if they do not run, let it be because they find themselves unable to do anything but crawl," Thor said, crossing his massive arms and looking particularly grim. It was impressive.

"There is a plan forthcoming, I presume." Ronan hefted his hammer and peered down at the holographic map of the planet.

"We're going to need to break the blockade," Captain America replied. "We're fairly certain they have complete control of the Peak, though."

"This orbital station may be formidable," Kl'rt said, "but surely a single outpost cannot house that kind of firepower." He seemed to be confident in his knowledge of the facility.

Spider-Woman was the one who answered. "Well, the first iteration of the station didn't," she said. Her time with the Skrulls—as an unwilling captive—had not made her a fan of the species, but she spoke with calm. "But Earth seems to have a consistent problem with alien invasions. So it got rebuilt… better."

Kl'rt considered the words, and then nodded.

"The good news is that we know the base," Bruce Banner said. "We have schematics, and we have personal experience inside the station. I've spent considerable time there. This is a job that can be done, and we have a pretty good idea of how to do it. Which is where all of you come in." He glanced around at the extraterrestrial portion of the contingent.

Kl'rt stared back with unmasked fascination. For a member of a race of shape-changers, he seemed particularly intrigued by the Hulk's other face.

Gladiator stepped forward. "Whatever the need, my Imperial Guard will be ready." Oracle stood at his right hand, Mentor at his left.

Mentor looked at Captain America. "So the station—a micro-problem needing a surgical solution. Then the blockade. A macro problem, met by our fleet, I would expect."

"Which leaves only the problem of your world," Oracle added.

"Yeah. Existing," Captain America replied. "We've got that one." He pointed to the display on the table they surrounded. "So here's what we're going to do."

CHAPTER 32

A GREATER PURPOSE

THE ships came out of the jump near Mars and moved steadily toward Earth. Captain Marvel entered the observatory where Captain America was waiting and nodded to Thor as she walked past him. He nodded back and remained where he was—a silent sentinel who, for the moment, seemed content to stare at the stars.

The view was spectacular. A Skrull battle cruiser drifted past on the left, and above them another Shi'ar ship glistened in the reflected light from the red planet. The place where so much of this had begun.

Carol stepped up and gave Captain America a quick report. "Jump's completed. We're on our final approach now. A forerunner has confirmed what the Shi'ar long-range scans told us. We're basically going to be crashing a blockade."

"As expected. Our numbers?"

"The council spared what ships they could in the hope we would overwhelm the pirates, send them running when they saw what was coming, but their numbers are equal to ours."

"They're also fresher than we are," Manifold said. "Rested. Not beaten. They'll hunt us like animals after wounded prey." His face showed clearly how defeated he felt.

"You okay, Eden?" Captain America responded.

"I'm tired," he said, wiping his brow with his palm. "I can't believe what I just lived through, and now I have to do it again. And this time with the lives of my family and people at stake. It seems futile and unending. How do you keep going, Captain? How do you make sense of it? Faith? Fate?"

Captain Marvel answered. "Don't over-mythologize it, kid. Believe whatever you want—just make sure you hit the other guy before he hits you, and that you knock his ass out." She understood the grief and the stress better than most. She had been a soldier for years, and had been fighting against alien invaders for much of that time.

Captain America stepped close to Eden. He was almost a head taller, and his expression was grim, but somehow his eyes were reassuring.

"Listen to Carol, Eden," he said, his voice calm but firm. "I'm not a believer in heroic quests undertaken by men and women of fate. There is no hero's journey." Captain Marvel watched Steve Rogers speak and again felt that odd sense of inspiration.

She was a seasoned veteran, and she was a power to be reckoned with, but this man was something more. He had a balance to him that defied the very words he was speaking. Captain America *was* a man of fate—or he seemed that way to her, at least. She could give orders, and they would be followed. But when Captain America gave orders, it was different. He inspired passion. She couldn't explain it better than that.

"There's just life and how we choose to live it." Cap put his hand on his teammate's shoulder. Eden straightened, squared his shoulders, and nodded. "So you know what you're supposed to do, Eden?"

"Yes," Manifold replied. "Wait until we're engaged, and then jump a team behind their lines. Open the door when no one's looking."

"That's right. Do your job, because we're all depending on you. That's all anyone can ask of you. Your best."

He turned. "Carol, we need to go check on the crash shuttle."

"It's in hangar seven."

"Out of what? Seven hundred? Want to show me where, Captain?" He smiled as he said it. Then he looked back at Eden one more time. "You okay?"

"Yeah."

"Hang in there. We're almost home."

EDEN MANAGED a weak smile. He was still tired, but he felt steadier than he'd been before. Captain America and Captain Marvel walked away together. He watched them go, then turned to peer out the viewport of the *Lilandra*.

He studied the ships moving around them, swarming above the curve of the planetscape below. The closest was a Skrull vessel. They were miracles of technology, and he was both thrilled to admire them and horrified by what they had done. The ships—all of them, it seemed—showed signs of the battles they'd fought and survived.

Manifold wondered whether he looked as scarred.

Suddenly Thor's reflection appeared next to his in the glass, and Eden jumped a little. It spoke volumes about how much his life had changed in the last month that he had forgotten a god was in the room.

"Steve Rogers and Carol Danvers are great warriors." Thor spoke softly, but with conviction. "I am honored to call them my friends," he said, his voice deep and resonant. "But they could not be more wrong." He pointed with his chin to the stars and the spaces between them. "Out there are gods and men and all creatures in between. They were all born, and they will die—but each one with a purpose."

The Skrull vessel began to move, accelerating at a frightening pace. The Shi'ar war cruiser above them followed suit. More and more ships appeared, until they were a swarm moving through the vacuum.

"Surely I tell you the universe has conspired to put the world in our very hands," Thor continued. "It is a test for titans." He turned his head to the left so he was focused on his companion. "Only we can save the world, Eden Fesi. That is your destiny. Your entire life has led to this day. You were born for this." Thor lifted his hammer as if it were his child. "As was I."

Around them the stars seemed to blur slightly as the floor beneath them vibrated with the now familiar feeling of the massive engines reaching full power. Thor smiled and pointed toward the distant shape of Earth, growing larger as they moved.

"Will you join me in teaching the oldest lesson of them all, Eden?"

How could he refuse a god?

"FLEET VECTOR linear," Ronan the Accuser announced. "We hide ourselves behind your moon."

"Why hide?" Warlord Kl'rt responded, sounding impatient. "They know we're coming."

"No one wants to get there faster than we do, Kl'rt," Captain America said.

"This has to be timed just right," Captain Marvel explained. "Otherwise it'll be a bloodbath."

"In what way, Captain?" Gladiator asked.

"While it might look peaceful, the Peak has enough firepower to take out this ship—and a lot more," Captain America replied grimly. "If we destroy the station from a distance, however, a lot of innocent personnel will die—and that's something I won't allow." As he watched, the *Lilandra*'s pilots ran their hands over glowing holographic displays. "Prepare the advance team," he said to Carol, then he turned to Gladiator. "Activate the fleet—get us into position just outside of the kill zone. The timing has to be perfect, or they'll know what we're doing."

The heavens lit up as the thrust engines moved their vessels away from the dark side of the moon.

EDEN FESI stood by with the Black Widow and Shang-Chi, and he waited. Whatever fear he had, whatever exhaustion pulled at him, it no longer mattered.

"Go," Carol Danvers said over the comm.

"Okay," he replied. A thrill ran through him. "Hold on tight."

His abilities flared—

—and a moment later they were aboard the Peak.

"Contact," the Widow said. "Manifold jump successful."

ON THE Peak, Black Dwarf waited as patiently as he could. He was rewarded with a series of warning signals and his new captain calling out in alarm.

"General! The proximity alarms! We have multiple signals... coming at us from behind the moon! We are under attack!" The new captain's ability to state the obvious was as egregious as his predecessor's, but so far there had been no insults, so he got to live and keep his command.

"Good," Black Dwarf responded, raising his mace in front of him. "We have waited long enough." He moved closer to one of the defense stations. "Are weapons batteries ready, Gunner?"

"They are fully charged, General."

"Then you have my leave. Open fire as soon as they are in range, and burn them from the heavens."

The Peak looked like a dagger poised inside a large ring. The ring itself had a dozen different batteries that could be used against incoming vessels. As the approaching fleet drew closer, they blossomed open in preparation. All around the station, the pirate ships of Thanos moved into position, as well, prepared to destroy whatever might come their way—even a ship as large as the *Lilandra*.

"Send them early to the hell we all crave."

The barrage of firepower that erupted was enough to shame the sun.

ABOARD THE *Lilandra*, klaxons sounded, and the ship rocked from the sheer number of explosions in close proximity. From her position at the communications array, Oracle called out.

"Majestor! We've lost the *Pinnacle* and *Kyrin's Pride*."

"The station's kill zone stretches farther than we thought," Gladiator growled. "Emergency actions! Deploy the Imperial Guard."

Captain America added his own instructions. "Avengers assemble!"

External feeds revealed the forces released from the *Lilandra*'s bay door. They wielded a terrifying level of firepower. Spearing through space, they destroyed a number of pirate vessels. Then they approached the Peak and a collection of weapons capable of destroying full-size battleships.

Before they could reach their target, one of the Imperial Guard was killed by a blast that cut him in half.

"We've lost Superguardian Titan," his teammate Manta announced over the comm. "The fire's too heavy to break through without significant losses. We await your orders."

"Heavier losses than expected, Majestor," Mentor said.

"Should we pull them back?" Oracle asked.

"No, Oracle, tell them to press forward," Gladiator said. "Move the *Lilandra* betw—"

"Hold on, Gladiator," Captain America said. "Anything, Carol?"

"They're in!"

"Acknowledged," he replied. Then to Gladiator, "Tell the guard to pull back just outside the kill zone. We'll have that station down soon, one way or the other."

WITH BLACK Widow in the lead they moved rapidly and quietly, the Widow leading, Shang-Chi a moment behind her. Manifold followed and kept his eyes alert.

He had family on the Earth, and Australia had already surrendered to Thanos. He would see all of the aliens dead before he would allow his family to be hurt.

Ultimately it came down to a simple decision.

His family mattered more.

He kept telling himself that as they proceeded.

"We should be able to use any of the access panels on the command level," Natasha said. "So, kiddo, what level is this?"

"I'm pretty sure Eden put us right where we need to be, Widow," Shang-Chi answered. "But I—*look out!*"

A concussive explosion sent the Widow slamming into a wall.

"THEY'LL GET the job done—Natasha knows what's at stake," Captain America said. "All the pieces are on the board except us; we need to get out there." He squared his shoulders and started toward the door. "Tell Hyperion to spin up the engines, Carol. We're on our way down." He paused and then said, "I'll be right behind you."

She nodded and then moved on. Steve Rogers looked back at the men standing in the command center. Gladiator, Ronan, Kl'rt, and Annihilus.

"You didn't have to…" Words were failing him. "What I mean is, I want to thank you all for this."

"Thank us when we've earned it, human." Kl'rt smiled at him. It wasn't an expression he'd ever seen before on the warlord. "What good is effort if we fail?

Do best efforts soak up the blood and bury the fallen?"

Kl'rt spread his arms and gestured toward the battle being waged just outside. There were warriors from all of their races fighting together, against a single enemy. There had been times when none of them would have thought it possible.

"If beaten, who remembers the conquered, Captain America? Not I. So save your thanks until we stand over the broken bodies of our enemies. Save them until we've won."

BLACK DWARF heard the voices outside his command center. They were spoken softly, but his hearing was sharp.

"We should be able to use any of the access panels on the command level." The voice seemed to be female. "So, kiddo, what level is this?"

Whoever responded was male. "I'm pretty sure Eden put us right where we need to be, Widow."

Moving quickly for his size, Black Dwarf threw open the command center's door and saw three humans. A pale woman with red hair, a darker male with wild hair, and a male who looked directly at him as he moved into the hall.

"Look out!" the male said. Black Dwarf swatted the woman aside. She tried to dodge but was caught off guard. The blow sent her crashing into the wall.

He loomed over the remaining two and sneered. "As I expected… like thieves in the night. Like cowards afraid of your own shadows." The female was already back on her feet. He was suitably impressed—he had not pulled his punch. Anyone slower would have been paste along the wall.

"You sneak in here to shame me once again," he continued. His hatred for the humans was a growing thing. The loss of his honor was a cancer, and one he intended to cut out. "You'll find the Black Dwarf hardier than that. More than enough for you to choke on." With that, he launched himself against the intruders.

"Manifold!" the woman cried out. "Get back to the ship. Tell them we're not going to get the field down in time." As she spoke she fired four projectile rounds into the warriors standing closest to him, and they died on the spot. She then tested her firearm against Black Dwarf's hide, and he smiled as the bullets bounced back.

"Bring backup!"

The one with the wild mane of hair disappeared. Black Dwarf scowled and swung at her, but she dodged successfully.

"Bring your reinforcements! I will kill all of them, too!"

EDEN FESI reappeared where he had last seen Captain America. Instead of the leader of the Avengers, he stared at the commanders of four empires.

"Critical harm to the *Benevolence*. Pulling the carrier back." That one was Ronan the Accuser. He spoke to the leader of the Shi'ar.

"Heavy losses on the right flank. I'm sending in three heavy frigates." That was the Super-Skrull.

"Should have let me bring drones." The nightmare with the vast demonic wings and the green head was Annihilus. He spoke and his voice sounded like the angry buzz of hornets. "They're good for fighting. Good for dying. Good for blockades and for sacrifices."

"Hold." Gladiator spoke, and for a brief moment Manifold allowed himself to be stunned by them. They were legends, and he was just Eden Fesi. "The humans will succeed in bringing down the station. It's their world they're fighting for. They have to win."

"No," Eden said, and the commanders turned, suddenly aware of his presence. "Have they already left? They have, haven't they?"

"They have." Ronan stepped closer. "Why are you here, and not on the station?"

"Uhhh... little problem." He bit back the part of his voice that wanted to laugh. It wasn't humor, it was hysteria, and he knew the difference. "One of Thanos' generals is there. We're not going to be able to gain control of the Peak quickly enough. They'll all get hammered going through the kill zone.

"What should we do?"

"WHY DO you keep standing, little one?" He stared at the male. The female was still up, as well, but she was wounded. He had hit her enough times to kill, but like the male she moved and brushed aside the worst of his attacks.

Black Dwarf did not duck or avoid blows. He thought he might have to examine their methods more carefully, later. For now he just wanted them dead.

"Does a tree fall from a slight breeze?" The insult was obvious. The male looked at him and shook away his apparent fatigue.

"You die well, human, but dead is dead, isn't it?" Black Dwarf said. "Farewell." He swept the mace around and positioned himself for the killing blow.

Sssshfamm!

Before he could bring the mace around he was knocked backward. Twin lines of fire burned into his chest. The pain was rare. Very little caused him harm. Even Thanos' beating was the first exception in many months, but this was a line of fire through his torso that seemed to peel back the layers of his dense hide. He let out a scream as he fell, still clutching his weapon. Painfully he raised his head.

Behind the two humans stood five more shapes. The wild-haired human had returned and brought support. Worse, he recognized them. They were among the most feared warriors in the galaxy.

The Majestor's eyes still burned. That was how Black Dwarf knew exactly who and what had hit him.

"Get your companions, human," the Shi'ar said. "Do your job. We will handle this."

Black Dwarf sneered, wiping blood from his mouth. "A Strontian prince. A Kree judge. A relic from a broken empire, and a dead thing from another time and place." He had fought alongside Thanos and knew the difference between a threat and a group of failures. He stood up and grinned a feral grin. "This is all you have? This is your best? What gods have you offended to die in such poor company?"

He held his mace out in front of him, and energies crackled from all of its spikes. The Shi'ar came for him first and he blocked his opponent's blow. The weapon was designed to shatter the hulls of ships. It would be more than enough to handle the likes of a Strontian.

Gladiator's bare-fisted strike shattered the head of the mace. Disgusted, Black Dwarf hurled the shaft, sending it soaring across the room. It was only a weapon, he told himself. He was better off with his bare hands.

"The day is almost done, villain." The Gladiator came for him again, and Black Dwarf hit him as hard as he could, sending him hurtling across the hallway. The Skrull caught his comrade before he could tear through the hull.

He also left himself open for a retaliatory strike.

"Villain?" With a backhand swipe he drove his fist into the Skrull's head, and felt the flesh yield to the unexpected force of his attack. "*Villain?*" he roared as he lashed out again. Another creature would have lost its head, but the flesh was malleable even at its hardest, and no bones were broken.

The shape-changer started to rise, and he hit it again.

"You are imperials," he growled, "enabling or even ruling hundreds—thousands—of worlds. And you speak as arbiters of… what? Justice?" He struck out at the insectoid from another dimension, Annihilus. "Fairness? Honor?" The creature struck back, and its hands were powerful indeed—but Black Dwarf was stronger. He smashed the creature backward and it squawked. Its wings fluttered as it tried to right itself, and he grabbed for it again.

"Good and evil?" he bellowed. The vile thing belched fire into his face. He was forced to let it go and close his eyes lest they be burned out of his head. Just the same he delivered a kick across its chest and sent it sprawling.

Abruptly he was staggered by a blow. The hand that hit him was rough and rocky, not at all like the hand of any of his enemies. The Skrull struck again. It was said that one of his race possessed the powers of several human heroes—this had to be him. The Skrull moved around him, wrapped him in pliable limbs, and pinned his arms. He pulled one arm free even as the Skrull's hide burst into flame.

Damn the shape-changer…

He bit back the pain that stung him, and with his free hand he hit the Gladiator again. The blow was solid and the man fell to the ground. Black Dwarf smiled grimly and used the same hand to grip part of the burning arm that held him. It stretched and he pulled harder, trying to tear the limb away. The Skrull let out a cry of his own.

Black Dwarf would not die this day. He would kill the enemies of Thanos and redeem himself in his master's eyes.

"Right and wrong?" he shouted into the faces of his opponents. Annihilus breathed fire down his back, and he grimaced. "What sort of person with real power speaks of such things? Who believes any of it?"

Then Ronan the Accuser was there. The Kree killer looked down upon him as Annihilus tried to destroy him from behind and the Skrull struggled to keep him pinned. Still he was winning—he knew he could kill all of them with ease, given enough time. Had he not already faced the wrath of Thanos?

"I do, Black Dwarf," the Accuser replied. "I speak of such things, and I believe them. You have been judged."

Ronan lifted his hammer up and brought it down with all of his considerable might. The weapon looked like a hammer, true, but legend claimed it also drew on the Power Cosmic—the very life force of the universe. When it struck, the hammer struck with the power to level buildings.

The Black Dwarf's head shattered.

He was dying and he knew it. His neck had broken in the impact, too, and he could not move. But he could hear them as they spoke.

"That was more entertaining than I anticipated," the Skrull said. "Now what?" The creature sounded shaken by the blows he'd been dealt, but Black Dwarf would have felt better about dying if he'd at least taken one of the bastards with him.

"We still have the pirate fleet to send running," Gladiator replied. He, too, sounded worse for his injuries. "So that is what we will do—while the Avengers fight for the Earth and battle to vanquish the tyrant who holds their world."

Black Dwarf wished he could be there. Wished he could help Thanos, and prove his worth. He died with that wish unfulfilled.

CHAPTER 33

TYRANT

THE ship was large enough to carry them and small enough not to be a target. Rather, it was a small target, and that helped. Even so, the hull sustained substantial damage after the shields failed and the controls got sticky.

"Listen, Carol," Cap said. "I can land us if you need me to."

How quaint, she thought, but she didn't say so out loud. "No. We're going to be close, but hopefully not close enough that they notice us."

"Close" was a little more than fifty miles from where they wanted to be, but it was a tradeoff—distance for secrecy. When they stepped from the vessel, they saw exactly how much damage had been done. Captain Marvel had piloted them home in little better than Swiss cheese. Hulk surveyed the wreckage and smiled. Thor didn't even seem to notice. Hyperion looked at Captain Marvel and nodded his appreciation of her skills.

"I should've gotten us closer," she said.

"Look around, Carol," Captain America responded. "It's Earth. Home. It'll do just fine." He climbed out and looked at the frozen land around them. It was cold and it was uninhabited, as far as they could tell.

"As for the target, the coordinates Iron Man gave us put that location—and Thanos—southwest of here. Call it 220.25 degrees." He looked in that direction and pointed. "Distance of about fifty-two miles. Hyperion?"

"I see it," Marcus Milton replied, scanning. "Looks like an excavated build-out—an in-ground structure. I can see five life-forms. One of them looks to be in some sort of containment field."

"That's likely the son," Cap said. "Okay. So, Hulk, can you head over there? Knock on the front door, soften them up a bit and distract them? We'll be right behind you." As the Hulk prepared to leap, Thor stopped him for a moment.

"Harness your appetite, Banner," he said. "Leave some for the rest of us." Thor smiled wryly as he said it.

Hulk looked at him and grunted.

Then he was on his way, powerful legs carrying him an incredible distance with just one leap. There would be more.

ABOVE EARTH, near the Peak, the ship-to-ship fighting continued. The pirate blockade broke, but it did so slowly. The Imperial Guard and a few of the Avengers continued their fight alongside the ships, and the Guard fought with unusual savagery as they mourned the loss of one of their own to the pirated weapons.

While the council rulers dealt with Black Dwarf, Black Widow, Shang-Chi, and Manifold continued toward their destination. They were brutal and effective, and at times Manifold felt like a third wheel as he watched the other two beating their enemies into submission. He did what he could, but he was tired and wasn't the skilled fighter they were.

"The level is clear," Shang-Chi said finally. The Widow joined Eden at the panel, and her fingers flitted over the controls. "Crack it if you can—otherwise we need to move on to the hangar and get back out there." As he spoke he dropped the last of the pirates to the ground. The man didn't even sound winded. It was embarrassing how much more in shape he was than Eden.

"No. I think we're good, Shang," Eden said. The digital readout danced as the access codes overrode whatever locks had been put in place. "We're in." The Black Widow looked over his shoulder and nodded.

"External monitors are online," she announced. "We've got an ops center."

"Putting everything on..." Manifold saw the

shape that hovered outside and almost forgot to speak.
"...the... screen..."

The boy was out there. Tall and thin, his hair
moving in the void of space as his hand glowed
brighter and brighter. Looking at him, even on the
monitor, was difficult.

Nightmask stood next to Starbrand, both of them
on the ring of the Peak. They did not float away. They
did not suffocate, or freeze, or bleed out from their eyes
and mouth. That was the sort of thing that happened
to people in the movies. Instead, Nightmask touched
Starbrand on the shoulder. The boy nodded his head
and waved his hand.

Around them the ships of the alien blockade
exploded, one after the other. Not all of them, but
a very significant number. They were tiny flares of
light against the vast luminescence coming from a kid
named Kevin Connor. The light around Starbrand was
brighter than the sun, and it was impossible not to see
the correlation between his gesture and the resulting
devastation. It was both beautiful and utterly terrifying.

"I am so glad he's on our side," Eden said.

"If he ever decides not to be," Black Widow said,
"I want you to put him on the other side of the Skrull
Empire's darkest moon." She stared at the monitors for
several seconds, and then spoke into the comm. "Am
I reading this right, Hawkeye? It looks like they're in
full retreat."

"Uh-huh," the archer replied. "Bugging out. We
won."

"Not yet," Natasha said.

"Any word from Earth, Widow?" Hawkeye asked.

"Patching in to Avengers Tower," she said. "Being rerouted."

THE WAR for the Golden City continued. Like the Avengers and their allies, the Wakandan forces—led by Queen Shuri—started pushing back. The invaders quickly discovered why Wakanda had never been successfully invaded.

T'CHALLA LOOKED at the gathered forces they had beaten down.

"That seems to be the last of the foot soldiers," he said to his fellow Illuminati. "They fought together better than I expected, as if they were coordinated and controlled."

"I believe they were," Reed agreed. "Attacking in waves, automatons, but that's a problem solved— they're all down for the count. How's our other one coming along, Tony?"

"Almost there." Iron Man worked at the control panel that offered access to the safe room where the antimatter bombs were kept. "Whoever changed the codes was very good... but I'm better."

"Yes, but is your armor picking up anything from inside the room?" the Beast asked anxiously. "The bomb?"

"It has to be powered on. The readings are off the charts." Iron Man confirmed the fears they all felt. Then he announced, "I'm in. Hopefully we're not too late." As he spoke, the door to the vault slid soundlessly to the side.

Black Bolt stood near the far wall; behind him was a tall, lean woman with blue skin and no hair. Her features were angular, and her hands were placed on Black Bolt's standing body. He was conscious—but as the old adage went, the lights were on and nobody was home.

"Too late for what?" She looked at the approaching figures and smiled. "To save me from whispering in the king's ear? To stop me from finding your bomb? Too late to save your world?"

The antimatter bombs were fully activated, and the air hummed with the potential for death and destruction. She peered in their direction, her expression one of pure malicious venom.

"Answer them, Inhuman. Let them know if they are too late to stop me."

Iron Man stopped in the doorway.

"He's not going to—"

"She has his mind," Namor spat. "Of course he is! Move back, Beast." The Atlantean moved quickly, shoving the Beast to the side as if he were weightless. "You won't want to—"

The shockwave that hit them sent Namor, Iron Man, and Reed Richards soaring backward. T'Challa narrowly managed to avoid the massive sonic detonation. Doctor Strange was protected from the destructive force of Black Bolt's voice by a quickly erected sorcerous shield.

The anger on his features was plain to see.

"The bomb…" Strange said. "Black Bolt… you servants of Thanos…." He had been made a fool by one of those very servants, and he had not forgiven that slight. "You have no idea what kind of arrogance it takes to think the power you are trying to control can be controlled at all." He continued forward and his hands moved, his fingers dancing in contortions nearly too fast to see as he summoned his power and cast his spell. "You push us all to the brink, and then over the edge.

"Very well, let me show you the abyss."

A blinding light shone from his left hand, while he used the right one to fashion glowing, interlocked rings. The effect was simultaneously mesmerizing and terrifying. Tentacles of energy materialized and lashed at the air. They became solid, vaguely reptilian, then wrapped themselves around the woman—and especially Black Bolt.

"Again, Inhuman," she said, fear edging her words. "Scream for me!"

Black Bolt screamed, and the tendrils that tried to wrap him into a package were shredded, as were the ones that had caught his puppet master. This time the sonic assault broke through Strange's defenses. He was knocked backward, a scream peeling past his lips, utterly unheard in the cacophony.

Suddenly new tendrils caught Black Bolt, wrapping around his face and cutting off his voice. These were fleshier, and the strands wrapped up both him and the woman. She screamed her frustration as she tried to break free.

"T'Challa, I can't hold them for long," Reed Richards said as he struggled with his captives. "Quickly."

"All I have is a rumbler," the Black Panther said, "but there's no way we won't be caught in the—"

"Use it!"

Holding down the safety T'Challa pushed the red button on his Vibranium sound grenade. The shockwave lifted all of them into the air, and the explosive noise shook their brains inside of their skulls. It left them stunned and half deaf.

The blue woman was the first to recover, and she stepped toward an antimatter bomb. T'Challa's suit had absorbed some of the impact, and he made it to his hands and knees a second later.

"Don't… don't do it," he said unsteadily. "Don't be a fool." He could feel cool air rushing over his flesh where his suit had been torn open. "There's only… a few seconds' delay. You'll kill yourself, along with everything else."

"Do you know where Thanos found me?" She peered down at him, and when she spoke it was as if she were talking to a child. "In an orphanage for the badly damaged, the unwell. The lost ones who had experienced so much horror at a young age that all they wanted was for life to end. Like all of the others, I had been tortured and abused. I was… different.

"My crib mate was Thanos' very first tribute," she continued. "I watched as he butchered his own child, and then I begged him to honor me the same way. He promised me he would, but only if I would help him kill all his other children—the other bastards he'd spawned. I gave him the only thing I had of value. I gave him my word."

She put her hand on the bomb. The energies cracked and sparked, but they were still contained, if only barely.

"Then I waited years for the tyrant to finish what he had started. Years for him to do what he promised. Now the last child of Thanos is on Earth." Suddenly, she wasn't speaking to T'Challa. She was speaking to her master. "And here I am, fulfilling my word. I am not afraid to die. This will be your end, as well, for making me wait."

T'Challa tried to stand. He had to stop her. His world and his people needed him. Still she hit the switch on the side of the bomb's casing, and the energy levels spiked higher. The very air around the device crackled and snapped with energy.

"The bomb is finally charged, and according to the knowledge I stole from the Inhuman king, all that remains is to activate the trigger—and then your world ends."

Again the king of Wakanda tried to stand, but his limbs wouldn't obey him. His arms quivered. His legs shook, then collapsed under his weight. All he could do was watch.

"Ahem…"

The blue-skinned alien looked toward the spot where she had thought to find the trigger mechanism. It was a large metallic box with two handles and a half-dozen safeties. And it wasn't there.

"Now normally, you're just my kind of crazy," Maximus said, a sly smile playing across his face. He sat on a pile of rubble. "But there are plans underway, and I'm invested in them, so… I find myself torn."

She held out her hand. "Give it to me." There was a flicker of light in her eyes, and T'Challa suspected she was trying to capture the man's mind as she had his brother's. However, his grin just grew wider.

"How about I give you what you want if I get what I want?"

"Which is?" Her frustration seemed obvious enough.

"The same thing I always want," he replied as if she should have known. "I want to look like the smartest person in the room. Believe it or not, with this crowd it isn't as easy as you'd think." She frowned.

"Deal?" he said. "Yes, let's call it a deal. So here's your bomb being triggered." He hit the switches, tapping them in the right order, and T'Challa felt his soul go numb. The world—the whole of it—and the madman was going to end it for the sake of his ego.

"And here's me telling you that you forgot about the most dangerous thing in the room."

The area around the antimatter bomb glowed for a moment, and Lockjaw appeared. The glow continued—

"No!" the alien woman cried out, then both she and the bomb vanished—as did the Inhuman teleporter. Maximus dropped the trigger and grinned. He looked directly at T'Challa.

"Really, why would the lot of you make a bomb like that?" he asked brightly. "That's the sort of thing I would do. You're supposed to be the heroes of the story."

THE WORLD warped, and an instant later the room in the Necropolis disappeared from her sight, to be replaced by a vast, unearthly frozen wasteland. Beside Supergiant the antimatter bomb whined at a high enough pitch to make the ice shiver beneath it.

"No."

She glanced around frantically, taken off guard by the change. The massive dog looked at her and said, "Woof."

And then it disappeared.

Faster than thought she was wrapped in a flash so bright it burned her eyes, followed by a detonation that consumed everything.

"ANYONE HOME?" The voice crackled in his ear.

Tony stood still for a moment, doing a full systems

check. Surprisingly, he was alive and his armor was functional.

"Natasha? Is that you?"

"It's me. We've locked down local space. What's left of Thanos' fleet suffered heavy losses and is in full retreat. The council ships are moving off. We're back to being on our own, Tony."

He looked around the room. The bomb was gone. Just plain gone. The Beast and Namor helped Doctor Strange get to his feet. Reed was helping T'Challa stand. The man's panther outfit was blown half away from his body. None of them looked very steady.

There were remnants of... tentacles? Some of them were still wriggling. All of them were bleeding a weird orangish goo. Black Bolt was free, and Maximus was right next to him, rubbing the side of Lockjaw's head.

"All right. Good," Stark said. "You've got overwatch. Pick the hottest of the hot spots and send reinforcements if you can. New York, Wakanda. I'm sending you the coordinates of where we're headed."

CHAPTER 34

WAR

THANOS walked among the ruins of Orollan and savored the sights that lay before him. Behind him, his son pounded the walls of the glowing golden energy tube that held him. By rights he should have already killed the boy. Thane was a threat. He was the stuff of nightmares.

In his youth Thanos had found many a woman to satisfy his urges. He also knew what the repercussions would be. Sooner or later his children would find him and try to kill him, to take his place. He had sought to end his father's existence, and the fact that he had thus far failed was a wound that would not heal. Something he would, in due time, seek to rectify.

His children could do no less.

And yet...

The boy had killed all of the people in the city around them, and he had done so without even trying. If Thanos could harness that power, if he could somehow make it his, it could aid him in his ultimate goals.

This was a tantalizing puzzle.

It was also the sort of quandary that might be used against him if he were not careful.

"We have lost contact with Black Dwarf and our agents on the Peak, Master." Corvus Glaive moved up behind him—cautiously, as it was unwise to surprise Thanos. "It seems the human heroes have returned here with significant support from other worlds. Our time runs short."

Thanos replied as if he hadn't even heard. "Don't you love chaos, Corvus?" He turned and looked at his second. "It's when the chaos comes that lesser creatures lose their mettle, submit to instinct and panic—but it's when those like you and I thrive." He looked past the man to the energy prison.

"I will kill my son now. Not as some reaction to the noise, but because it pleases me to do so." All around him he found death, and it was good. "Maw, release the boy. Let him do his best against me before he dies." Before any of them could move, the ground shook under their feet. It was a minor tremor, but it was there just the same, accompanied by a brief pounding sound.

"What is this?" He turned in the direction of the sound. A small figure appeared, rapidly growing larger, aimed at him like a missile.

The Hulk roared as he descended.

Simple physics state that a falling body cannot control its descent, and it cannot change direction. Thanos was ready. He struck the Hulk, combining his own strength with the green behemoth's momentum. This sent his attacker hurtling backward into one building after another, shattering stone and destroying the structures in a chain reaction that left a trail of destruction. The wall of the Eternal Chasm stopped him, but only after he broke away a portion of it.

The Hulk was a powerful beast, but it would not be alone. There was no reason for it to seek him out if it hadn't been directed to do so by someone else. It wasn't in the monster's nature.

"Do you see, Corvus?" As Thanos pointed, the green monster regained his feet, groggy and dazed as he was. "All life is noise. All life is a distraction Therefore it has no real value and must be treated as the diversion it is. Kill this beast for me. Make it suffer."

Corvus Glaive and Proxima Midnight both responded, launching themselves at the Hulk as their master watched them. With another Earth-shaking vibration, the Hulk returned the favor, hurling himself in their direction and landing with an impact that nearly knocked them off their feet.

"He's fast, my love." Proxima leaped to the side as the half-ton of green fury crashed into the ground where she had stood just a moment before. Corvus dodged the assault, but barely.

Spinning in the air, she hurled her spear, and it broke into three separate missiles. The weapon had been forged from a sun trapped in distorted space-time. It had been a life-giving new star and a blazing supernova. She had earned it from Thanos long after he had taken it from its maker's corpse.

The three missiles hit their target and burned into the Hulk's flesh. At her command, black tendrils writhed around him. The spear's parts grew heavier, enough to make even the Hulk groan and fall forward to catch himself on hands and knees.

"Do you feel that, monster?" she crowed. "It's the weight of a star holding you down."

His blood flowed green from wounds that tried to heal, yet could not as the pieces dug deeper. While he struggled, the blade of Corvus Glaive slid to his throat and cut into jade flesh, drawing more blood.

"A thick hide on this beast, Proxima, but even super-dense skin cannot stop my blade," he said, wearing a cruel grin. "My glaive can cut atoms, beast. It can cut you, too. I'll hang your head above my mantel, and watch it as it glows above the fire. I'll look up at it and—"

A metal disc slammed into the side of his head, and he was thrown back. The weapon was well known to Thanos. It was wielded by one of the Avengers.

"Ah." Thanos looked up into the sun. "Now this is more what I expected."

Captain America caught the shield in midair on the rebound. Coming down from the sky behind him were three more: Captain Marvel, the would-be god Thor, and a red-haired figure wearing a cape. That one he did not know.

Captain Marvel caught Proxima by her arm and threw her. As she hurtled through the air, however, Proxima summoned her spear; the three burning stars of energy tore themselves away from the Hulk's body in an effort to obey their mistress. As they did, the Hulk staggered to his feet... and began to shrink. He let out a roar of fury that dwindled into a gasp of shock. The man who remained looked at Proxima.

"How did you do that?"

She answered him with a savage backhand that knocked him unconscious.

"I can do so much worse, fool."

Not far away Ebony Maw whispered to Thanos' son. The words were too distant to hear.

Corvus swung his blade at the leader of the new arrivals. Captain America deflected it with his shield, which he then used to bash him in the face. Corvus had grown complacent and cocky, Thanos mused.

It is time for him to learn a lesson.

The red-haired man in the blue and gold stepped closer and braced himself, ready for a fight. Corvus' lessons, it seemed, were about to begin.

"ARE YOU watching, Thane?" The Ebony Maw looked at his prize and smiled softly. He gestured to the newcomers who fought against Thanos and his Black

Order. "They are here, your last chance at salvation. The human heroes of Earth. They are your only hope."

One of the newcomers summoned lightning from the skies and cast the bolts at his father, who barely seemed to notice them. A woman joined his efforts and launched energy blasts from her hands. The energies sprayed ineffectually off Thanos, and he knocked her back with twin beams from his eyes. Turning quickly he did the same to the warrior with the hammer, striking the man so squarely that he flew back until he vanished from sight.

"Do you think they can save you?" the Maw continued. "I do not. You've likely spent your entire life believing how all of this should be. You probably were taught to cherish life. To lift up the unfortunate. Be honorable and, above all, be a good man. Do these things, and the universe will reward you in some way."

Proxima joined her husband in his assault on the shield-wielding man, pounding her restored spear into the ground. The explosive concussion knocked all of their opponents off their feet.

Ebony Maw shook his head and frowned. "It's an ethos—and a noble one at that. Believing in hope. But listen to me, boy." The newcomers tried to stagger to their feet, with little success. "All hope is fleeting in the face of Thanos."

Thane peered at his father, a man he hadn't met until a short while ago.

So much to process in so little time…

"Your father plans to kill you, Thane," the Maw

said frankly. "That is his goal, and that is what will happen—if he has the chance."

"What are you telling me?" the son of Thanos demanded. "That I should give up? That there isn't a chance? I don't believe that. There's always a chance."

"Not at all," the Maw replied. "At least not in the way you mean. Not in any way you would imagine." A momentary lull ended and the fight raged again as the red-haired warrior shot eye-beams toward Proxima. "There is light and there is darkness, Thane. Both exist. There is no unwritten law that says good men will always win, and so they don't."

Glaive struck from behind, cutting into the shoulder of Proxima's opponent. For all the strength the man appeared to possess, he bellowed in pain. It had to be excruciating.

"In the end, Thane," the Maw continued as if everything else was just a distraction, "all that remains are the whispered prayers of the condemned, and the hope that there is a god listening."

"CAROL... GET up," Captain America said. She was still stunned from the blue woman's assault. Hyperion struggled with the figure in the tattered cape. Thor was nowhere to be seen. "We've got to—"

"Steve, behind you," Captain Marvel said, and he spun. Proxima Midnight drew back her glowing spear, energies crackling where she gripped it.

"Two great captains," Proxima said, "doing what

all captains do best." She hurled it, and the weapon separated. "Farewell, humans. You were weak and deserved such a humble ending."

"Get behind my shield, Carol—" Cap said, then all three missiles struck. Two careened off the shield, but a third one caught him in the midsection, causing him to cry out in pain.

"Impressive—he deflected two of—" Proxima said, then, "No. No!" The two gleaming bolts came at her husband from behind, driving into him and through him. He only had time to grunt. Yet he never dropped his weapon, and still it cut his opponent.

"Tell me, monster, does it sting?" Hyperion said, grabbing the glaive and pulling it free. "Does it burn? Because this is your end."

Blood pouring from his face, Corvus Glaive replied, "You cannot threaten someone… with what they want."

"Call it a gift, then," Hyperion said. The energies that came from the man's eyes were as bright as the sun and when they struck, Corvus burned as if he had fallen into the sun's very heart. The light blasted through him, searing meat and bone alike into a blackened ash.

"Corvus!" Proxima Midnight screamed.

"CORVUS!"

She reached for his weapon. "I have it," she said. "I have you." Before she could grasp it, however, Captain Marvel struck with a two-handed burst of energy, knocking her back.

"Get up," Carol Danvers said as her opponent did just that. Energy danced around her hands and turned her hair to fire. "We're not done here. We haven't even starte—"

A massive fist struck Captain Marvel and knocked her twenty yards through a solid stone wall. She disappeared behind mounds of rubble. Thanos stood over Proxima as she gripped her husband's weapon, and then fell to her knees where his ashes began to dissipate with the wind.

ABRUPTLY THE wind stopped blowing, and Thanos frowned. An instant later the air around him exploded in electrical discharge.

KRAK-A-THOOM!

The sky roared and lightning danced across his body, arced from his form to hit the ground, boiling sand into glass and roasting the bones of the dead. The assault was massive, but he was Thanos and had endured far worse.

He looked to the skies and smiled.

"Do it again, thunder god."

Thor obliged. KRAK-A-THOOOM!

This time the light was enough to blind, the sound enough to deafen. The lightning came upon him and continued for what seemed like an eternity. Debris leapt into the air. The pain was a living thing.

Finally the worst was done, and the glazed ground around him cooled enough for him to move his feet.

"Is that all?" Thanos said, his form smoldering. "Or do you have something more?"

Thor leapt to the challenge, and Mjolnir came down in a broad arc. The hammer slammed into Thanos' skull and sent him to his knees. Lightning arced between them, and sent daggers of pain across his side and his face.

Sometimes he forgot that others held true power, as well. Thor was powerful indeed, and Thanos suspected he was capable of killing if the mood struck him. He had lived for thousands of years, and he wielded the power of the storm. He brought Mjolnir around a second time and slammed Thanos to the ground.

"One of us will die here today, Thanos," the thunder god pledged. "One of us dies now!"

He swept Mjolnir over his head and brought the hammer down. Thanos knew then he had been right. His opponent's intent was no less than destruction. Thanos blocked the blow and caught the head of the hammer with his hand.

When he struck back it was with the same intent.

"DON'T YOU love chaos, Thane?"

The Ebony Maw squinted against the glare of the lightning that was raining down upon Thanos. He spoke as calmly as before.

"It is in times of chaos that lesser creatures lose their mettle and submit to instinct, to panic. They run. Yet some, the best of us, thrive on these moments."

He found a button at the base of the containment device. A moment later an arm rose from the device, displaying a small control panel. He tapped a series of commands into the panel, and it was only a matter of seconds before the containment field faded away.

"So as you witness Thanos, refusing to be beaten by mortal or immortal, I release you."

"Why?" Thane asked. "Why would you?" Thane was not a fool. He stepped away from his temporary prison.

"To see if you are truly evolved." Again that kind smile that belied the man's actions. "I want to see if you will run."

They watched together as Thor was cast backward by a massive energy blast. The Titan was battered, yes, bruised and bloodied, but he was still strong, and his enemy looked little better. Thanos struck again, smashing Thor into the ground and then blasting him backward.

"You've spent your entire life running from who you are," the Maw continued. "Trying to be that good and noble man." He leaned in closer. "Well, here is your chance for one final good act. You can save all of them. You can save the people who came here to fight for you, but in doing so you become what you have resisted for so long." The Ebony Maw whispered into the young man's ear. "You have a decision to make, Thane. Will you reach out and take what is yours?

"Are you the son of Thanos?"

Not far away, Thanos channeled energies into

his fists until they were white-hot. His enemies were down. They were defeated. The look on his face was of raw, unbridled fury, and it was clear in that moment that the Mad Titan knew nothing of mercy. He had come to kill someone, simply for the act of being born.

"Yes. I am Thane. Son of Thanos."

He reached out.

"I am the son of Thanos."

His clawed left hand had killed before. If he used it, his father would die as any other would die.

But his right hand? That one also glowed, at first with a golden light, and then white-hot like his father's. His right hand was living death.

Ever wary, Thanos turned toward him at the moment the hand made contact. The very air around the Titan crackled and bled. The air itself screamed in agony as Thane touched his father. The ground shivered; the air froze. The tyrant let loose a scream no one would ever hear.

"What have I done?" Thane said.

"If you've wondered what would be worse than death, now you know," the Ebony Maw said. "Thane, son of Thanos. Greater than his father could ever hope to be. Greater than a world like this one. No single world can contain what you will become." As he spoke, they were enveloped in a glow and began to fade away.

"After all, what is one world for a man who could have many?"

"BAD DREAMS?"

Steve Rogers opened his eyes and looked up at the armored face of Iron Man. The air around them was a cloud of dust and darkness. Every part of his body ached; in a few places the pain was enough to make him want to say so. At least it was a friendly face he saw as he awoke.

"That depends," Cap replied. "What kind of world am I waking up to, Tony?"

"Ours."

"Then I guess the dreams are okay."

Iron Man offered him a hand, and he took it. Not a dozen feet away, Hyperion also was rising to his feet. He had been caught in the backlash of the battle between the thunder god and Titan, and the damage added to what he had already endured. Captain Marvel was on her feet, but looked a little unsteady.

The next thing he saw was the destruction—ruins of a city he'd never known existed, and the bodies of the countless dead. The completeness of it, the savagery with which it had to have been accomplished, bordered on the unimaginable.

"What happened?" Captain America asked. "You and the cavalry arrive in time to save the day?"

"No." Iron Man shook his head. "It wasn't us. Near as we can figure, it was the son." Thor stood nearby, his armor blasted away from his body. Even in his current condition, scraped and bruised, the thunderer stood straight and true. "He appears to be quite a gifted boy," Tony continued. "If he had a hand in the decimation of this city, then he's definitely his father's offspring."

Not far away, Bruce Banner stood looking at something. The smoke cleared, and Cap was stunned to see Thanos. The Titan stood perfectly still, his arms up in a defensive posture, frozen in a block of amber. Proxima Midnight stood by his side in the translucent prison.

"Not really sure how he did it, but it looks like he took out his father." Cap and Tony moved closer. "No idea what that stuff is, either—it looks like amber, but it's much tougher. Not in any database I can access. I'd say it's as unbreakable as your shield, Steve."

Steve Rogers looked into the eyes of Thanos, and saw something he never expected to see. Fear.

"So did we win here, Steve?" Tony's words were calm, but there was a hint of uncertainty.

"We're alive, and Thanos has been beaten," Captain America said. "Let's call that a victory."

CHAPTER 35

FROM THE ASHES

DEEP in the Himalayan mountains, the brothers met.

It was just the two of them for the moment, with Lockjaw, but soon enough they would begin gathering their people together again. The Inhumans were not dead. That, at least, they had seen to successfully. Everything else about the future remained uncertain.

Black Bolt held out his hand, and Maximus looked at him for a moment before reaching into a protected pocket and pulling out a glowing red gem-like device.

"This feels positively ceremonial, brother," he said. "Is it our funeral? I think it should be."

He frowned, and saw that Black Bolt frowned, as well.

"Well, I mean, really, what could the royal

family—or any of the Inhumans at large—believe except that you and I are dead? That you were killed by Thanos, and I perished in the fall of Attilan."

Black Bolt looked at the glowing ember in his hand. Then he studied the ground beneath him. The spot where, for endless seasons, Attilan had rested before their king deemed it necessary to move on.

"Oh, they will mourn us—you more than me, I imagine—but they will mourn us, and rightly so," Maximus said, and then his expression turned to concern. "We're not going back to them, are we?"

The ground changed. The same light that burned within the ember began to ripple, to shift and send patterns across the snow.

"Why else would you be leaving the Codex here?" Maximus continued. "Where it has been hidden before, to be found by whoever would take up your mantle?" Maximus shook his head, and for a moment a familiar haunted expression came across his face. "I can't help it—can't stop the spiders from crawling through my mind, weaving the same question in their webs. Why? Why the trickery? Why the nature of the bomb? Why sacrifice the city?" he said. "Why are we here, Black Bolt? Why do these things, unless…

"Unless…

"Oh."

Black Bolt held up one finger and placed it before his lips. On the ground around them, the red light continued to glow and spread, witnessed only by the three of them. At six different points, the stone began to rise. In a place where human eyes could not see, where the clouds around the mountains hid the truth from any eyes looking down, Attilan began to rebuild itself.

It would not be the fastest process, but it would take hold, and the city would rise again as it was always meant to be. For humans the term was nanotechnology, but when the original planners of Attilan had designed the secrets hidden within the Codex, they likely used a different phrase.

Maximus, who thought he knew the ways of his brother, laughed in delight.

"Ah, Black Bolt, who is the mischief-maker now? You were always going to scatter our people, weren't you? Like seeds… because Thanos or no, you were always going to detonate the bomb. I was so wrong." He laughed and spread his arms. "I thought you were giving us the last of the Inhuman age, but this? This is the dawn of a new one!"

Black Bolt smiled silently, and his brother laughed for the both of them. Around the planet, new Inhumans would be awakening, the results of Terrigenesis. Some of them might remain scattered, but most would be found in time, and they would be offered what should have been offered to them in the past. They would be invited into the Inhuman family. Some might say no, true. But most, he suspected, would say yes.

Soon the Inhumans would gather again, and they would gather in Attilan, which rose slowly from the ground even as Maximus laughed madly.

THEY STARTED on Whaan Prime. The Ex Nihili gathered to mourn the passing of their brother, Jerran Ko, who brought death when his time to leave the universe was forced upon him.

They mourned, yes, but they did more than that. They rededicated themselves to what they were always meant to be: a force for life and change in the universe. They started on Whaan Prime, changing the dead world and bringing back what had been stolen away.

As they concentrated and offered portions of themselves, the once-rich land grew fertile again; life began and quickly evolved. Grass grew, algae formed, plants came back, and trees rose in forests. In time more life would arise. The seeds were scattered and tasked to flourish.

When they were done, they would move to another world destroyed by the Builders. Some were dead and others scarred, but the Ex Nihili would work to restore the balance that had been taken whatever the case. Their sister, the last of the Abyssi, would watch over them to judge their efforts.

Once again in their existence, they had a purpose that made sense.

ON CHANDILAR, the Shi'ar throne world, Gladiator looked at the data files presented to him and nodded. His head hurt from absorbing information, and not for the first time he wished for a simpler life of hitting things and leading his elite forces into combat.

We seldom get what we wish for the universe, he mused. Mentor stood nearby and sipped at a warm drink.

"I can feel your frustration from here."

"When did you become a telepath?"

"I didn't." Mentor smiled. "I can just read the expression on your stony face."

"We lost so very much."

"We kept what matters," Mentor replied. "We have an empire. We maintained our core beliefs. You led us well through what was a hellish situation at best." He held up his cup in salute. "Long live the Majestor."

"We have to rebuild the fleet."

"Of course we do."

"We need new members of the Imperial Guard."

"Naturally."

"I mean sooner rather than later."

"We're already searching for a replacement for Titan. We've dispatched an honor guard to his homeworld to properly show our respects. Rest assured, Kallark, we are well at work on this. All of what you are saying is in the reports I presented to you."

"There are a great number of reports, Mentor."

"Yes. That is why I presented you with the summary."

"That fact terrifies me more than the possibility of another invasion." He stood and moved away from the reports. "Whatever the case, the top priorities are rebuilding the fleet and bolstering the Imperial Guard."

"As you say, Majestor."

Sometimes he wondered whether the praetor was merely humoring him.

HALA, AS with so many other worlds, was recovering from the war. In a ceremony broadcast across the planet, Ronan the Accuser stood before the Supreme Intelligence as attendants completed repairs to his containment tank, and listened to the litany of sins he had committed. The word "treason" came up several times.

The other Accusers stood with him. They had left with Ronan to fight the war against the Builders, and those that survived fully understood their fates were tied to his.

When he had listened long enough, Ronan raised a hand and spoke.

"I do not come here to surrender myself to your justice, Supremor," he announced. "I come here as an Accuser. I come here as the Head Accuser, and I offer myself in that position to the Kree Empire, which we have brought back from defeat."

The Supreme Intelligence grew silent. The amalgam of a million years of Kree history contemplated the words for a moment, and then responded.

"In that spirit, and in that context, you are welcomed back into Kree society and back to your post on Hala." There was a moment of silence as Ronan nodded his head, and then the artificial intelligence added, "All charges of treason will be forgiven and removed."

"That would be for the best," Ronan said.

Inwardly, he seethed.

AT PRAXIS-2, the stargate did not close. It was not converted to its original purpose. The vast hole between universes stayed exactly as it was when the drone army of Annihilus began to swarm the planet. Vast armies of the insectoids swept the landscape. Those few people assigned to posts there fled in terror.

They were permitted to leave.

Praxis-2 became Annihilation World. There was no one left on the planet to disagree.

ON TARNAX II, the Skrulls gathered and celebrated their victories. There were feasts aplenty and orders to rebuild. Their armies and fleets were heavily depleted.

Long before the feasts were finished on Tarnax II, the Council of Warlords agreed to crown a new emperor. There was little discussion. Warlord Kl'rt was one of the greatest warriors in the history of the Skrull people, and his abilities as a commander were beyond reproach. Past defeats were forgotten, and the Super-Skrull was placed upon the throne by unanimous decree.

As his first order of business, he stated that—for now at least—Earth was no longer to be considered a target. Many thought that a wise choice, as the planet had, thus far, refused to be conquered. Others remembered that the Avengers had led the way to victory over the Builders.

Still others muttered that Kl'rt continued to lick the wounds of his past, as Earthers had beaten him on several occasions. They were not, however, inclined to say it too loudly. Those who did had a tendency to disappear.

Throughout the Skrull Empire, a reward was offered for all technologies found from the Builder and Shi'ar fleets. The munitions plants were active night and day, as were the shipyards. Skrulls were born with conquest in their blood, and expansion was their birthright.

ON SPARTAX, a close neighbor of the Skrulls, the celebrations were more modest. The Skrulls had deemed the people of Spartax "traitors to the cause," and though no one attacked, no warships came for them, the people there soon understood the term "to sleep with one eye open."

Shape-shifters made for terrifying enemies, and Spartax received no assurances they would remain safe from attack.

ON TITAN, a tyrant grew.

He had started his life believing in fairy tales, in the possibility of mercy and peace, but Thane no longer held to those childish notions. The time had come for him to grow up and take his place in the grander scheme of things. The Ebony Maw stood by his side and offered advice on all things of importance.

The Maw was a good instructor, and Thane listened, intent on becoming all that his father had been and more. He wanted to be a fitting match for a universe that he learned was dying.

CHAPTER 36

LOST KINGDOMS

DOCTOR Strange looked at the rest of the Illuminati, focusing on Iron Man. Tony Stark removed his helmet and held it in front of him.

"What did you tell the others?"

"That I would take care of it."

"And they believed you?" Hank McCoy looked his way and raised one eyebrow.

T'Challa responded, "Why would they not? They see the world as they want it to be, not as it is."

Reed Richards frowned at the words. "No need to be fatalistic, T'Challa. Anthony built the current Avengers team to handle the impossible—and look, they did. They exist to build hope, so we can build the unthinkable. You know how it is. Different machines are made with different tools."

Namor growled. "And cemeteries are littered with dead men who died still believing they would live. Our world is dying. What are we going to do about it, gentlemen?"

Tony Stark stared at his helmet for a moment, looking at the distorted version of his face that peered back from the reflective metal surface.

"We continue—and though it may cost us our very souls, we gather the proper tools necessary." He rose from his seat and walked over to the newest residents in their prison—the frozen forms of Thanos and Proxima Midnight.

"We build," he said. "And we prepare for the unthinkable."

IN WAKANDA, the queen made her way to the Necropolis, pausing to observe the reconstruction that had begun to take place. She brought with her an escort of twenty Hatut Zeraze, for the chance always remained there would be more of the pirates left. There was also the possibility that the conversation she was forced to have would go poorly.

"Where are you, T'Challa? Come out." The Necropolis was a place of memory, a spot where the dead were supposed to rest and be remembered. She looked around, but did not see her brother until he wanted to be seen.

"You make it sound as if I was hiding, Shuri." He walked through an archway from shadows where she would have sworn nothing had been hidden. "I can smell the smoke from the fires that still burn. Birnin Zana needs her queen. What brings you here to the dead city when the living one calls to you?"

"Dead Wakandans," she responded, lowering her head. "The enemy broke the walls and poured into the capital. From the dead bodies, they made piles to stand on while they taunted us." She stepped closer to him and looked hard into his eyes. He did not want to look back, but had no choice.

Though they both wore the garb of their totem, she was his queen, after all.

"And look how they fell, Shuri," he said. "They were no match for the queen."

"What took you so long to come to our defense, T'Challa? Where were you?"

He gestured around him. "I was here. This place was overrun by the armies of Thanos, as well. I came as quickly as I could."

"I think he lies, my queen." The soldier in white pointed at T'Challa as he spoke. "I think without his crown he has become a coward. Maybe he was always a coward."

Without warning the Black Panther struck, knocking the man aside with a savage backhand. The soldier lay groaning on the ground as T'Challa stood over him.

"Your queen rules Wakanda, but here I am king. Speak thus again at your own peril." He turned to Shuri. "I am sorry, sister. Yes, the walls were broken, but the city stands. We will rebuild again."

She looked at her older brother, and then shook her head. She had to ask, though she feared the answer.

"T'Challa, what have you been doing in this place?"

He was silent for a moment. "The Necropolis does not concern you, Shuri. What happens here is of no matter to the kingdom."

"Lies."

He turned his head to see who spoke, and found the Dora Milaje entering the courtyard in which they stood.

"He lies, Queen Shuri."

T'Challa pulled away his mask. The Dora Milaje were the elite of the Wakandan forces and answered to the queen. They had served him faithfully, and he knew that very well. It was Aneka who spoke, the very woman he had appointed to lead the elite force.

"What is the meaning of this?" he demanded. "How dare you?"

"We loved you more than our lives, my king," Aneka said, her rage written in her expression. "But no more." She looked upon T'Challa and broke her spear over her knee before tossing the remains toward him.

Behind her, the other members of the Dora Milaje stepped forward.

"You have lost your way," one said—and she, too, broke her spear.

"You have lost your soul." Another broken spear, cast at his feet. The entire time, he stood stock still.

"What is going on here, brother?" Shuri gave him

a chance to defend himself, uncertain he had earned even that.

He was silent.

"Well?" Her word was a demand.

"Don't do this." His words were a plea.

She looked to Aneka. "Tell me." Her brother would not answer, and that was not something she could accept.

"Namor," the warrior said.

"What?" Shuri stared hard. There was a name she never wanted to hear again. There was a man who was reviled.

Aneka pointed at T'Challa, her face a study in anger and betrayal. "The prince of Atlantis has been here many times since he attacked our city. While Wakanda has been at war with Atlantis, the Sub-Mariner has been here!" She stomped her foot to indicate that the City of the Dead was the place she meant. "Many, many times." She glared at T'Challa, and Shuri could see the pain of the words.

"They consort with one another."

"Shuri, please." T'Challa looked her way. "You do not understand."

The queen studied the man she had admired and loved for all of her life, and felt a cold pit where that love should have been. She had been queen for only a short time, but he had failed her time and again. She overlooked that because he was her older brother, but now she could not allow the ties of blood to influence her.

"Then explain it to me," she demanded. "Tell me why." She fought back the tears. She held back the anger. She would give him this one chance.

"I…" He looked away. "I cannot."

Shuri stared for a dozen heartbeats while she considered his words. Then she turned away.

"We are leaving." Her words were a command, and no one misunderstood that fact. Least of all, apparently, her brother.

"Shuri, wait." He reached for her. "It's not what you th—"

"Get your hands off me!" She slapped his hand aside. The anger bloomed into a bitter rage. "You are no longer welcome inside the city, brother." Her eyes looked him over, and the rage grew hotter still, but she kept herself as calm as she had to. She was a queen and had to act that part, even if she wanted to stab out his eyes.

"And this is not done, T'Challa," she continued, "but there are funerals I must attend, friends I have to bury." She started away again and covered a dozen paces before she turned back to him. She stopped, but her escort continued on, knowing they were not wanted at that moment.

Some things had to be said without witnesses.

"You once told me this is a sacred place. That it is holy. The goddess walks here."

He nodded. "I did."

"Then you are a damned fool, T'Challa, to betray your people in her presence."

She walked away and felt his eyes upon her the entire time.

She did not cry. She would not allow herself that luxury.

T'CHALLA FELT his face burn with shame. His little sister had crushed him under her heel, and he could do nothing. He watched her go and wanted so desperately to explain… about the Illuminati, about why he fought to save the world rather than fighting beside her to save Wakanda.

The problem with secrets was that they had to be kept, or they were no longer secrets. And how would he explain the weapons he'd hidden so close to her kingdom, when he could barely justify it himself after all that had gone so very wrong?

There was a slow, sharp clap.

Then another… and another.

The applause caught him by surprise. The wind shifted, and he smelled Namor before he saw him. The Sub-Mariner walked down a series of stone steps from the broken landing above.

"Very well done, T'Challa." He continued to clap his hands, slowly.

"You cannot be so bent as to think this is the time to taunt me, Namor. You simply cannot be that stupid." The man's arrogance was legendary, but to do this now, when his world was ashes?

"Oh, I am not taunting you, T'Challa," the fishman said. "I am applauding your bravery." The words were made a lie by the smirk on the man's face. "And it is bravery. I did not know it myself until recently, but I am fully capable of seeing it now."

The Sub-Mariner was a powerful man. He was capable of bending steel with his hands, and so much more. He had taken the brunt of a blast from Black Bolt and remained conscious even as the walls around him were shattered. Just the same, T'Challa started considering where to hit him to cause the most damage.

"I am seeing so very clearly these days." His lip pulled back in a sneer. His eyes studied T'Challa with cold and merciless intent. He, too, was considering where best to strike at his enemy. He, too, restrained himself. Of that, T'Challa was certain.

"See, now you know what I know," Namor continued.

"And what is that?" The Panther tired of the Atlantean's games.

"What it's like to face death having lost everything you hold dear." Namor stopped directly in front of him, close enough that T'Challa could have struck. "You spent your entire life building a perfect kingdom, and now you have been cast out." He peered around the area for a moment, and then looked back at the Black Panther.

"You could have told her many things. The truth of what we are doing, the nature of you and I. You could have said, 'Namor is here now—I can give him to you.' But you did not." He smiled a cold smile. It was not a kind expression, but a distillation of his contempt for the former king of Wakanda.

"You did not, because you know what we used to call life has very little meaning these days. You know that the world itself is on the edge of collapse, and you would protect her from that even as she sends you away. Thus she repays you for the kindness of omission." He laughed and rose into the air, the small wings on his ankles holding him easily.

"Welcome to the edge," he said. "It is the perfect place for kings who have lost their kingdoms." A moment later he was gone, soaring into the air and heading for the sea.

IN GREENWICH Village lay a house no one could see unless he wanted them to see it: the Sanctum Sanctorum of the Sorcerer Supreme, a man who liked his privacy. There were exceptions. Wong advised him and cared for his needs. Stephen Strange would be lost without the man, and they both knew it—though neither spoke of that fact.

"There is something different about you, Doctor. I can tell."

Strange stared out the window and contemplated the city. Outside of his private sanctuary, it was rebuilding again. That almost always seemed to be the case.

The world, the very universe, continued to change.

"How hard is it to see a blood moon in the night sky?" He did not turn to look at Wong as he spoke. He continued to study the night and the stars. "For a very long time, I liked to think of myself as a man with a foundation, with a purpose, not someone defined by living on the periphery. Not someone catering to the needs of others." Finally he looked to his friend and companion. "Different, Wong? Yes. Very much so."

He had things to do, and he did not trust that he could do them with Wong by his side. Not this time.

"I want you to leave this room, Wong," he instructed. "Bar the door. Do not enter. Do this regardless of what you might hear, or what you think might be happening. If I have not emerged from this room in three days' time, summon Reed Richards. Tell him that this room— that the whole of the Sanctum Sanctorum—must be dispatched from this plane of existence."

Wong looked at him and considered speaking, but in the end nodded instead.

"I plan to use the Blood Bible."

"Master, the cost is too—"

"Do it now, Wong. Time grows short, and I am tired of watching others make choices of consequence while I do nothing."

Wong left the room and locked the door, following his friend's orders.

"If I am to be damned by these decisions," Strange said to himself now, "then let it be while using all the resources available to the Sorcerer Supreme. For I am not a pawn. I am a doctor, and it is time to find out what ails the universe."

A moment later he turned the pages in his Blood Bible and studied the spell he thought would be the best to answer an impossible question. He began the incantation, doing his best to ignore the fear that made him want to hesitate. Energies began to crackle around him, and bizarre forms flitted and danced in the arcing lights. There were sounds, strange and terrible, far beyond human hearing.

There was no place for cowardice, not with a universe at stake.

THE ILLUMINATI gathered. Or some of them did. Iron Man. The Beast. Mister Fantastic. The others were nowhere to be seen.

"You notice it's the royalty who are absent?" Stark said.

"True," Richards replied. "It's almost as if they have to stop and take care of their own worlds for a while. I'm rather surprised you have the time yourself, Tony. You have an empire of your own."

"Sometimes it's best if I let Pepper handle the details," he admitted. "She's better at it than I am."

"Terrigenesis," Hank McCoy said, breaking through the banter. "It's a happening thing right now, gentlemen. The cocoons have been found on every continent and in pretty much every nation. Some of them are already opening." He sighed as he dug for an apple in his backpack. "They've been pulling the rubble of the Inhuman city out of the harbor and checking for bodies. Not one so far that doesn't belong to one of Thanos' thugs. I can't say that news hurts my feelings."

"That's a disturbing fact, in and of itself," Richards said. "Given the records Black Bolt shared with us, the spike in the Inhuman population could very well rival the spike in mutant births over the last two decades." He glanced at Hank. Just to be safe, he clarified. "That means a massive potential for unexpected powers, uncontrolled abilities, and a panicked response by the persons who aren't transformed."

Hank finished a bite of his apple before responding. "I think the wisest thing you could do, Dr. Richards, in order to keep the populace safe, is either destroy the information you were given or blatantly lie to any government officials asking about it."

"You are not mistaken, Dr. McCoy."

"I can't believe I'm saying this," Stark remarked, "but I have to agree."

"This poses other problems that are all new," McCoy said in between bites. "Existing methods used to scan for mutants aren't likely to register Inhumans. That's going to make it difficult to locate or quantify these newer super-powered beings. Despite the fact that—as we have seen in the past—Inhumans don't always look, well, human."

"One nightmare at a time," Stark said. "We don't know how long it will be before the other members of our group will be available. In the meanwhile, there are still cities to rebuild, panicky people who need to be reassured, and alien technology that's just waiting to fall into the wrong hands."

"Most likely S.H.I.E.L.D. will be doing its best to

handle that last part." Richards offered a small smile. "I've already dodged a couple of calls from Nick Fury. I'll answer the next one."

Tony nodded in agreement. "He's been trying very hard to get in contact, and my people have been good at keeping him out of my hair. Maybe I should show him some mercy, as well."

Hank smiled around a piece of apple. "See? I don't get calls from Nick Fury. Do you know why? Because I keep a low profile. Kitty Pryde gets calls. You gentlemen get calls. But everyone assumes I'm just a jovial, blue-furred mutant, and no one tries to draft me."

"Says the guy who used to sport an Infinity Stone," Tony responded.

"Keywords: used to. And what sort of trouble did that cause? I continue to maintain, Mr. Stark, that a wise man keeps a lower profile."

"That would never work with my image."

Richards stood. "If it's all the same, gentlemen, we need to adjourn. I'm off to the Baxter Building to study a few probes I've sent out. There hasn't been any extraterrestrial activity since we defeated Thanos, but that can't last for long."

"Agreed." Beast stood up, as well, and tossed the apple core in his hand into the wastebasket halfway across the room. "I have to get back to teaching my students. Let's worry about saving the universe next week. For now, let's just bask in the glory of the latest victory."

Tony nodded.

"Amen to that."

ACKNOWLEDGMENTS

NO ONE works alone on a book like this, and a lot of times the driving forces behind the scenes get missed. To that end I'd like to acknowledge the people who have, through their efforts, made this book better than it would have been otherwise. Heartfelt thanks to Vivian Cheung, Nick Landau, Laura Price, Paul Gill, Cat Camacho, and the superhuman Hayley Shepherd from Titan Books; and to Jeff Youngquist, Caitlin O'Connell, Sven Larsen, and John Nee from Marvel Comics.

A heads-up to C. B. Cebulski, because once upon a time he helped me more than he knows. Glenn from the Comic Book Palace, in Haverhill, Massachusetts, was a lifesaver when it came to research, and I thank you kindly, sir.

And, of course, Steve Saffel from Titan, who has to work with my drafts and make them coherent, is an unsung hero, as well. Thank you, Steve, from the bottom of my heart. Doubly so for letting me play in my favorite sandbox. The original graphic novel, *Infinity*, was written by Jonathan Hickman with Nick Spencer. It was illustrated by Jim Cheung, Jerome Opeña, Dustin Weaver, Mike Deodato, Stefano Caselli, Leinil Yu, Marco Rudy, and Marco Checchetto. I hope I managed to do your works justice. Thanks very much for the ride!